DEAD TO RITES

White Jade Books

Brannigan Mysteries

Secrets of Silvergrove

Forget-Me-Nots and Forgotten Graves

Blue Iris, Blood Morning

Lotus, Lillies, and Last Courses (Fall 2026)

Roses are Red, Violets are Murder (Winter 2026)

Summers Rose Investigations

End in a Dead Heat

So Easy It's Criminal

Tacos, Sunsets, and Murder

The Drowned Duck (Spring 2026)

Cascade Agency Thrillers

Warm Taipei Rain

New Delhi Monsoon (2027)

Oxonia Chronicles

The Smoked Glass Murders

The Phantom on Platform 9 (Fall 2026)

Science Fiction

Samarqand: Prelude

Samarqand

Lost and Fallen (Summer 2026)

Redeeming Lost Pegasus (Fall 2026)

Bloodwine Warriors Trilogy (2027)

DEAD TO RITES

P. J. Kozeman

Published by White Jade Publications LLC
June, 2026

DEAD TO RITES

Cover Art and Design by M R White.
Interior Text Design by M R White.
First Electronic Edition: June, 2026
First Paperback Edition: June, 2026

ISBN 978-1-967892-12-9 Electronic
ISBN 978-1-967892-13-6 Paperback

To the NovelCrafter Crew on Story Hackers,
who wanted to see it done fast.

"Handle a book as a bee does a flower."

— John Muir

"The busy bee has no time for sorrow."

— William Blake

"That which is not good for the bee-hive cannot be good for the bees."

— Marcus Aurelius

Table of Contents

The Giving Season....1
Names and Challenges....15
Wednesday Preparations....27
A Beautiful Fall Day....39
Dead to Rites....51
An Early Arrest....63
The Theory of Bees....75
The Living and the Dead....85
Interview and Caution....95
Obsession....105
More Bad News....115
Thieves and Vandals....125
Team and Truth....135
Confrontation and Confession....147
The Clouds Fade....157
First Principles....169
5:47....181
Deliverance....191
Changes....203
A New Balance....215

Dead to Rites

The Giving Season

The lock clicked open under Mel's key, and she pushed through the double doors of The Giving Spoon into the familiar scent of cardboard and disinfectant. October morning light slanted through the high windows, turning dust motes into lazy spirals above the distribution tables. She flipped the switches, and fluorescent bulbs stuttered to life overhead.

First things first. Mel crossed to the walk-in cooler and hauled the door open.

Empty wire shelves gleamed back at her where the dairy delivery usually stood three deep. No milk. No cheese. No yogurt. The weekly protein staples that rounded out the dry goods and produce: gone.

She pressed her palms against her temples. Mrs. O'Keefe would be first through the door in ninety minutes, and a dozen families after her, all depending on those calcium-fortified gallons and blocks of cheddar that stretched tight grocery budgets into something workable.

Her phone was already in her hand. Arthur Pumble answered on the second ring, his voice rough with early morning gravel.

"Mel. What's happened?"

"The dairy truck never came. I need protein options, and I need them now."

A pause. Arthur's breathing came in labored pulls, each inhale catching somewhere deep in his chest. "I'll call Bruce. And I can bring honey. Two cases of the crystallized stuff. Easier to portion. Give you some sweetener variety at least."

"You're a lifesaver."

"I'm a beekeeper with inventory problems." His attempted laugh turned into a wet cough. When he spoke again, the strain had etched deeper into his words. "Legal troubles with the neighbor. Travers. He's claiming my hives encroach on his property line, threatening to sue for damages to his organic certification."

Mel gripped the phone tighter. Arthur's operation was already hanging by threads; the colony collapse had devastated his production, and now this. "What does he want?"

"The hives moved. But there's nowhere left to move them that has sufficient forage."

A pause stretched too long. Then came a cough, deep and wet, the kind that catches in the chest and won't let go, and she heard him pull it back.

"I'm too old to start over." His voice was quieter when he came back to the line. "Forty years working this ground. Started farming it long before I thought about keeping bees — the apiary's only eleven years, but this land goes back to my father. I built every frame myself." He stopped. "Bernie's already taken most of what was worth having, little by little. He just couldn't take that too."

His voice gave out on the last word.

"I'll have the honey to you within the hour," he said, as if none of it had happened.

The line went dead.

Mel stared at the empty cooler shelves, then shut the door and turned to survey her distribution area. The morning crowd would arrive expecting the usual setup; the dignified selection process she'd fought so hard to establish, where donors could choose their items rather than receiving a predetermined box like charity cases.

She grabbed a rolling cart and headed for the dry goods section.

Twenty minutes later, she'd rearranged the distribution tables into a U-shape that disguised the gaps. Canned tuna and salmon moved to prominent positions. Dried beans: black, kidney, navy, pinto; filled decorated baskets at each station. The peanut butter inventory stretched across the center table with small cups of sample crackers beside each jar variety. Not ideal, but it maintained the selection dignity that mattered more than the items themselves.

The front door chimed. Mrs. O'Keefe shuffled in, her canvas shopping bags already draped over both forearms. New lines creased the corners of her eyes, deeper than Mel remembered from last week. The older woman's gaze swept the tables, paused at the prominent bean display, then softened with what looked like relief.

"Morning, Melissa." Mrs. O'Keefe's shoulders dropped half an inch. "I wasn't sure I'd make it this week. The electric bill came, and—" She cut herself off with a quick shake of her head. "But look at all these choices. You've outdone yourself."

Mel's throat tightened. "We're featuring pantry staples this week. Those navy beans make excellent soup."

"Ah! My mother's recipe used navy beans." Mrs. O'Keefe moved toward the display with careful steps, her arthritic fingers already reaching for the packages. "I haven't made it in years."

The door chimed again. Leo Cortez shouldered through with a clipboard under one arm and his phone pressed to his ear, his dark hair still damp from a rushed shower. He raised one finger in greeting to Mel, mouthed an apology, then turned back to his conversation.

"No, I understand the timeline. Yes, I received the email. I just need—" His jaw tightened as someone on the other end interrupted. "Right. Yes. I'll confirm by Monday."

He ended the call and shoved the phone deep into his jacket pocket, then crossed to Mel with the clipboard extended. "Delivery schedule for the week. I moved the Riverside Lutheran donation to Thursday since they're doing their Harvest Festival collection on Wednesday."

"Perfect." Mel accepted the clipboard but didn't release Leo's gaze. His eyes held a distracted quality, something unfocused and elsewhere. "Everything all right?"

"Fine. Yeah." He cleared his throat and gestured at the rearranged tables. "What's with the new layout?"

"Dairy delivery fell through. We're improvising."

Leo scanned the setup with the quick assessment of someone who'd spent three years learning food distribution logistics at her side. His expression shifted to approval. "Smart. You've made the selection process even more personalized. Looks intentional rather than reactionary." He paused. "Arthur bringing honey?"

"Within the hour."

"Then we'll be fine." Leo pulled a marker from his pocket and began labelling the bean baskets with recipe suggestions in his careful, culinary-school handwriting. His phone buzzed against his ribs. He ignored it.

The vibration came again. And again.

Mel touched his wrist. "You need to get that?"

"Nope." The marker kept moving, forming perfect letters across the card stock. "Just scholarship spam. Nothing important."

The lie sat between them, obvious and uncomfortable. But before Mel could press, Mrs. O'Keefe approached with her arms full of selections, and the moment dissolved into the morning's rhythm.

The morning rush left the distribution floor empty by ten-thirty, and Mel's lower back ached with the particular burn of three hours on her feet. She retreated to the cramped back office where Leo had already spread across the desk with his laptop and a collection of ingredient labels.

"You're making recipe cards again." Mel dropped into the desk chair and rolled her shoulders until something popped.

"Mrs. Liao asked how to use chickpeas beyond hummus." Leo's fingers flew across the keyboard. "I'm giving her three options. Mediterranean style with olive oil and herbs, a coconut curry variation, and a simple mash for sandwich filling." He angled the screen toward Mel. "Look at the photography. I sourced images that match our typical pantry ingredients so donors can recognize what the finished dish should look like."

The cards displayed professional-level layout and food styling. Each recipe broke down into clear steps with prep times and nutritional information highlighted in easy-to-read callouts. In the corner of each card, Leo's logo, a simple spoon wrapped in a ribbon, marked the design as his.

"These are gorgeous." Mel leaned closer, scrolling through the variations Leo had created for seventeen different pantry staples. "You could sell these."

"I'd rather give them away." But pleasure flushed his cheeks. His phone buzzed again from his jacket pocket, draped over the spare chair. This time the vibration continued for a full ten seconds.

"Persistent spam." Mel raised an eyebrow.

Leo's flush deepened. He closed his laptop with careful deliberation and met her eyes. "The Culinary Institute sent their fall acceptance decisions early. I got in."

The words punched through Mel's brooding. Joy and loss arriving in the same breath. She forced her voice steady. "Leo, that's incredible. When do you start?"

"I haven't confirmed yet."

"Why not?"

His gaze slid to the office door, toward the distribution floor beyond. "Because accepting means leaving mid-semester. Three weeks from now. Right before the holiday rush when you need me most."

"We'll manage."

"You shouldn't have to manage. Not when I made a commitment to be here through December."

Mel pressed her palms flat against the desk. The old wood grain was smooth under her fingers, worn down by four years of grant applications and donor tracking forms and quiet moments stolen between crises. "This is your dream. You don't defer dreams for convenience."

"It's not about convenience. It's about responsibility."

Before Mel could answer, the mail slot in the front door clattered. Leo unfolded from his chair and disappeared into the distribution area. When he returned, he carried a short stack of envelopes and the weekly grocery circulars.

Mel accepted the pile and began sorting. Bill, bill, donation receipt, grocery ad, official-looking envelope from the Possum Gap County Administrative Office.

She slit the official envelope open and pulled out a single sheet of county letterhead.

The words arranged themselves into shapes she recognized but struggled to accept: Notice of Compliance Audit. Her name appeared in the addressee line. Below that, a bulleted list of allegations:

- Inconsistent donor intake documentation
- Unclear accounting practices regarding financial donations
- Potential misuse of grant funds allocated for food purchasing
- Failure to maintain adequate records for state reporting requirements

The letter showed an audit date, scheduled for the second week of November. The letter requested full financial records dating back eighteen months, donor intake logs, and itemized receipts for all food purchases.

Mel read the paragraph twice more, but the meaning remained unchanged. Someone had complained to the county. Someone had flagged The Giving Spoon for investigation.

"Everything all right?" Leo's voice pulled her back to the office.

"Fine." She refolded the letter and tucked it into her desk drawer, beneath the grant applications and tax records that proved her accounting was meticulous to the point of obsession. "Just routine bureaucratic nonsense. The county loves their paperwork."

Leo's expression suggested he didn't believe her, but he was too polite to push. Instead, he returned to his laptop and pulled up the delivery schedule. "We've got the Riverside Lutheran donation Thursday afternoon, and Arthur's bringing another honey delivery next Tuesday. I can stay late both days to process the intake if you need."

"You should be working on your acceptance letter."

"I haven't decided yet."

"Decide yes."

His jaw tightened. Before he could argue, his phone erupted again. This time an actual call that he pulled out and silenced without checking the screen.

Mel tilted her head. "Who keeps calling?"

"The Institute. They want confirmation by Monday."

"Or?"

They'll offer my scholarship to the waitlist." He pocketed his phone. "If I don't answer, maybe I won't have to choose."

"That's not how decisions work."

"I know."

Outside the office window, autumn wind scattered leaves across the parking lot. Mel's desk drawer seemed to gain weight, the audit letter adding bureaucratic gravity.

Three weeks. Leo would leave in three weeks, and she'd face the county audit alone. The holiday rush would arrive without his organizational genius. The pantry would continue, because it had to continue, but something essential would change.

She pushed the thought aside and pulled the delivery schedule across the desk. "Show me Thursday's logistics. If we're receiving the Lutheran donation at three, we'll need to clear space in the dry goods section by noon."

Leo's shoulders dropped with relief at the subject change, and they bent together over the clipboard, mapping the week ahead as if planning could hold back all the disruptions gathering at the edges.

The Historical Society occupied a converted Victorian on Maple Street, its gingerbread trim painted in shades of cream and burgundy that Eleanor Vance herself had researched from period catalogues. Mel climbed the porch steps at two o'clock with a cloth bag full of preserved goods donated by Mrs. Gaskins for the society's Autumn Fundraiser. Jams, pickles, chutneys.

Eleanor met her at the door in a cardigan covered with embroidered autumn leaves, her enthusiasm already at full voltage. "Mel! Perfect timing. You have to see the new exhibit before it opens tomorrow." She grabbed Mel's free hand and hauled her past the formal parlor-turned-reception-area into the back archives.

"I brought donations from Mrs. Gaskins." Mel raised the bag. "Three dozen jars of—"

"Yes, wonderful, set them on the counter." Eleanor waved toward a prep table without breaking stride. She pulled Mel through a doorway draped with velvet curtains into a room transformed by spotlights and museum-quality display cases.

The exhibit spread across three walls: Possum Gap Harvest Traditions Through the Decades. Photographs showed historical fall festivals, canning collectives, and community celebrations dating back to the 1920s. In the center of the room, period decorations dressed a harvest table: dried corn husks, woven wheat bundles, antique preserving jars filled with replica foods.

"That's beautiful." Mel moved closer to examine a photograph from 1952 showing the town square packed with vendors. "Your restoration work on these images is impressive."

"That's not even the best part." Eleanor crossed to a glass case displaying tournament programs and chess sets. Mel's gaze moved to the pieces arranged inside:

ivory and ebony, formal and perfectly still. A small card in Eleanor's careful hand read: The pieces are the ritual. The ritual is the community. Something in the phrasing settled wrong, though Mel couldn't have named the reason.

"This year marks the hundredth anniversary of the Possum Gap Chess Tournament. We're documenting the entire history." She lifted one of the programs, a glossy booklet printed on heavy stock. "You're coming Saturday, right?"

"I don't play chess."

"Nobody cares about chess!" Eleanor's laugh carried an edge of something sharper than humor. "The tournament is about community. Tradition. Everyone attends, players or not. It's practically mandatory civic participation."

Mel studied her friend's face. Eleanor's usual scattered energy had focused into something more intense, almost brittle. "You're unusually invested in chess attendance."

"It's the centennial." Eleanor returned the program to its display with excessive care. "Historic moments require witnessing. Besides, the tournament has all these elaborate traditions. The opening ceremonies, the ritual challenges, the specific rules about player conduct and spectator etiquette. It's fascinating from an anthropological perspective."

"You sound like you're describing religious rites rather than a chess game."

"Isn't that what tradition turns into? Secular ritual that binds communities together?" Eleanor's fingers traced the edge of the display case. "Bernie Travers is organizing the whole event this year. He's been invaluable with the historical documentation."

The name gave Mel a start. Bernie Travers. She'd heard it around town recently, always in contexts that suggested money, influence, and civic authority. "I didn't know Bernie was involved with the Historical Society."

Eleanor's expression shifted, something shuttering behind her eyes. "He's not. Not officially. He just has an interest in preserving certain historical records." She turned toward another wall display. "Come see the business history section. I found incredible photographs from the town's economic development in the eighties."

Unease itched between Mel's shoulder blades. Eleanor's evasiveness felt out of character for someone who often overshared every historical detail.

The business history display covered Possum Gap's brief industrial boom. Factories that had arrived in the late seventies, promising jobs and growth, then dissolving through the eighties, leaving empty buildings and economic depression behind. Photographs showed ribbon-cutting ceremonies, optimistic crowds, smiling men in suits shaking hands before brick facades.

Eleanor stopped at a photograph from 1976. Five men stood before a manufacturing plant, holding champagne glasses in a toast. The caption read: Quantum Adhesives Grand Opening — Partners Celebrate Innovation.

Mel leaned closer. The man on the far left wore thick glasses and an uncertain smile that didn't match the celebration around him. Something about his features tugged at recognition.

"That's your father." Mel pointed to the figure. "I didn't know he was involved in Quantum Adhesives."

Eleanor's hand shot out and adjusted the display placard, blocking Mel's view of the photograph. "Minor investment. Nothing significant." Her voice had gone flat. "I just remembered I have a preservation board meeting in fifteen minutes. We're discussing climate control for the archive storage."

"Eleanor." A beat.

"I really need to prepare. Thanks for dropping off the donations. Mrs. Gaskins's preserves will be perfect for the fundraiser." Eleanor moved toward the exit, her cardigan sleeves fluttering with the speed of her retreat.

Mel followed, confusion giving way to concern. "Is everything all right?"

"Fine! Wonderful. Just busy." Eleanor held the front door open, her smile fixed. "See you Saturday at the tournament? Please say you'll come. It would mean a lot."

"I'll think about it."

"Don't think. Just come." Eleanor's fingers tightened on the door frame. "Trust me, Mel. You need to be there."

Before Mel could ask what that meant, Eleanor ushered her onto the porch and closed the door with decisive finality.

Mel stood on the Victorian's steps, replaying Eleanor's reactions. The evasiveness about Bernie Travers. The strange intensity about the tournament. The photograph of her father. The abrupt dismissal.

Autumn wind scattered more leaves across Maple Street. Somewhere in the distance, a dog barked. Mel descended the stairs, but Eleanor's final words circled through her mind: You need to be there.

Not want. Need.

The low afternoon sun turned The Giving Spoon's parking lot golden and deceptive. Mel twisted her key in the front door lock while Leo carried the last box of sorted donations to his sedan.

"Thursday's delivery is going to be tight." Leo set the box in his trunk. "The Lutheran church is donating twice their usual amount for the holiday season. We might need to reorganize the entire dry goods section by Wednesday."

"We'll make it work." Mel pocketed her keys and faced him. "What's really going on?"

He closed his trunk with careful precision, then studied the cracked asphalt. "The Institute's scholarship is full-ride. Everything. But they need me by November eighth. If I defer to spring, I lose it entirely."

Right before Thanksgiving. Right before Thanksgiving, when the pantry's distribution volume doubled and desperate families lined up hours before opening. Mel put on her social face.

"That's wonderful. You have to accept."

"I can't abandon you right now. It's your busy season."

"I've been running this pantry for years. I managed before you arrived, and I'll manage after you leave."

Leo's hands curled into fists. "You shouldn't have to manage alone."

"I'll figure it out. Mrs. Liao's nephew might need volunteer hours." She managed a smile. "We'll make it work."

A rusted pickup truck pulled into the lot, engine rattling. Arthur Pumble climbed out with careful movements, his face grey beneath his beard.

Mel crossed to him. "Arthur. You didn't need another trip today."

"Had the honey in the truck already." He lowered the tailgate, revealing two cases of jarred honey.

They transferred the cases together. Arthur moved with stubborn determination, but tremors shook his hands. He braced against the truck bed between each lift.

Before he lowered the tailgate, Arthur held a jar of late-season honey to the fading light. Deep amber, nearly red. The last of the season's flow. "Forty years of harvests," he said. "Started farming this ground long before I thought about keeping bees. The apiary's only eleven years, but the land goes back to my father." He turned the jar slowly in his hands. "Might not see many more like this one."

Mel asked: "You mean the weather?"

Arthur set the jar carefully in the box. He didn't answer.

"You're coming to the tournament Saturday?"

Mel hesitated. "I don't play chess."

"Neither do half the attendees. It's tradition." Arthur's smile was tired. "Bernie Travers is running the whole show this year."

The second mention of Bernie in one afternoon. Mel filed it away with Eleanor's evasiveness and the audit letter.

"Maybe I'll stop by."

"That's what I like to hear." Arthur climbed back into his truck, each movement calculated against pain. Through the passenger window, Mel caught a glimpse of a prescription bottle rolling loose in the cup holder, the pharmacy label catching the last of the afternoon light. She looked away before he could notice.

"See you both Wednesday."

The truck's engine coughed to life and Arthur pulled away.

Leo waited until the truck disappeared. "He looks worse."

"I know."

They stood together as the autumn sun sank toward the horizon. Leo's phone buzzed again.

"You're confirming by Monday." Mel kept her voice firm. "Not asking. Telling."

"Yes, boss." Relief softened his smile.

"Good. Now go draft your acceptance letter. Make it professional."

"What about you?"

"I'm going home to drink tea and pretend I don't have a county audit to prepare for."

Leo's expression sharpened. "That letter this morning wasn't routine."

"No. But it's nothing I can't handle." She climbed into her truck before he could press further. "Monday, Leo. Or I'm calling the Institute myself."

His laugh followed her as she started the engine. Mel sat for a moment, wondering what bothered Leo. And with that chess tourney. She shook her head and turned to the street.

Names and Challenges

Leo stood in the door to the Spoon's kitchen when Mel arrived, his delivery clipboard under one arm and his phone open to an email he hadn't sent.

He showed it to her without preamble. She read it.

"Send it."

"I wanted you to see it first."

"I've seen it. Send it."

He sent it. His phone made a faint swoosh, the sound it made for coupons and dentist reminders, completely unequal to what it meant. Leo looked at the screen for a moment, then slid the phone into his pocket and picked up the clipboard.

"Two weeks' notice," he said. "Even though I'm not technically required."

"You're not required."

"I know. But it's the right thing."

"That's why you're doing it."

He handed her the clipboard. The week's delivery schedule, updated in his careful block printing. He'd moved the Riverside Lutheran donation to Thursday; their Harvest Festival was Wednesday and he'd worked around it. He thought of things like that. It was one of the reasons the scholarship made sense.

They opened the pantry.

Tuesday ran its usual rhythm, quieter than Monday. A different set of families with different patterns. The Cortez family came early, before school, for the milk they stretched through the week. Mrs. Gaskins came at nine-thirty, always with her preserves to donate and an opinion about town governance to offer for free.

"Bernie Travers filed an objection to the Cochran Street Garden expansion," she said, arranging three jars of pickled okra on Mel's counter with the care of someone presenting evidence. "Foot traffic concerns, he says." She didn't elaborate on whose foot traffic. She didn't need to.

Mel had heard about the Cochran Street proposal, a vacant city lot adjacent to the lower-income blocks near the pantry's supply routes. A community garden, properly maintained, would serve forty families. Maybe more if the soil tested well.

"What kind of objection?"

"The bureaucratic kind. He files papers and waits." Mrs. Gaskins's voice carried the particular flatness of someone who has been frustrated by a thing for so long it has become a feature of her face. "Things die quietly when he does that."

After she left, Leo set down his recipe card and looked at Mel.

"How many times now?"

"Third time I've heard his name this week."

Leo went back to his card. "Consistent," he said, which was more restrained than the situation deserved.

Near eleven, while they were restocking the dry goods section, Leo mentioned Cheswick. Almost incidentally. The kind of information that surfaces naturally when you've spent the morning talking about chess centennials and planning commissions and the particular way civic power concentrates in small towns. He'd been in the hardware store yesterday and gotten cornered by a man from the chess club.

"David Cheswick," Leo said. "One of the best players this region's produced. Hasn't competed in years. Coming back Saturday for the centennial."

"Against Bernie?"

"That's the drama. They have history. Something about a state championship ruling years ago. The hardware store man was not fully coherent on the details." Leo paused. "He was very coherent on the part where he said those two should never be in the same room."

Mel wrote the name in her notebook. Then, looking at the page, she realized she'd already written Bernie Travers twice this week without meaning to.

Three times in two days.

She tore the page off and tucked it under the counter. Nothing to do with it yet. But she'd started keeping it.

The man who came through the Giving Spoon's door at two-thirty on Tuesday afternoon was not what Mel had been picturing.

She'd pictured bureaucracy: clipboard, county lanyard, the harassed efficiency of someone with four more sites before five o'clock. What she got was a man in a pressed jacket who paused at the threshold and took in the room with an expression of genuine appreciation.

"Ms. Hunter." He crossed the distribution floor with the ease of someone who had been in a hundred similar rooms. "Bernard Travers. I serve on the County Oversight Board." He offered his hand.

His handshake was correct: firm without force, released at the exact right moment. He had the kind of face that made people feel looked at.

"You received the audit notification last week," he said. Not a question.

"I did." She didn't offer what she'd thought of it. "Would you like to see the records?"

"I'd love to see the pantry, if you'll indulge me. The audit itself is administrative — your records are in order, I'm sure of it." He said this with the warmth of someone doing you a favor by assuming the best. "I prefer to have a sense of the operation."

She showed him around. She had nothing to hide and she knew it, which should have made the tour feel routine. It didn't. He was genuinely interested in how the distribution tables worked, in how she'd designed the selection model to preserve dignity for the families who came. He asked questions that proved he'd read the grant documentation before arriving. He remembered a donor name from her 2024 intake summary, which she hadn't expected.

"Remarkable," he said, at the cooler section. The way he said it meant something other than remarkable.

At the back of the floor he paused at the donor-receipt board; the photographs of families served, the handwritten thank-you notes Mel pinned beside them in rows. He studied one photograph for a moment. A grandmother and three small children in winter coats, holding paper bags.

"Your record-keeping is unconventional," he said.

"Photographs beside intake forms." Mel kept her voice even. "The families appreciate knowing the pantry sees them as people rather than numbers."

"Of course." He nodded, still looking at the photograph. "The county auditors prefer numerical summaries. More portable. Easier to assess across multiple sites without — local context." He turned back with his full attention restored. "I mention it only so you're prepared. They're excellent at their work, but they're most comfortable with standardized formats."

He thanked her for her time. At the door he turned back with the timing of a man who had learned exactly when to turn back: "I think what you've built here is genuinely impressive, Ms. Hunter. Possum Gap is lucky to have it."

She said the appropriate things and watched him cross the parking lot and get into his car.

Then she stood in the middle of her distribution floor, the photographs, the four years of meticulous records, the families' names documented with more care than the county would ever require, and felt the particular cold of being assessed and filed by someone who had already decided what to do with the information.

She had nothing to hide. That hadn't made her feel any safer.

The planning commission met in a room in Town Hall that smelled of old carpet and fluorescent-light flatness, the specific atmosphere of rooms where civic decisions were made reluctantly. Folding chairs. A podium. A horseshoe table where the commissioners sat with the careful neutrality of people who had learned not to have opinions before the public comment period ended.

Mel came because Mrs. Gaskins had mentioned it, and because she'd heard Bernie Travers would be there, and because she had started, without quite deciding to, paying attention.

The Cochran Street Garden proposal had been in consideration for eight months. Tonight was the formal comment period before the vote. The lead advocate was Janet Philpott, retired schoolteacher, long-time pantry volunteer, patient and meticulous in the way of someone who had spent decades navigating systems that nobody designed for her. She presented the proposal in twelve minutes: soil analysis, cost projections, comparable programs in similar communities, a petition with three hundred signatures from Possum Gap residents.

Bernie Travers arrived five minutes into her presentation. He sat in the front row. He took out a notebook and wrote something.

When the comment period opened he was the first to raise his hand.

He was polite. Mel had expected something else; she had steeled herself for bluntness and received instead something that took longer to name. He asked clarifying questions, each one phrased with apparent admiration for the proposal. He thanked Ms. Philpott for her thoroughness. He noted that the community need she described was genuine and important.

Then he opened his notebook.

"I notice that the petition includes a signature from Harold Blanchard of the Zion Hill Road address," he said. His kept voice measured, mild. Helpful. "Mr. Blanchard passed away in March. I didn't want the commission to be working from inaccurate information."

The room went still.

One name. One signature out of three hundred. Bernie continued at the same measured pace, certain it was an honest administrative error. He simply wanted the record to be complete, he thought the commission deserved accurate information before voting. He said he looked forward to supporting the proposal once the paperwork reflected reality.

He thanked everyone for their time and sat down.

The council tabled the pending petition review. December, at earliest.

Janet Philpott said nothing. The commissioners moved to the next item. Bernie made another note in his notebook and capped his pen.

Mel watched him. And while she watched him she became aware of someone watching him the same way. A man in the fourth row, near the aisle, sitting very still. Late forties, maybe fifty. Unremarkable clothing, unremarkable posture, except for the quality of his attention. Focused, unhurried, absolutely without distraction.

He was watching Bernie the way you watch a clock. Not waiting for something to happen. Noting the time.

She couldn't see his face clearly from her angle. She filed him anyway.

Bernie left after the following agenda item. At the door he paused and his gaze swept back across the room: the reflex of a man cataloguing what he was leaving. His eyes found Mel. They paused there for two seconds, precise and deliberate, before he was gone.

Mel realized she had stopped breathing. She started again.

In the row behind her, a woman said: "That man."

The woman beside her said nothing. Which was the same thing.

The Historical Society's back archive room smelled of old paper and cedar and the stillness of things no one had moved in years. But someone had been moving them recently. Mel could tell from the pale rectangles on the shelving. Shifted boxes had disturbed dust in a pattern that didn't match the careful arrangement. And from Eleanor herself: a faint smudge of archive dust on her cardigan sleeve, and a new box placed exactly where an old one had been, Eleanor willing the seam to be invisible.

Mel had stopped by on an errand, returning a centennial exhibit pamphlet Eleanor had asked the printer to deliver care of the pantry. The kind of small neighborly transaction that accumulated, over four years, into something called friendship.

"Come look," Eleanor said, and her voice had the particular brightness of someone who has been waiting for a reason to show someone something.

The tournament display occupied the center of the archive room, with properly lit cases, placard labels in Eleanor's careful calligraphy, a hundred years of Possum Gap chess arranged with the same care Eleanor gave everything she loved. Grainy photographs of bearded men at cafe tables. A hand-drawn bracket from 1952. A color portrait of this year's competitors.

"The white queen," Eleanor said. She gestured toward a glass case where a single chess piece rested on dark velvet. Ivory, yellowed at the edges, larger than playing size — the kind of object that had a ceremonial weight separate from its function.

"Every opening match since 1935, the champion has held this piece while the tournament clock is set. It predates the formal rules. No one decided it. It's just what we always do. One of the rites." A small pause. "Bernie carries on the tradition beautifully."

Mel looked at the piece for a moment. "Dead to rites," she said, without meaning to say it aloud.

Eleanor blinked. "Pardon?"

"Nothing. I was thinking about tradition. How it becomes —" She stopped. "Never mind. It's beautiful work, Eleanor."

Eleanor's enthusiasm resumed. She moved to the next case, the next panel. Mel walked beside her and listened, and while she listened she noticed the box on the shelf that wasn't quite flush with the ones beside it, and the smudge on Eleanor's sleeve, and the way Eleanor had positioned herself between Mel and the back corner of the room.

Bernie Travers's name appeared on three placard panels, the tournament's longtime organizer, his photograph beside a list of past champions.

"I saw him last night," Mel said. "At the planning commission. The Cochran Street Garden discussion."

Eleanor's hands went still on the edge of a display case. "Oh."

"He tabled it."

A pause, half a breath too long. "Bernie takes civic process very seriously."

Something in the sentence was accurate and something else was doing work. Mel waited. Eleanor had turned to straighten a placard that was already straight.

"Eleanor." She kept her voice even. "Is everything all right between you and Bernie?"

"Of course." The smile arrived a moment after it should have. "We collaborate professionally. The centennial required his organizational expertise. We have our differences, as colleagues do, but the work is what matters."

She held her hands together. Not fidgeting. Controlled.

"His connections to the older families in town were invaluable for the business history portion," Eleanor continued. "His knowledge of the companies from the eighties especially. He opened doors I couldn't have opened on my own."

Again: every word true. Every word in service of another purpose.

Mel picked up the pamphlet she'd brought and said she should get back. Eleanor walked her to the door, the guide-tour warmth restored and running perfectly.

At the top step, Eleanor touched Mel's arm. "Mel. Be glad you're going on Saturday."

Not I'm glad you're going. Be glad. As if it were instruction, or warning, or both.

"Why?" Mel asked.

Eleanor smiled, and the smile was the end of the conversation. "Because it's the centennial. The hundredth year." She paused. "Some things only happen once."

Mel thought about that sentence all the way home.

The Giving Spoon transformed on Community Table nights in a way that always surprised people who only knew it as a distribution center. The shelving units folded back. Mismatched tablecloths, donated over the years from estates and attic clearances, covered the folding tables Leo brought from storage. He cooked for two days before these evenings: tonight's menu was chicken and rice soup, skillet cornbread, a squash dish he called experimental. Everyone else called it good.

Arthur arrived before the doors opened, two jars of honey under his arm, and settled in the corner with Bruce Parmalee, retired now after coaching the high school chess team for twenty years. A man who could reconstruct any game he'd ever played from memory. They were doing exactly that when Mel arrived to start the setup, Bruce's finger tracing moves on the tablecloth while Arthur watched and nodded.

Mel moved through the room with the ease of seventeen repetitions. She knew who would arrive early and be gone in thirty minutes, who would need the leftovers packed with care, which children would drift to Leo's side of the kitchen. She knew Mrs. O'Keefe would sit with the Cortez family, and that the Liao children would need something to do with their hands.

Noreen would have been working the far end of the room, drawing people out, producing names from her memory like gifts. Her absence had a shape.

Tim Renshaw arrived at six-fifteen. He brought a jar of chutney from the Methodist Church fall sale. Good provenance, a genuine donation. He set it on the table with a slight self-consciousness, the manner of someone not sure of the protocol. His father had come to every Community Table until his health made it impossible. The tradition had apparently waited three years for the son to find his way back to it.

"First one for you?" Mel asked.

"My father described them differently. More formal."

Mel glanced at the mismatched tablecloths, the soup, the children. "More formal than this."

"Much." He looked around the room. "This is better, I think."

He found a seat and stayed for the soup and the second round of cornbread. He had a way of listening to people that was genuinely present — no drift in the eyes, no management of the conversation toward himself. Mel noticed this because she spent a great deal of time noticing what people gave other people, and this quality was rarer than it should have been.

The tournament came up near the end of the meal, as it always did in October. Bernie's name followed, as it always seemed to this week. The centennial. His organizing role. The significance of a hundredth year.

Bruce Parmalee said, to the tablecloth and his imaginary chess board: "David Cheswick hasn't answered my last two emails."

Arthur said: "He'll come."

"He's said that for three years."

"He'll come this time." Arthur moved an invisible piece. "He has to."

The table moved on. Mel filed it with the rest.

Arthur left early, earlier than usual. He came to find her near the kitchen and said goodnight with a specificity that felt meaningful, not the warmth of leaving a party but the warmth of someone who had meant to say something and hadn't quite.

At the door his hand rested on the frame a moment.

"Big week," he said.

"For the tournament."

He looked at her. Just for a moment. "Sure," he said. "For the tournament."

The October air came through the open door, sharp and clean, smelling of the season's end.

By nine o'clock the tables were folded and the floor swept and Leo had gone home carrying the leftover soup. Mel sat at the desk in the back office with the audit documentation spread before her.

Four years of quarterly summaries. Donor intake logs. Itemized receipts for every purchase and every donation received. She had kept records this carefully not because she anticipated review but because the work required it, because the families who depended on the pantry deserved to have their names and circumstances documented with the same care the pantry gave their dignity.

She did not open the audit letter again. She knew what it said.

Leo texted at nine-thirty: **confirmed. start date nov 8. thank you for not letting me defer.** Then, after a pause: **you'll be fine.**

She typed back: **I know.** Then: **go pack.**

Her notepad had two lines on it, written without intention during the evening's paperwork.

Bernie Travers. Three times in two days. Four times now, counting this one.

Below that: Gregory Dowen. She'd gotten the name from Bruce Parmalee at the table tonight. Chess player, Cambridge-educated, part of the centennial guest roster. Arrived in Possum Gap three weeks ago. Quiet man. Walks a dog every morning.

She looked at the two names for a moment. Then she turned the pad face down.

The audit deadline was nine days away. Leo left in two weeks. The tournament was Saturday.

She turned off the desk lamp. The window showed the parking lot in the October dark, the same lot where Arthur had driven away Monday with the prescription bottle rolling in his cup holder. She stood there for a moment with her hand on the switch.

Some things only happen once.

She didn't know what Eleanor had meant. She suspected, driving home through the stripped maples, that Eleanor hadn't known either, that the words had slipped out from somewhere deeper than intention, from whatever it was Eleanor was protecting in those archive boxes she'd hurried to cover.

The October dark was complete and cold and still.

Saturday was three days away.

Wednesday Preparations

The festival was becoming itself.

Mel could feel it the moment she turned into the Miller's Hollow Park entrance Wednesday afternoon: the particular energy of a town preparing to be more than it usually was. A white canvas pavilion was going up along the park's midsection, two workers on ladders fighting the aluminum poles into their sockets while a third held the canvas out of the leaves. Vendor stakes were already in the ground along the main path, orange marking flags where the food stalls and craft tables would stand. Someone had brought a riding mower across the grass even though the grass was already short; they were just doing something useful with their hands.

Eleanor had asked Mel to drop off a box of exhibit pamphlets at the tournament registration tent. The centennial programs, four-color, printed on good stock, smelling of fresh ink. Mel balanced the box and found her way to the tent without much difficulty; it was the largest white structure at the park's east end, positioned against the cedar screen that ran along the park's boundary.

She hadn't paid attention to that tree line before. It was worth paying attention to. The Eastern Red Cedars stood in a row along the park's eastern edge where the maintained lawn ended, dark and dense, planted close enough together that you couldn't quite see through to the other side. The smell of cedar came off them in the October air, clean and resinous. A natural wall.

"Arthur."

He was at his assigned space, a folding table twenty feet from the registration tent, already draped in burlap, six rows of honey jars arranged in the careful pattern he used at every market. He was checking the labels with reading glasses he wouldn't admit he needed, running his finger along each one. His hands were steady today. No tremor. A good day.

He looked up and his face did the thing it did: the full-body arrival of warmth, as if Mel's appearance was exactly what he'd been hoping for.

"Come see this." He gestured at the cedar screen. "This is my favorite part of this park and nobody knows it's here."

They walked to the tree line together through a gap where two trees stood slightly farther apart. A planting mistake or a decision, now decades old She could see to the other side: rough meadow, autumn-brown, and beyond it the glint of water through willow branches.

"Mashburn Creek," Arthur said. "My hives are right along the bank. South-facing rows. Three acres of wildflower ground between the cedars and the water." He looked through the gap with the expression of a man looking at something he has built over a long time. "Maybe a quarter mile from here to the nearest colony. A good quarter mile."

Mel looked through the gap. She couldn't see the hives. She could just make out the creak of the creek and the far rustle of asters still holding their purple at the water's edge.

"Bees need water?" she asked.

"Bees need water." He nodded at the creek. "And shade, and late-season forage. They've got everything they need over there. They have no reason to come here."

He said this with the same matter-of-fact pride he brought to all his apiary knowledge. Mel stored it without knowing why she was storing it. Sometimes you kept things because the person telling you clearly meant you to keep them.

Back at the registration area, two men from the chess committee were in a low-grade dispute about the master's table. It was a specific table, brought in for the occasion. Heavier than the others, wider, the kind of table that announced itself as the important one. The dispute was about position: under the pavilion center or at the east end, closer to where the cameras would be set up for the centennial documentation.

"The light's better at the east end," said one.

"Tradition says center," said the other.

"The light," said the first man, with the finality of someone who had already won.

They moved the table to the east end of the pavilion, facing the cedar screen. Mel watched them settle it on the soft ground, adjust it twice, and declare it correct. The ground near the cedar screen had a slight give to it; the turf management crew had aerated it last week, and the soil hadn't fully recovered. The table's legs pressed small, neat impressions into the grass.

She left the pamphlets and walked back to her car through the park's increasing organized noise. By Saturday this would be a community event. Right now it was a rehearsal.

He came from the north entrance with a uniformed officer and a clipboard, which was standard, and with the bearing of someone who trusted his own assessment, which was not always standard.

Mel recognized Miles Corbin from town events the way you recognized useful civic fixtures, present at the right moments, not intrusive, doing his job without requiring an audience for it. She knew his name. She'd seen him at the Giving Spoon fundraiser two years ago, nursing a cup of coffee and watching the room with the same attentiveness he was applying to the festival grounds now.

He found Eleanor first. She was coordinating near the registration tent with two members of the parks committee, and he went directly to her with the manner of someone who had worked with her before and found it efficient.

"Detective." Eleanor's voice was steady, professional. "The east path is still soft from the aeration. I'd recommend routing foot traffic along the main path until Saturday morning."

"Noted." He wrote it. "The woods access?"

"The cedar screen has one gap, about twenty feet south of the registration tent. We'll have a rope line there for the weekend."

"Good."

Then he spotted Arthur Pumble.

Something in Corbin's bearing changed; not relaxed exactly, but warmer. He excused himself from Eleanor and crossed to Arthur's table with the stride of a man going somewhere he actually wanted to go.

"Mr. Pumble." He offered his hand.

Arthur took it with both of his. "Miles. You look thin. Are you eating."

"I'm eating."

"You don't look like you're eating."

"The festival always makes me forget lunch." Corbin looked at the honey jars. "How's the yield this year?"

"Late season surprised me. Good amber. I brought the crystallized stock — better for portioning at events. You should take a jar home."

"I'll take two. My mother's been asking."

They talked for another minute, about the festival turnout projections, about whether the chess matches would run long, about the specific location of Arthur's table and whether it had adequate shade for the honey. It was the conversation of two men who knew each other's rhythms from years of the same small-town calendar.

Mel was standing close enough to hear. She wasn't eavesdropping; she was waiting to return a borrowed dolly to the equipment shed, and Corbin and Arthur were between her and the shed. So she heard "Miles" and "Mr. Pumble" and the specific warmth between them, and she stored that too.

Corbin noticed her on his way from the table.

"Ms. Hunter." He said her name with the precision of someone who had looked it up when he arrived and wasn't going to pretend otherwise. "Miles Corbin. We've crossed paths at the Giving Spoon fundraiser. The fall one, two years ago."

"I remember." She did. He'd come alone, stayed an hour, talked to four people with genuine attention, and left without taking anything from the dessert table, which she'd noticed because almost everyone took something from the dessert table.

"Good event," he said. He meant it. "The pantry does important work."

He did his security walk. She watched from across the grounds: orderly, unhurried, checking exits and access points and the distance between the parking area and the pavilion. At the cedar screen he paused for longer than anywhere else. He looked through the gap to the meadow beyond. He made a note on his clipboard.

Whatever he wrote, he didn't share it. He capped his pen and moved on.

Arthur appeared at Mel's elbow with a jar of honey wrapped in brown paper. "For you," he said. "The dark amber. Better than the other kind for baking."

"Thank you, Arthur."

"He's good, isn't he." He said it looking after Corbin, who was completing his circuit near the pavilion. "Best detective this county's ever had. Knows how to listen. Doesn't assume."

"He seems thorough," Mel said.

Arthur nodded, as if thorough was exactly right. "Go home at a decent hour," he said, which was his way of saying goodbye.

She drove past the entrance on her way out and saw Corbin making one final note at the park's north gate, writing something in the October late light with the focused attention of a man who believed the notes would matter. They would. Not in the way he expected.

The out-of-towners had started arriving.

Mel noticed them at the Giving Spoon when she opened Thursday morning, not at the pantry but at the neighborhood generally, the way you notice that a street has changed overnight when new cars appear in the usual parking spots. The Shady Lane Motor Court must have filled up; she passed it on her way in and the lot was busy by seven-thirty. Chess people, mostly — they had a particular way of carrying themselves in public spaces, an inward quality of attention, as if the external world were a problem they were assessing for moves.

Bruce Parmalee came in just before nine, not for distribution but to drop off a case of canned tomatoes from his church's harvest surplus. He stayed for coffee and talked.

"Your man Dowen came to the chess club practice last night," he said, in the way he said most things — without preamble, as if the conversation had been going on for ten minutes already. "Sat in the back. Didn't play. Didn't speak to anyone. Watched three full games without taking his eyes off the boards."

"Is that unusual?" Mel asked.

"For a spectator? Not especially." Bruce considered. "For a man who plays at his level, a bit. He'd see everything the players were doing wrong. Must take discipline to just observe."

"You knew him before?"

"Knew of him. He's in the chess world. Cambridge graduate, published some theoretical work, good competitive record before he stopped playing. No reason to stop that anyone knows." He looked into his coffee. "No reason to show up here three weeks early, either, for a centennial tournament he's not entered in."

Mel added this to her running account of Gregory Dowen. It fit the shape she was building but didn't resolve it.

"And Cheswick?" she asked.

Bruce's expression shifted. "Not here yet. I've been watching the lot at the Shady Lane since Tuesday. His name's on the bracket. Tournament committee says he confirmed." A pause. "He's done this before. Arrives late or not at all."

"You think he might not come?"

Bruce wrapped both hands around his coffee mug. "I think David Cheswick has very good reasons to be in that room Saturday and very good reasons not to be." He finished his coffee and stood. "Bernie usually wins these arguments with him. One way or another."

Mel watched him go. The pantry filled with its usual Thursday rhythm, different from Tuesday's rhythm, different again from Monday's, each day of the week its own specific character. She distributed and sorted and noted and managed. She was good at this work and she liked doing it and it asked everything of her attention, which is usually enough to quiet a busy mind.

It wasn't quite enough, this Thursday.

On Thursday evening, Mel drove through Possum Gap the long way home.

The Historical Society's light was on in the back archive room at seven-thirty.

She drove past slowly. The front of the building was dark; the back window glowed a soft amber, the kind of light that meant a desk lamp and concentrated work. Eleanor's car was the only one in the side lot. Whatever she was doing in those archive boxes, she had come back to do more of it.

Mel almost pulled over. Then she thought about Eleanor's face at the top of the porch steps — *be glad you're going* — and the smile that ended the conversation, and she drove on.

The lights were on at Possum Gap High School for extracurricular activities. Mel stopped to drop off surplus canned goods for the school's food cabinet and walked the main hall with a box under her arm.

She heard the chess club before she found it. The particular quiet of concentrated game play has its own acoustic signature, all near-silence broken by the occasional slide of a piece on a board. The room was the old home-economics room repurposed: long tables, good overhead lighting, twelve students in pairs at boards, one student at a demonstration board up front.

The student at the demonstration board was a boy Mel didn't know. Seventeen, she estimated. He moved like someone older who had been doing this one thing for a very long time. The demonstration was precise, showing a sequence of moves, explaining each in a low, clear voice, pointing at the board with a certainty that wasn't arrogance, just accuracy. He knew this. He had known this for years.

She stood in the doorway a moment longer than she meant to. The boy finished his sequence and made a small observation that made two students laugh and one sit forward with sudden interest. He had a teacher's instinct, she thought, even if he didn't know it yet. Then his posture returned to the flatness of someone who has agreed to be here and renegotiates the agreement every time.

In the back of the room, a woman sat with her phone in her hand but her eyes on the boy. Small, gray-haired before her time, composed in the way of someone who had learned to be very still in rooms where others made decisions about her. She was watching the boy's hands on the pieces, not his face. Something in the precision of her attention, directed at a specific thing, tracking a specific measure, resolved itself into something Mel recognized: a woman calculating what her child was worth.

She left the canned goods at the office and drove on.

The Sunflower Cafe had two men from the chess club in the corner booth. She stopped for coffee and sat at the counter where she could hear without leaning in.

They were talking about David Cheswick.

"His record-keeping was better than the committee's," one said. The tone of someone describing a grievance they'd heard many times and come to believe entirely. "Every move documented. Every judge's note. He had the whole state championship in a binder, annotated. He could prove Bernie cheated."

"So why couldn't he get anyone to listen?"

"Because Bernie was Bernie. And because proving cheating in a chess tournament requires the tournament committee to cooperate, and the tournament committee was—" He moved his coffee cup. "Cooperative, in the other direction."

"He called Eleanor about it. For years."

"Eleanor knows what she knows."

"She protects what she protects."

A long silence.

"Should be something," the first man said finally, "seeing those two across a board again."

Mel paid her check. She drove past the Shady Lane Motor Court on her way out; the lot had grown since morning, ten or twelve cars now. Out-of-towners, chess people, the contingent from the county seat. She looked at the lot without quite knowing what she was looking for. Cheswick had confirmed. Cheswick wasn't here yet.

She drove toward Haven Terrace.

She hadn't planned to stop. She'd planned to drive past, confirm the address, file the geography, leave.

She parked at the curb outside Haven Terrace before she had quite decided to stop.

The October dark was complete by eight o'clock. The complex's exterior lights were amber and slightly insufficient, the kind of lighting that defined spaces without fully illuminating them.

She almost missed him because the dog moved first.

A small dog, black and white, moving at the end of a lead with the purposeful energy of an animal that takes its exercise seriously. Then the man: unhurried, coated against the cold, walking with his hands at his sides in the particular ease of someone for whom this is the most natural hour of the day. He came around the corner of the nearest building and turned onto the sidewalk that ran along the street where Mel's car waited.

She knew the face. Fourth row, planning commission chamber, watching Bernie Travers note the time.

She knew the name now. Gregory Dowen.

He walked without looking at anything in particular. Not at the cars, not at the lit windows of the complex, not at the street ahead of him with any obvious purpose. He was simply out with his dog in the evening, which was what people did. The dog moved ahead of him, nose sweeping left and right, cataloguing the October grass with the focus that dogs bring to smell.

At the sidewalk end, the dog paused. Its ears went up. It turned its nose toward Mel's car, directly and with the certainty of an animal that knows what it's detecting.

Dowen didn't follow the dog's gaze. His hands remained at his sides. He waited for the dog's survey to conclude, and then they turned onto the residential street running south along the complex, Aster Lane, an ordinary block of ordinary houses, the kind of street a man walks because it's his route, not because of anything that draws him there. They turned right at the corner and were gone.

Mel sat for a moment. A quiet man and his dog, out for an evening walk. She'd confirmed a face and learned that the animal was a Cavalier King Charles Spaniel, black and white with small orange markings at the brows, trim and alert and clearly accustomed to this particular walk.

She'd also learned that the morning walk went south on Aster Lane. She didn't know yet why that would matter.

She pulled away from the curb and drove home.

The rain came in the early hours of Friday morning, just as the forecast had promised.

Mel heard it start at three o'clock, a light tapping on the bedroom window that she registered in the half-sleep awareness of someone who has been waiting for something to begin. She got up and looked at the street. The maples were moving. The parking lot had gone dark and wet and reflective. The October air through the cracked window was colder than it had been and smelled of the season turning for good.

She stood at the window for a minute, hands on the sill.

Friday. The rain would soften the festival grounds, which was not ideal. The setup crew would lay down board runners. The chess pavilion would hold. The tournament had survived worse in its hundred years.

She thought about the master's table at the park's east end, its legs pressed into the aerated turf. About the cedar screen behind it, dark and dense, holding the line between the park and the meadow. About the glint of water she'd seen through the gap Wednesday afternoon, and Arthur's hives in their south-facing rows along the bank.

She thought about a woman in the back of a chess room watching her son's hands. She thought about a man who walked the same route every morning, early, while the grounds were still empty and the ground was still soft. She thought about Cheswick, somewhere between his confirmed hotel reservation and the tournament bracket, choosing whether to arrive.

None of it connected yet. She was watching separate things.

What she couldn't have said was that everything she'd observed since Monday was moving in one direction, patient as a chess player waiting for the board to open.

The rain was light and did not stop.

Saturday was two days away.

A Beautiful Fall Day

The park had become what it had been promising to become all week.

Mel parked at the north entrance Friday morning and stood for a moment before getting out of her truck, taking in the transformation. The white pavilions shown in the morning light, their canvas sides tied back to let the October air through. Harvest decorations, dried corn and woven wheat bundles and the particular autumn orange that Possum Gap did well — ran along the fence lines and the vendor stalls. The chess tables stood in precise lines, ready for the mock military campaigns. Additions stood on each table, as Eleanor's centennial demanded: nameplates, scorebooks, the ceremonial clock at the master's table. Three TV camera crews from the county news station were running cables across the grass.

Eleanor met her at the gate with a clipboard and the look of someone who had slept well for the first time in weeks.

"The centennial banner needs repositioning by two feet," she said. "The camera angle is wrong. And someone needs to tell the honey stand to move six inches south so the afternoon light doesn't glare off the jars."

"Good morning to you too."

Eleanor's mouth did something that was almost a smile. "Good morning." She looked at the park with open satisfaction. "Isn't it wonderful."

It was. Mel had lived in Possum Gap for four years and she'd been to the Fall Festival every one of them, but she hadn't understood until this moment that Eleanor had been building toward something, that the centennial was the point toward which three years of careful work had aimed. The park looked like a place that knew what it was for.

She found Arthur at his honey stand before she went to do Eleanor's centering work. He had arrived early; his table dressed with a burlap runner, a chalkboard sign he'd lettered himself, and six varieties of honey arranged in a careful gradient from lightest to darkest. Spring clover at the left, winter wildflower at the right, and in the center a small reserved sign over four jars labeled late-season aster, this harvest only.

He was adjusting the sign's angle when she came up. His hands were completely steady. His color was better than it had been Monday.

"Good morning," she said.

"Good morning." He stepped back from the table and looked at it the way a painter steps back from a canvas. "What do you think?"

"I think you should charge more."

He laughed, the full one, the one that went all the way through him. "The aster honey is twenty-two dollars a jar. My wife would have said I've lost my mind. She'd also have said she was right."

They talked for a few minutes about the morning's setup and the expected turnout. She watched him while they talked: his ease with the jars, his satisfaction with the arrangement, the way he touched each label once as if confirming the honey was real. Whatever was wrong with him, this morning it wasn't visible. This morning he was simply Arthur Pumble at his honey stand in October, which was one of the things he was most entirely himself doing.

The festival setup continued around them in the organized chaos of community effort. Mayor Coldwell moved through the grounds with two aides and a practiced expression of civic pride. The TV crew repositioned a light stand, briefly losing power, fixing it on the third try. Two chess officials had a disagreement about whether the master's table needed a second microphone; they resolved it in eight minutes, which was efficient.

Bernie Travers arrived at eleven.

He came with a small group, two members of the tournament committee, someone with a tablet, someone with a camera, and moved through the setup with the energy of a man for whom this event was a personal production. He conferred with the TV crew. He approved the table positions. He reviewed the bracket display board, made two adjustments, and stepped back satisfied. He said something to a passing vendor that made the vendor laugh.

From across the park, in the ordinary commotion of festival morning, he was impressive. The thought came to Mel unbidden and she noted it: this was how he operated. Full competence, full charm, the cruelty stored for private use.

She turned back toward Eleanor's centering task and didn't look at him again.

The volunteer coordination table was near the east pavilion, and by two o'clock on Friday afternoon it had become a minor social hub, people stopping to check their assignments, pick up name badges, return clipboards, ask where they were supposed to be. Mel had been there three times already with various Eleanor-related errands, which is how she came to be reaching for the sign-in clipboard at exactly the moment someone else reached it from the other side.

"Sorry —"

"No, go ahead —"

They both stopped. The clipboard sat between them on the table.

He was tall, which she noted peripherally, and he was looking at her with the attention of someone whose default mode was presence rather than distraction. Sandy brown hair, a watch that was old money rather than new, the relaxed posture of someone who had made peace with taking up space. The handshake he offered was reflex, not performed, just what his hand did when it was near another hand.

"Tim Renshaw."

"Mel Hunter." She took the clipboard.

"The Giving Spoon," he said. Not a question — a recognition, warm and specific.

"You know it?"

"I handle the finances for two of your donor organizations." He said the name of his business without emphasis. "Your quarterly reports come through my office. They're very thorough."

"More so than the county requires."

"I noticed that quite specifically." The corner of his mouth moved. "It's unusual. Most nonprofits do the minimum documentation the regulations require and call it good. Your records show you are someone who actually cares about what happens."

"Someone does. Someone needs to."

She was signing in as a festival volunteer; he was doing the same. His assignment showed the spectator seating area near the chess pavilion, something his family had probably underwritten at some point, she thought, and then thought it wasn't her most charitable observation about a man she'd known for approximately ninety seconds.

"You follow the chess circuit?" she asked.

"Poorly and with enthusiasm." He accepted the clipboard back from her and wrote his name in a clear, decisive hand. "I played in college. The key word there is 'played.' I use it generously. I can move the pieces correctly and explain the rules to a patient audience. Beyond that it gets complicated." A slight pause. "My father followed the tournaments for twenty years. I kept the habit."

"Your father was involved?"

"Attended, mostly. He thought civic participation was a form of gratitude." Something in the sentence was past tense in a way that ended that line, and he moved past it without making a production of it. "He would have appreciated this centennial. Eleanor's done something real here."

"She has."

They were both holding clipboards, which meant neither of them had a natural reason to move. The afternoon light came through the pavilion canvas at a long October angle, the kind that is generous without being dramatic. Twenty feet away someone was adjusting the centennial banner's left edge for the fifth time.

He asked about the Giving Spoon's information table near the main entrance. She explained what they were distributing: programs for the region's food bank network, information about the pantry's monthly schedule, a sign-up sheet for the Community Table. He listened while she spoke in the way that she had noticed in people occasionally: without the slight interior lean that meant someone was waiting for their turn to speak. He was simply present to what she was saying, his hazel eyes on her face, and when she finished he asked a specific follow-up question that proved he'd heard the specific thing rather than the general shape of it.

She became aware that she was noticing this.

"The information table is usually Noreen's project," she said. "She's traveling."

"Is she back for Saturday?"

"Sunday." Mel looked at her clipboard. "Leo and I are managing it today."

"Leo Cortez," he said. "Culinary school bound, I think I remember correctly."

"He confirmed this week."

"Good for him." He said it with the genuine quality of someone who had no stake in the matter but found it genuinely pleasing. "Good for you, too, for not talking him out of it." Something in the sentence suggested he knew more about the Giving Spoon's situation than a casual acquaintance would; the donor organizations, their quarterly conversations about the pantry's finances. She found she didn't mind.

"I should get back to Eleanor," she said.

"Of course." He stepped back from the table, giving her the natural exit. "It was good to meet you, Ms. Hunter."

"Mel." She said it without deciding to.

He nodded once. "Mel."

She turned toward Eleanor's area and walked back through the festival afternoon. She was halfway across the park before she realized she'd said his name in her head. Tim. Just once, not attached to anything particular. Then she was back at Eleanor's side and there were fourteen things that needed doing.

She was moving toward the Giving Spoon's information table at three-thirty when she became aware of Bernie Travers moving in the same direction from a different angle.

He reached her position first by several steps, not accidentally, she thought later. He had good spatial awareness, the quality of a man who always knew where other people were in a room.

"Ms. Hunter." He stopped at the right distance. Close enough for conversation, far enough for propriety. "I'm glad to have a chance to speak to you today."

"Mr. Travers."

"I wanted to say, regarding Tuesday's planning commission meeting —" He paused in the way of someone who has planned a sentence carefully. "I hope you understand that my objection to the Cochran Street proposal was purely procedural. The garden itself is an excellent idea. The county should absolutely expand community agriculture access. I'm a strong supporter of the principle."

"Of course," Mel said.

"It's the documentation that matters. The commission can only act on accurate information. A petition with inaccurate signatures creates legal exposure for everyone involved." His expression was thoughtful, even regretful. "Ms. Philpott's proposal will be better for the review. Stronger."

"I'm sure it will be."

He looked at her for a moment in the way he'd looked at her at the planning commission, the assessing, cataloguing quality she'd noticed on Tuesday. He did it openly, which was its own kind of message.

"You were at the commission meeting. I don't often see Giving Spoon staff at civic planning sessions."

"I find it useful to know what's being planned."

Something moved in his expression, not quite approval, not quite surprise, something in between. "So do I." He offered his hand again. "I hope the festival goes well for you. The pantry's information table is an excellent community resource."

She shook his hand. His grip was the same as Tuesday: correct, released at exactly the right moment.

She watched him walk away. He did not look back.

What she felt, standing in the October afternoon with the festival running its cheerful noise around her, was the specific cold of suffering a review twice now by the same person. On Tuesday, in a planning commission chamber. Today, in a park, in public, with a hundred people around.

He had come to her this time. She hadn't decided yet what that meant.

She went back to the information table and told Leo, who was managing it, that she needed five minutes. She walked to the east edge of the park and stood with her back to the cedar screen and looked at the master's table under the pavilion canvas and breathed the October air until the cold feeling settled.

Then she went back to work.

By mid-afternoon the tournament registration desk had the low-grade tension of people managing a problem they didn't know how to name.

David Cheswick's nameplate sat at the masters' bracket table. His hotel had confirmed his Thursday check-in. He had paid his entry fee two months ago. His name was in the centennial program, in the full biography Eleanor had written from his competitive record, his wins, his style, the state championship twenty years ago that everyone in the chess world knew about and the tournament record reflected ambiguously.

He was not here.

Mel found Bruce Parmalee at the side of the registration tent, in conversation with two older men she didn't know, visiting players from the county seat and the university club, men who'd been coming to Possum Gap for the tournament for decades.

"He always comes Thursday," the taller visitor was saying. "In thirty years I've never seen him arrive after Thursday evening. He likes to settle in."

"He settled in Thursday," Bruce said. "He checked in. Someone from the hotel saw his car in the lot Thursday evening. That's all anyone's seen."

"Did someone call the room?"

"Multiple times. Nothing."

A silence.

"He does this," the second visitor said finally. His voice was neutral, reportorial. "He works himself up to attending and then can't make himself walk in. Coming here means seeing Bernie across a board again. Means everyone knowing what happened. He might have decided he couldn't face it."

"He's not a coward," the taller man said sharply.

"I didn't say coward. I said it might not feel worth it." A pause. "Bernie has a talent for making enemies and David just can't let it go the way others have."

Others have. Mel filed the word.

Eleanor arrived, moving efficiently through the registration area. She passed the conversation and slowed at the name.

"David has called the Historical Society a number of times over the years," she said. Her voice was careful in the specific way it had been on Wednesday at the archive room. "He was interested in tournament historical documentation. Particularly the state championship records."

Bruce: "What did you tell him?"

"That the records exist. That we maintain them. That historical documentation has protocols for access." She moved on before the next question could form.

The taller visitor watched her go. "Eleanor knows things she's not saying."

"That's not news," Bruce said.

Mel thought about the archive boxes Eleanor had been moving on Wednesday. She thought about the photograph from 1976. She thought about what happened at a state championship twenty years ago, and who the officiating arbiter had been, and whose files might document what actually happened.

"His history with Bernie," she said to Bruce, after the two visitors moved toward the bracket board. "The state championship. What exactly happened?"

Bruce looked at her with the expression of someone deciding how much to say. "Bernie won on a technicality that David has never accepted. The arbiter had declared that Davig had followed the wrong clock procedure. Or so David says. The ruling arbiter was someone with existing ties to Bernie's organization." He was quiet for a moment. "David is not an easy man. The grievance has not improved his personality. But he is also not wrong: What happened at that championship was not clean."

She drove past the Shady Lane Motor Court on her way back across the grounds. The parking lot had grown since morning, with all the out-of-towners arriving for Saturday. Cheswick's rental car was still in the same spot it had occupied Thursday night. She recognized it by position and by the empty quality of a car that belonged to someone who hadn't been back to it.

The car was there. Cheswick was not.

The vendors had begun to close by five o'clock, folding their displays back into boxes and bags, the park gradually quieting from the organized optimism of the afternoon into the still expectancy of the evening before. The TV crew broke down their rehearsal setup and left. The tournament committee did a final walk-through and declared themselves satisfied.

The park at dusk was a different thing from the park at noon. The crowd noise was gone and the October evening came in: cooler, quieter, smelling of leaf fall and the cedar screen along the east boundary. The white pavilion canvas moved in the evening breeze. The harvest decorations held their color in the last light: orange and rust and brown, a season at its peak. The day they would all remember that something dramatic happened here.

Eleanor found Mel near the registration tent as the light was going.

"Good?" Mel asked.

Eleanor looked at her park: the placement of everything, the hundred small decisions of three years' work assembled and complete, and nodded. "Good." She said it quietly, with the satisfaction of someone who knows the word is sufficient.

"You did something real here," Mel said.

Eleanor touched her arm briefly. "Thank you for being part of it." Then she went to find her car.

Mel made her way slowly toward the north lot, stopping at Arthur's stand where he was boxing up the reserved honey, the four jars of late-season aster that had been under the sign all day.

"Good sales?" she asked.

"Sold out of everything except these." He touched the sign and then began carefully lifting jars into a box he'd lined with an old towel. "I'm taking these home. They're for specific people."

He reached under the table and produced a jar wrapped in brown paper.

"Late-season wildflower," he said. "I set it aside this morning. I was going to give it to you then and forgot in all the setup." He held it out. "For a good neighbor."

The jar was still slightly warm from the afternoon sun. She held it with both hands.

"Thank you, Arthur."

He waved the thanks away; the embarrassed wave of a man who means a gesture and finds gratitude for it beside the point. He picked up his box with careful deliberateness and made two trips to his truck: the box, then a small cooler, then the chalkboard sign wrapped in a moving blanket. Each trip planned out, each movement deliberate. She watched him without being obvious about it, this man who had agreed to be at his best today, and had succeeded.

He raised a hand as he drove out. She raised hers back.

She stood alone in the park for a moment. The last of the evening light was orange-red in the maple canopy. White cloths covered the chess tables for the night. The master's table stood at the eastern edge of the pavilion, facing the cedar screen, Bernie Travers's nameplate still in place beneath its cloth.

Something made her look east. Not a sound, just the pull of the direction, the habit she seemed to be building all week. The cedar screen was dark against the sky, the gap where she and Arthur had stood on Wednesday barely visible at this distance. She looked at the tree line, at the particular density of it, at the way it held the park on one side and whatever was beyond it on the other.

Nothing there. October evening. The bees in their south-facing rows a quarter mile away, settling in for the night.

She turned toward her truck.

Tim Renshaw's name moved through her mind on the north path — just the name, easy and unasked-for — and she let it go before she reached the gate.

The honey jar went in the cupholder beside her.

She drove out of the park and through the residential blocks and past the turnoff to Arthur's place, which she didn't take. The maples were nearly bare and the October night was clear and cold and the forecast said clear for Saturday, all day.

Tomorrow was the festival.

It would be a good one.

Dead to Rites

The Fall Festival arrived on a Saturday that Possum Gap had ordered from the universe specifically for this purpose.

The sky was clear and hard and October-blue above the pavilion canvas. The maples at the park's edges were at their peak, orange and crimson and gold, the specific extravagance of a Tennessee October before the cold makes everything sensible. By nine o'clock the grounds held a steady crowd moving through vendor stalls that smelled of kettle corn and cider and the last harvest of the year. Eleanor's Historical Society booth near the registration tent had the longest line.

Mel came with Leo. He had a camera because Eleanor had asked him to photograph the Giving Spoon's information table for the annual report. He took it as an opportunity to document everything else too. He moved through the crowd with the focused energy of someone trying to look at everything before it ended. Mel understood this. She was doing the same thing.

Corbin stood near the youth division boards at ten o'clock, watching something with the expression that passed for a smile on a man who didn't smile publicly. She followed his sight line to a girl of about eleven who was completely destroying her opponent with the focused calm of someone who had been doing this for years. His daughter, she guessed. He looked like a man proud of something he hadn't made and couldn't take credit for.

Agnes Moskov was in the spectator area with her hands wrapped around the rail. Derek started at a board in the youth section; the arbiter moved him up to fill a late withdrawal in the open section. He played with his back very straight, his notation quick and precise.

Gregory Dowen was on a bench near the east side of the pavilion, a book open on his knee. His eyes moved between the page and the activity around the master's table at intervals too regular to be casual.

Arthur was at his honey stand. His hands were trembling today.

Not badly. A fine tremor, the kind that came from fatigue or pain managed at the edge of its tolerance. He had it controlled; anyone passing quickly would miss it. Mel saw it because she was looking for it after Friday's good day, the way you look for the return of something you'd briefly stopped expecting.

She walked toward the chess pavilion with a stack of centennial programs Eleanor had given her. The festival ground was soft here, close to the cedar screen; the Thursday rain had done its work and the turf hadn't fully recovered. She slowed as she passed the master's table, already dressed for the afternoon match: the ceremonial clock, the felt-lined box for the white queen, Bernie Travers's nameplate at the champion's seat.

The ground beside the table had small, neat prints in the soft earth, a dog's, certainly, too small for a retriever. She glanced at them without quite stopping. One set of prints was odd: a paw impression showed five toe-pad marks instead of four. She looked at it for a moment: the extra mark, the asymmetry; and then moved on. Dogs everywhere at a festival.

Halfway across the pavilion she noticed a faint smell, sweet and floral and chemical, like something between perfume and a garden product. She attributed it to one of the vendor stalls. She kept walking.

At the registration tent, Tim Renshaw was helping reposition a sponsor banner. He saw her across twenty feet of crowd and nodded once, warm and brief. She nodded back. Leo, at her shoulder, made a small noting sound.

"Who's that?" he asked.

"Insurance," she said.

"Of course."

Arthur's honey stand was doing good business by mid-morning. The late-season aster had moved out by eleven; the spring clover was half gone. He worked the table with his left hand mostly, keeping the right one in his pocket when he wasn't using it.

She bought a jar of summer wildflower she didn't need and stayed.

"Good morning," he said. "You didn't have to—"

"I wanted the wildflower. The summer kind."

He found her one that satisfied him. While he wrapped it he talked, the way Arthur talked: continuously, cheerfully, with the occasional detour into something serious before returning to cheerful without announcement.

"Forty years of keeping bees, and every harvest still surprises me," he said, holding a jar of the late-season aster to the light before boxing it. "Might be the last time I get to say that."

"Because of the legal situation?"

His smile stayed in place, but something behind it did a different calculation. "Bernie's lawyers sent another letter Wednesday. They want to know if I'm prepared to negotiate relocation terms." He set the jar down with care. "There's nothing to negotiate. There's nowhere to go. The forage here is what makes the honey worth anything — the late asters along the creek, the clover fields north of town. You move the hives to a different soil profile, a different flowering calendar, and you get different honey. It wouldn't be mine."

"What happens if they force relocation?"

He was quiet for a moment. A couple came to the table; he served them with the full warmth of a man who was not having this conversation, and then they left and he was again.

"Some fights you lose before they start," he said. "I've been in this one long enough to know what it is."

Mel looked at his hands. The right was out of his pocket now, steadied against the table's edge.

“I’m going to help,” she said. She said it without knowing exactly how she meant it. Just that she did.

Arthur looked at her for a long moment with the expression he used when he knew someone meant something and was deciding whether to receive it. “Thank you, Mel,” he said finally. Accepting it. Which was harder for him than dismissing it.

He sold another jar. She carried hers toward the pavilion and thought about Bernie Travers’s lawyers and the words *relocation terms* and the particular way Arthur had said *the forage here is what makes the honey worth anything.* As if the place and the thing were inseparable. As if moving one was the same as destroying the other.

At twelve-thirty, Eleanor’s voice came over the festival’s sound system.

“We have an administrative matter to address regarding the masters’ bracket. David Cheswick, registered challenger, has not presented for the tournament. Per tournament bylaws, the defending champion may demand a substitute challenger or accept a forfeit.”

The chess community’s reaction was immediate and recognizable, the compressed murmur of people who knew exactly what this situation meant and had several opinions about it.

Bernie Travers, standing near the master’s table, spoke without raising his voice, and somehow the crowd made space for the words anyway: “We’ll play. The tournament committee will identify a suitable substitute.”

He said *suitable* the way a man says a word when he’s already decided its contents.

The committee deliberated for nine minutes. The substitute produced was Derek Moskov, the youth division’s strongest player, already on the grounds, seventeen years old and ranked high enough that the bylaws permitted it under the centennial’s exhibition rules. Eleanor made the announcement with the careful neutrality of someone managing a decision they had not made.

Agnes Moskov's grip on the spectator rail whitened at the knuckles. Derek, when told, gave no visible reaction. He simply closed his game notebook, rose from his seat, and walked toward the master's table. He had the posture of someone who had been performing other people's expectations for long enough that the performance had become indistinguishable from his gait.

On the bench across the pavilion, Gregory Dowen's book closed.

He didn't mark his page. He set the book on the bench beside him and rested his hands flat on his knees, and he watched the activity around the master's table with the quality of a man watching something he has been expecting. Not surprise. Not satisfaction. Something more precise than either: the patient attention of someone who has arranged a situation and is now observing its first movement. His breathing was steady. His posture was easy. He looked like a man at rest, except that men at rest don't watch things quite that carefully.

Mel was standing thirty feet away and she saw this. She didn't know what she was seeing, really.

Bernie settled into the champion's chair with the ease of a man at home. He opened the felt-lined box and removed the white queen, ivory, old, larger than the playing pieces, the ceremonial piece that held the rites of every opening match since 1935. He cupped it in both hands, breathed on the carved surface, and polished it with the chamois cloth from his jacket pocket. Slow circles. The piece held to the light, examined, polished again. He transferred it from hand to hand, rubbing the cloth across his palms, and set the queen on the board at its opening square with the precise deliberateness of a man performing a rite he has performed a hundred times.

Mel was close enough now that she could smell it: the sweet floral-chemical smell from the morning, stronger here, associated now with the master's table and the afternoon light over the pavilion. She couldn't isolate it. She didn't try. Fall flowers, she thought.

Derek sat down across the champion and moved his opening pawn.

For the first forty-five minutes, Derek held.

He played the Sicilian Defense — the choice of someone who has studied their opponent carefully and committed to making him work for every exchange. Bernie won material steadily but not easily; Derek was precise and fast, his notations clean and his expressions neutral. He played chess the way he'd played it in the demonstration Thursday night: with technical certainty, without visible joy. The crowd settled into the respectful quiet of people observing something real.

What was real: at seventeen, against a player who had held a regional title for eleven years, Derek Moskov was making him work. The chess community around the pavilion realized this with the specific language of their world: slight forward leans, quiet notations of their own, the occasional murmur of something respected. He was good. Even the people who knew nothing about the game could see that he was good.

Bernie saw it too. His commentary began in the second hour.

It was not loud. That was the first thing Mel noticed; the cruelty operated at a conversational level, as if what he was saying was simply chess analysis. "Interesting choice," when Derek played his knight. "I might have done that differently at your age. But then, at your age I had better coaching." A pause. "Your mother must have high hopes."

Silence.

"She's watching?" Bernie glanced toward Agnes without seeming to look. "How encouraging."

The crowd's quality of attention changed. The respectful quiet became the uncomfortable quiet of people witnessing something they couldn't stop. Mayor Coldwell shifted in her seat. Corbin, at the pavilion's edge, frowned at his clipboard.

Derek's notation hand paused for exactly one second. Then he wrote his next move.

"Brave," Bernie said.

Agnes's knuckles were white on the rail. Derek played on — correctly, methodically, without looking up.

Bernie took the initiative in the third hour and drove the middle game with the efficiency of a man for whom this was maintenance, not effort. He made observations as he played, always about chess, always accurate, always with the specific edge of a man who understood exactly how to make a technical observation land as an insult.

At two-fifty he leaned forward in the champion's chair and reached for the white queen, his palms closing around the carved piece.

"Your mother must be so proud," he said. Just the one sentence, quiet, precise, the way a scalpel is precise.

Derek Moskov's eyes filled.

He didn't make a sound. His face stayed composed — the composed face of someone who has had a great deal of practice — and two tears ran straight down and he wrote his notation in the same clean hand he'd been using for two hours. The crowd held very still.

Mel, standing at the pavilion edge, heard something begin.

A sound from the direction of the cedar screen. Low, harmonic, the sound of a great number of small things moving together with direction and purpose. She turned toward it without knowing why.

Three things happened at once, which is not how it seemed afterward.

The hum became a roar.

The swarm crossed the cedar screen in a mass that moved the way fast weather moves, low and directed, with the focused coherence of something that knows exactly where it is going. People near the east edge of the pavilion scattered and the crowd noise changed from ambient to urgent. Mel heard Leo say her name.

Bernie Travers looked up from the chess board.

The swarm arrived.

It did not attack the crowd. It did not sting the people running past it or the chess officials diving for cover or Agnes Moskov throwing herself in front of Derek as he pushed back from the table. It moved through the crowd without touching it, through the gap and chaos of a hundred people in sudden motion, and it arrived at Bernie Travers with the specificity of a thing guided.

Mel smelled the sweet chemical smell suddenly and intensely, present and close and completely without context, and then the sound was everywhere and she was backing away without deciding to back away and Leo's hand was on her arm.

Arthur Pumble rose from behind his honey stand. His hands came up halfway. An instinctive gesture, the beekeeper's gesture, the motion of someone who has spent forty years communicating with colonies through breath and stillness and the slow translation of their language. His hands came up halfway as if to call them back. Then they dropped to his sides.

He stood very still and watched. The bees did not touch him. They moved past him without deviation, without interest, and they hit Bernie Travers the way water hits the lowest point of a drain — with the indifference of physics, with the inevitability of something that has found exactly what it is looking for.

Corbin's voice over the chaos — not a bellow, something more effective than a bellow, the voice of professional authority: move back, move away from the stand, give them room to disperse. He was already moving through the crowd, creating space, which was the right instinct and too late to help.

Ninety seconds. The swarm dispersed back toward the cedar screen in the same directed fashion it had arrived, following a geometry that had nothing to do with random flight. It crossed the tree line and was gone.

Bernie Travers was on the grass beside the master's table. His right hand grasped a white queen.

Dowen was not at his bench. He was twelve feet away, standing at the pavilion's edge in the afternoon light. He had risen from his bench and stepped back; not run, not hidden, just stepped back in a slow, deliberate movement while everyone else was moving fast. His face held an expression Mel would not be able to name until much later. A man waiting.

She did not consciously notice this. She realized it later, in pieces, the way you surface details you had no reason to notice at the time and every reason to remember afterward. The moment passed.

The EMTs arrived in eleven minutes. They were professional and swift and there was nothing for them to do.

Corbin was already running yellow tape when they confirmed what the crowd already knew. He did it while following a system: tent stakes in the soft ground, the tape running at the correct distance from the master's table and expanding outward to include the full perimeter of the immediate scene. His hands did not shake. His voice was level on the radio. He was doing his job well, which was what he always did, and it was the right thing to do.

Mel and Leo were on a bench near the registration tent. Eleanor sat beside them, her centennial program clutched in both hands. She had not said anything in forty minutes. The centennial program's cover showed two chess pieces, a king and a queen, and Eleanor's careful annotation of the tournament's hundred-year history inside. Mel didn't look at it. She looked at the yellow tape and the activity beyond it.

The grounds had cleared the way festival grounds clear when something has gone wrong: the vendors quiet, the crowd held at the perimeter by equal parts Corbin's instructions and their own uncertainty about what to do next. Someone was weeping audibly somewhere behind them. A child, separated from a parent briefly and reunited; still stood together near the gate with the stillness of the recently frightened.

Arthur Pumble was near his honey stand. The swarm's passage had knocked two jars from his table; they'd broken on the hard-packed earth at the stand's edge, and the bees that were always around his inventory were working the spilled honey with the indifferent efficiency of creatures that do not understand tragedy. He stood beside this and did not look at it. He looked at the yellow tape and the covered table beyond it and did not move.

The officer keeping the perimeter didn't let Mel cross to him. She stood at the tape and Arthur looked up across the distance and they held the look for a moment before an EMT moved between them.

Corbin completed his perimeter at the master's table. He crouched for a moment at the table's edge, looking at the ground — the soft earth, the prints she'd noticed this morning. He wrote something in his notebook.

"Animal tracks consistent with small domestic dog, proximate to master's table," she heard him tell the young officer. "Festival attendees with pets present throughout setup. Note it and move on."

The officer noted it. He moved on.

They sat in Leo's truck for forty minutes while authorities processed the scene.

Leo didn't speak for most of it. He was looking at the back of his hand, which had gotten tangled in a vendor's rope during the scatter and was slightly abraded. He kept looking at it with the focus of someone working through a problem.

"It didn't sting anyone else," he said finally.

"There are stings," Mel said. "I heard they're treating a few people at the first aid tent."

"Not from the main swarm. From the edges, the disruption — people stepping on them, probably, during the scatter." He was still looking at his hand. "The main swarm hit one person. One specific person. In a crowd of a hundred."

Mel said nothing. He was working through something and he needed to work through it.

"Swarms don't target. They defend, or they follow the queen's chemical signals, or they disorient and sting generally in a defensive zone. What just happened —" He turned his hand over. "That swarm crossed a cedar windbreak and a quarter mile of meadow and moved through a crowd of people and stung one of them. Specifically. While ignoring everyone standing next to him."

Corbin knocked on the passenger window. Leo rolled it down.

"I'll need formal statements tomorrow," Corbin said. He said it with the professional economy of a man who had done this before. "For now — what you saw, where you were standing. We have your contact information." He looked at them both. "It was a tragedy. The festival must be suspended, maybe canceled. We'll have answers shortly."

"What kind of answers?" Mel asked.

"The kind that explain what the hive was doing. It's unusual behavior, but noise and movement can agitate bees near large crowds. We'll have the apiary assessed." He was already stepping back from the window. "Thank you both for staying."

He walked back toward the master's table.

Leo was quiet for a moment. He turned his hand over one more time, then put it in his lap.

"And Arthur," he said. "Did you see him? During the attack. He raised his hands."

"I saw."

"Like he was calling them. And then he stopped."

Mel thought about Arthur's face during the thirty seconds the swarm was present. The grief in it. Not guilt — grief. The specific grief of a man watching his life's work do something he knew was wrong.

Leo watched him go. "He's wrong," he said. Not accusing — observational, the voice he used for chemistry problems he hadn't yet solved.

"Yeah," Mel said. "I think he is."

She pulled out of the parking lot twenty minutes later. The yellow tape was still going up as she drove past the park entrance. In the rearview mirror: the cedar screen dark against the sky, the pavilion with its covered chess tables, the honey stand with its spilled jars. Arthur Pumble was still beside his stand, looking up at the sky where the swarm had gone, his hands at his sides.

Three days to prove his bees were innocent.

She didn't know that yet. She was three days away from knowing it.

She drove toward home through the stripped October maples, the festival honey jar in the cupholder beside her, and she thought about what Leo had said.

That swarm crossed a cedar windbreak and a quarter mile of meadow and moved through a crowd of people and stung one of them.

One particular person.

An Early Arrest

Monday came in gray and stayed that way.

Mel had the coffee going early and the biscuits in by quarter to eight, and the small machine of the morning ran the way it always ran. Her hands knew the work. The rest of her was somewhere behind her hands, catching up.

The Giving Spoon's Monday crowd was usually a dependable dozen by eight-fifteen. Today it was four. Mrs. O'Keefe came in with her canvas bags and took her usual two minutes deciding between the canned peaches and the canned pears, and took both, which she never did, and didn't joke about it, which she always did. At the corner table two men from the feed store sat over coffee with their caps still on, talking in the low tone the whole town had been using since Saturday. Somebody had left a supermarket flower arrangement on the front counter overnight, carnations and a ribbon, with a card reading FOR THE TOWN in ballpoint capitals. Nobody knew what to do with it. Mel had moved it twice and put it back twice.

Bernie Travers had been dead not quite two days, and Possum Gap was conducting its grief the way it conducted everything, at the feed store and the church and the counter of her pantry, in voices that dropped when the door opened.

Leo was at the prep station with the cutting board and the morning's onions, and beside the cutting board, open and face up, a textbook. Thick, used, the spine cracked white. He hadn't said anything about it. He read while he worked, a paragraph at a glance between cuts, and his knife never slowed. Mel watched him do it for a moment and decided she wasn't ready to ask. Whatever he was building in there, he would bring it to her when it held weight.

Mrs. O'Keefe paused at the counter on her way out, bags loaded. "You heard, I suppose." She said it kindly. She said everything kindly. "They took Arthur in. That's what they're saying at Hutchins'. Took him in last night, and charging him today."

"They're saying a lot of things at Hutchins'," Mel said. "Arthur didn't do anything."

"Well." Mrs. O'Keefe adjusted her grip on the bags. "I hope you're right, honey. He's a good man."

"I'm right."

It came out with more iron than she'd intended, and Mrs. O'Keefe smiled a little, the way you smile at confidence you'd like to borrow, and pushed out into the gray morning.

Outside, a car door slammed. Then a taxi trunk slammed, unmistakably a taxi trunk, and a voice Mel knew, thanking somebody at an unhurried length.

Noreen came through the door towing a carry-on with one bad wheel, wearing a tan she had not left with and the expression of a woman sixty minutes off a regional flight and already composing the account of it.

"I want it noted," she said, by way of hello, "that the Chattanooga airport confiscated my guava jam at security and waved through the man ahead of me carrying what I can only describe as a machete in a golf bag. Eleven days I'm gone. I have thoughts about the jerk chicken at a place called Miss Verna's that I intend to share at length, because I took notes, actual notes, and the short version is that everything I have ever cooked is an apology. So I'll need coffee, and I'll need to know why Royce at the taxi stand looked at me like I'd come home for a funeral, and—"

She stopped. Mid-sentence, one hand still on the carry-on handle.

She looked at the men in their caps at the corner table. At the carnations with their ballpoint card. At Leo, who had set down his knife. Then at Mel.

"Mel," she said, in a different voice. "Whose funeral did I come home for?"

Mel gave her the short version. Saturday, the festival, the masters' match. The swarm that came over the cedar screen and went through a hundred people to reach one. Bernie Travers dead on the grass with the white queen still in his hand. And the thing Mrs. O'Keefe had carried in from Hutchins' this morning: Arthur, taken in.

Noreen listened the way she did, perfectly still, her eyes narrowed behind the dark-rimmed glasses, absorbing it with the focused intensity she usually reserved for cataloging rare books. When Mel finished she was quiet for a moment.

"Three questions," she said. "Who found him first? Has anybody talked to the beekeepers, the association people, anyone who actually knows what a swarm does and doesn't do? And what does Corbin think happened?"

"The whole pavilion found him at once. I don't know. I just don't know."

"That's a poor showing for two days." Noreen set the carry-on upright by the counter, parked it with a small precise motion, and unzipped the front pocket. "Well. We can't leave Arthur in a cell."

She didn't say it like a proposal. It came out like a fact about the week, the way you'd say the rain was supposed to start Thursday. And she meant *we*; the *we* included Mel as if it had never occurred to her that it might not.

From the front pocket she produced a package in parchment, dense and dark, and set it on the counter between them. "Black rum cake," she said. "From a woman in Ocho Rios who is now my correspondent for life. I bought it for the three of us, so I'm glad to see they didn't arrest anybody who works here."

Leo came around the prep station, wiping his hands. "Hi, Noreen."

"Leo." She looked at him, then at the textbook lying open by the cutting board, and did not ask. "You've gotten taller. It's rude."

It went the way it always went when the three of them stood in a room, and Mel watched it happen, and the morning loosened a notch. Leo carried the facts. Noreen carried the questions. The two of them had simply begun, without a vote, without waiting for her.

"The festival," Noreen said, pulling off her field jacket. "Before all this. Anything worth telling? You were dreading the information table."

"It was fine. Eleanor's booth did well. I met Tim Renshaw, he was helping with the banners." Mel turned for the coffee pot. "Arthur's lawyers got another letter Wednesday, that's the thing to focus on. The legal pressure was already at full."

Behind her, a silence happened.

She didn't have to turn around to know that Noreen had looked at Leo, and that Leo had looked back, and that they had conducted and filed an entire correspondence.

"Renshaw," Noreen said, unhurried. "Mm. We'll come back to that one."

Detective Corbin arrived at ten-thirty.

He came in the way he did everything, with economy, and stood at the counter with his hat in his hand rather than on the rack, which told Mel the visit had a fixed length before he opened his mouth. Noreen offered him coffee. He declined it politely and looked at the three of them and visibly decided that telling it once to all of them was the efficient version.

"Arthur Pumble was formally charged this morning," he said. "I wanted you to hear it from me and not from Hutchins."

The room did something. Mel set down the cloth she was holding.

"Charged with what, exactly," she said. It wasn't a question.

"You know with what." Corbin's voice stayed level. "I'm not going to argue the case at your counter, Ms. Hunter. But you'll hear it all anyway, so. Motive: Travers spent the better part of a year dismantling that man's livelihood, and Arthur's been telling people all fall that Bernie took everything worth having and couldn't take the bees too. His words. We have them more than once." He paused. "Method: they were his bees. Nobody in three counties knows them better, and nobody else could have made them do what two hundred people watched them do. Opportunity: he was forty feet from the table all day, and he was at that apiary alone Saturday evening when my people came out. It's a straightforward case. I'd be derelict if I didn't bring it."

"It's a bad case. Wrong," Mel said. "You stood there Saturday. You saw his face."

"I saw a man whose bees killed somebody."

"Detective." Leo had come forward, and his voice had the careful pace it got when he'd rehearsed something in his head against an imagined argument. "Swarms don't target. They defend a queen, or they defend a hive. What happened Saturday was a colony crossing open ground past a hundred people to reach one man. The only way that happens is a chemical signal. I talked to my father yesterday, he's a biochemist, he's worked with insect signalling. He says you can buy synthetic queen pheromone from research suppliers. Put it on an object and a colony will defend that object like it's the queen herself. Anyone could have done it. It didn't have to be the beekeeper. It only had to be somebody with a credit card and three weeks of reading."

Corbin listened all the way through, which Mel acknowledged to herself as a point in his favor, and then said: "Did your father examine these bees?"

"No, but—"

"Has anyone found this chemical on anything?"

Leo's jaw set. "Has anyone looked?"

"The state lab has what the county sent them. If there's something to find, they'll find it." Corbin turned his hat over once in his hands.

"It's a theory, son. It's not a bad one. Bring me a fact attached to it and I'll treat the fact with respect."

Mel tried her idea. "Have you thought about whose dog was near the tournament?"

Corbin sighed. "Dog? They were everywhere. Maybe a couple dozen. Not important.

Mel chose silence. She had no way to contradict him.

"The timeline, then," Noreen said. She had not raised her voice all morning and did not now. "Bernie handled every piece himself before the match. Polished them. He sat down at half past two, and the bees came at a quarter past three. If something was on that queen before the first move, your killer is Bernie's own ritual. If it got there during the game, your killer was in front of two hundred witnesses and you have a hundred photographs. Either way I'd want to know which before I charged an old man. That's not an opinion about Arthur. That's an opinion about sequence."

"And it's noted." Corbin said it without irony, which was somehow worse. "The case goes forward. I'm sorry. I know what he is to you, all three of you, and I'm sorry."

He put his hat on, which meant the visit had reached its fixed end, and moved for the door. With his hand on it he paused, half turning, a man remembering an errand.

"There's an emergency council session tonight. They're taking up what to do with the hives while this gets sorted." He said it the way he'd have mentioned a road closure on Route 9. "Thought you'd want to know."

The door closed behind him.

Nobody said anything. The coffee maker ticked. Out on the street a truck went by, and the carnations on the counter stood in their ribbon, for the town.

Mel washed the mixing bowl.

It didn't need washing. Her hands did it anyway, around and around under the warm water, and she stood at the sink with her back to the room and let the thing assemble itself in front of her.

Marisol Vega's strawberries set fruit in May because Arthur's hives worked her rows in April, and the difference between a good May and a bad one was whether Marisol's girls got school clothes that didn't come from the church box. The Hendersons' orchard. The clover fields north of town, leased for forage, money that went into pockets she could name. Honey jars at the farm stand and the Saturday market, eleven dollars at a time, in a town where eleven dollars was a tank of gas measured out to Friday. She stocked Arthur's honey on her own shelves and watched what people's faces did when they took a jar, because it wasn't charity if it came from up the road. It was the town feeding the town.

The twenty-second of November was nothing yet. She didn't know the date yet. What she knew was what it would take with it: if they destroyed those hives, it would not be a line item. It would come out of kitchens. It would come out of Marisol's rows and the orchard and the ledger at Hutchins' that nobody called a credit ledger. And Arthur would sit in the Redbud County jail while the county killed the only witnesses that couldn't lie, and a man who had done this thing, who had stood in a crowd and done it, would watch it happen and be safe.

She turned off the water.

Leo was sitting on the prep stool with the textbook closed under his flat palm, watching her. He'd been watching her think, she realized, for a while.

"I've been reading about synthetic pheromone lures," he said. "Since last night. Papá sent me three papers and a supplier catalog. I have a list of compounds."

That was all he said. That was Leo saying *I'm with you.*

Noreen didn't say anything at all. She took the spare apron off the hook by the walk-in, the one that had been Carol Anne's before Carol

Anne moved to Knoxville, and put it on, and tied it behind her back in a bow she didn't check.

That was Noreen saying *I'm with you.*

Mel dried her hands on the towel and hung it straight.

"I need to go see Arthur," she said.

The Possum Gap police station had converted its one holding cell into desk space years ago, a fact the town told on itself with some pride at council budget time. There had never been anyone to put in it. So anyone actually charged with something went to the county, and that was how Mel came to be sitting at two o'clock in the visiting room of the Redbud County Sheriff's holding facility, twenty minutes up the state route, in a building the color of weak tea.

It wasn't brutal. It was worse in a smaller way: it was bleak, rundown, and used to itself. Linoleum, a clock in a wire cage, a deputy who was perfectly kind and called her ma'am twice. They brought Arthur to a plastic chair across the table from her, no glass, no cuffs, just a county-issue shirt a size too big and a man inside it she almost didn't recognize.

At the apiary, Arthur was a fixed point the world organized itself around: the hives in their rows, the bees in their lanes, everything in relation to him. In the plastic chair he was a thin old man with a tremor in his right hand and nothing anywhere around him that was his.

"Mel." He tried to make it sound like a welcome. It came out like an apology.

"I'm looking into it," she said. "I want you to know that. Me, and Leo, and Noreen's back. We're going to find out what happened on Saturday, the actual thing that happened, and we're going to get you out of here."

Arthur looked at her, and for a moment she wasn't sure the words had landed anywhere. His eyes had a tired middle distance in them, and his right hand moved on the tabletop, slow circles of the thumb against the fingers. An old motion. It took her a second to place it: it was the motion of a man rolling a frame's wax foundation smooth, working a thing he wasn't holding.

"I'm too old to start over," he said. "Too sick."

He didn't explain the sick. The clock in its cage clicked.

"If they destroy that colony… I want you to understand something. Those bees have been with me for eleven years. I built every frame myself." He looked at the wall behind Mel's head. "Bernie took everything else from me, little by little. He just couldn't take that too."

His voice gave out on the last word. He didn't say what he would have done if Bernie had succeeded. He didn't have to.

Mel reached across the table and put her hand over his, over the slow circling thumb, and it went still under her palm. The deputy by the door looked at the ceiling with professional tact.

"That's not going to happen," she said. "None of it is going to happen. You hear me?"

"You always were sure of things." A ghost of the honey-stand warmth crossed his face and was gone. "It's a good quality. Don't spend it all on me."

On the drive back down the state route, the gray afternoon going to an early dusk over the stripped fields, she replayed it. *Too old to start over. Too sick. He just couldn't take that too.* A man measuring himself against what he had left to lose, and finding the arithmetic short. Grief, she thought. Exhaustion, and grief, and that terrible tenderness about the frames he'd built. Anyone could hear it.

She heard a man afraid of losing his life's work. She drove home sure of it, both hands on the wheel.

It did not occur to her, that afternoon, that there was a second way to hear it. That would come later, from a man with a level voice and a file folder, and when it came she would remember this room and this table and understand exactly what the true meaning was.

The council chamber smelled like radiator heat and old paper, and by the time the gavel came down it held more of Possum Gap than it had in years.

Mayor Patricia Coldwell ran the session from the center of the oak crescent with the brisk, careful neutrality of a woman who knew a packed room was a packed room of voters. Vince Abraham sat to her right, drumming his fingers. The secretary read the agenda item aloud: *public safety: disposition of the Pumble apiary pending resolution of legal proceedings*, which was a great many syllables, Mel thought, for *killing the bees.*

It went the way she'd been afraid it would. The word *menace* appeared from the floor. A man from the east side described his grandchildren's swing set in relation to the flight path with a cartographer's relish. Sheriff's counsel said the word *liability* four times. Somewhere in the third row a voice said what everyone was circling: nobody could feel safe with a hundred thousand of those things up there and their keeper in a county cell.

Mel stood up.

She had never once spoken at a council session. She knew it, the room knew it, and Coldwell's eyebrows accepted it even as the mayor recognized her with a courteous nod.

"Those hives are evidence," Mel said. Her voice came out steadier than the inside of her felt. "Whatever you believe happened Saturday, it's the subject of an open murder case, and those colonies are part of it. Destroy them and you've burned the evidence before anyone's read it. And separate from that, and I'd ask you to weigh this, the apiary pollinates half the growing operations on the east side of this county. Marisol Vega's berries. The Henderson orchard. That's not Arthur's livelihood, that's a dozen livelihoods, some of them at tables I feed. You're not voting on an insect problem. You're voting on whether this town eats a little worse next year to feel a little safer this month."

The room rustled. Coldwell let it settle.

"Ms. Hunter, thank you. The chair notes the concern." And the chair did, Mel could see it, noted and weighed and filed against fifty constituents with swing sets. "But the council is bound to respond to a demonstrated public-safety question. The motion before us sets a date certain, allowing time for the legal process Ms. Hunter describes to run its course."

The motion set the date certain at Wednesday, November 22. Resolved comfortably before Thanksgiving, Abraham observed, so folks could have their holiday with this behind them. It carried, four to one, the one being a councilwoman whose name Mel resolved to learn.

Outside on the steps the night had turned cold, the first hard cold of the season. Mel stood with her coat open and did the arithmetic the council had just handed her.

Three weeks. Twenty-three days to the twenty-second. Said out loud, in the radiator warmth of that chamber, it had sounded almost generous, time enough for the process, time enough for the truth, time enough. A date certain, far enough away that nobody had to feel like an executioner tonight.

Plenty of time. She buttoned her coat. Above the courthouse roof the sky was scoured and starless, and somewhere east of town, in their rows in the dark, a hundred thousand witnesses waited out the first night of the rest of their lives.

The Theory of Bees

The kettle-corn vendor remembered the smell of the day better than the order of it.

"Burnt sugar and rain coming," Paku Brownlie said, walking a folded table up the ramp of his trailer. Twenty-one years old and he ran the kettle rig like a man with a mortgage. "That's a Saturday I'd have called a good one, right up till it wasn't."

Mel stayed out of his path, hands in her coat pockets. Around them she saw Miller's Hollow Park taken apart a piece at a time. A county flatbed idled near the bandstand, two men in safety vests stacking folding tables on its bed, and tire ruts ran through the rain-soft grass in long brown curves. Someone had set a pumpkin on the bandstand rail for Halloween. Nobody had carved it, and nobody had come back for it. The town didn't have the heart this year, and the pumpkin sat there knowing it.

"You had a sightline to the chess pavilion," Mel said. "Your stand was, what, forty feet out?"

"Closer to fifty." He latched the trailer gate and gave the pavilion a look. The tent still stood, white and wrong, with yellow tape sagging between two garden stakes at its entrance. Two stakes and a prayer. That was the county's whole opinion of the ground in there. "I watched the crowd more than the chess, tell you the truth. Crowds buy when they're happy. They were happy right up to three o'clock."

"Anything before three? Anybody near the tables who didn't belong near them?"

"Ma'am, it was a festival. Everybody belonged everywhere." He scratched under his cap. "I remember a kid dropped a candy apple and cried like the world ended. I remember Eleanor Vance's banner come loose at one corner and a tall fella fixed it. The rest is just faces."

It was the fourth version of the same answer the morning had given her. Everyone had watched Saturday happen. No one had seen it.

Noreen stood at Mel's shoulder with a small reporter's notebook open against her palm, the spiral kind, half the pages already written in. She had produced it from her bag an hour ago without comment, the way another woman might produce reading glasses, and the sight of it raised a question Mel was saving for later. How long had Noreen owned a notebook like that, and what was in the front half?

They worked down the row of remaining vendors and got nothing better. At the end of the row, Arthur's honey stand stood exactly as he'd left it Saturday, jars in their ranks, the hand-lettered price card gone soft at the corners from two nights of dew. Neither of them said anything about it. Mel straightened the card without choosing to, the way she'd square a crooked place setting, and moved on.

The setup volunteer found them, rather than the other way around. She was a stout woman in a booster-club windbreaker, coiling an extension cord elbow to palm, and she'd heard from Paku what they were asking.

"I'll tell you the one odd thing, and it isn't very odd," she said. "I had the tables up by half past six Saturday morning. Hardly a soul out yet. There was a man walking a little dog over by the chess area, just walking it, back and forth like you do. Black and white, the dog. Little thing."

"What did the man look like?" Mel asked.

The woman thought about it and came up empty-handed. "A man. Jacket, I want to say. I was counting chairs, honey, I wasn't taking attendance. Dogs everywhere at a festival anyway. By ten there must have been twenty of them."

"What time did he move on?"

"Couldn't say. I went for the second cart and when I came back it was just tables."

Noreen wrote it down. "You saw him yourself," she said. "This isn't something Carol or Doris handed you."

"Saw him with my own eyes, for what little they did me."

"Half past six in the morning, the chess area, a small black-and-white dog." Noreen put a period on it like a pin through a moth. "Thank you. That's the first primary-source anything we've had all day."

The woman went back to her cords looking modestly pleased, a witness to history at last.

It was nothing. Mel filed it the way you file a receipt you'll never look at again, and the two of them walked the long way out past the pavilion. At the tape she stopped. Through the tent's open side she could see the masters' table still in place, the folding chairs cocked at the angles two hundred people had left them in, and the trampled ground all around going green again at the edges. No one official had knelt on that ground. No one had photographed it, gridded it, read it. Near the table leg, where the crowd had not pressed in, the soft ground still held its Saturday-morning prints: shoe treads, one boot, and a small dog's paw, the left front one toe too many, five pads where four belonged. Mel looked at it once and moved on. The county had what the county wanted, twenty minutes up the road in a cell.

Her knees wanted to do it themselves, right there, tape or no tape.

"Not yet," Noreen said, watching her. "Not without knowing what we'd be kneeling for."

The Spoon closed by six, the ovens ticking themselves cool, and Leo stood by the prep counter the way a general claims a map room.

His notes ran the length of the steel in three neat ranks. The chemistry textbook lay open with its cracked spine flat, and beside it a printed paper wore his block capitals up both margins. Somewhere off toward Maple Street a knot of trick-or-treaters shrieked and faded, the town's children keeping Halloween alive at a distance, in some other world where the worst thing abroad was a rubber mask.

"There are three compounds worth knowing," Leo said. "Geraniol. Citral. And one called 9-ODA. Everything I'm going to say is those three."

Mel pulled a stool to the counter and sat. Noreen had the end seat, notebook open to a clean page, glasses pushed up her nose.

"Bees talk in smells," Leo said. "When scouts find a good home site, they fan out a scent that says come here. That scent is mostly geraniol and citral. You can buy a synthetic blend of it from any beekeeping supplier in the country. It's called a swarm lure, and it's legal, and it's cheap, because all it does is attract scouts to an empty box. It can't move a colony anywhere. It's a suggestion, not an order."

"And the third compound makes it an order," Mel said.

"The third compound is the queen." He set his finger on the printed page. "9-ODA is the spine of queen mandibular pheromone. It's the smell that means the queen is here, she is real, she is yours. A colony will organize itself around that smell. Defend it. Travel to it." He looked up. "Papá walked me through the papers twice. Geraniol and citral say come look. Add 9-ODA and it becomes she's over there. The whole colony, moving with intent, to a point."

He took a paper bag from the stack by the register, tore it flat, and drew while they watched. The hive rows. The line of Mashburn Creek. Then the cedar screen, cross-hatched, and on the far side of it a small rectangle. The pavilion. His pen moved the way his knife moved, nothing wasted.

"Three hundred meters, give or take. Saturday's breeze was out of the southeast, which is the helpful direction." He set the pen down. "A blend like that, applied to something at the masters' table, and what two hundred people watched happen is just chemistry doing what chemistry does. The bees weren't wrong. They were aimed."

"According to whose catalog?" Noreen said. It wasn't a challenge. It was a librarian checking the spine before she shelved the book. "Walk me backward. The synthetic blend with the queen compound. Who sells that, and to whom?"

"Research suppliers. Pheromone houses that serve entomology labs, mostly. Papá says you'd want a credit card and patience, and you'd want to know the words to search for. Three weeks of reading would get you the words." Leo said it evenly, a boy quoting his father with the citation attached. "It's not over-the-counter. It's not restricted either."

"So not the beekeeping aisle at Platt's."

"No. But not a locked cabinet anywhere, either."

The kitchen held the quiet a moment, bleach-water and cold onions and the tick of the cooling ovens. Mel had stopped moving some sentences back. She stood with her palms flat on the steel and let the thing finish assembling in front of her, the way she'd watched it start to assemble at her sink on Monday. Aimed. Every objection she might have raised stepped up, looked at Leo's map, and sat back down.

"So this wasn't an accident," she said. Not a question.

"It was a very deliberate accident."

Nobody put a name in the room. That was the discipline of it; there was no name to put, and all three of them knew the difference between a mechanism and a man. But the outline of him stood at the edge of the lamplight anyway. Someone with a credit card. Someone with three weeks of patience and access to a chess table. Someone who had stood in a crowd of his neighbors on a bright Saturday and watched his chemistry arrive on schedule.

Noreen closed the notebook on her pen. "Now I want to see where they came from," she said. "The bees. I want to walk it."

"Tomorrow," Mel said. "We'll walk it."

The gap in the cedar screen was a body's width, worn through by years of Arthur's shortcuts, and stepping out the far side of it was like stepping into the back room of the crime.

The apiary lay in morning light. White hive boxes in their south-facing rows, paint weathered to chalk at the corners. Mashburn Creek ran shallow behind them under the willows, past the last purple rags of the asters, and the air over the whole field carried a low working murmur, fewer wings than summer but wings all the same. Mel turned once and looked back the way they'd come. Through the gap, framed in cedar, the white peak of the pavilion tent. Leo's paper-bag map, walked on her own two feet. Three hundred meters and a favorable breeze.

"Inspection's not till Thursday." A young man came up the row between the hives with a feeder pail in one hand. Early twenties, sandy hair under a watch cap, and a brass key swinging on a bootlace around his neck. He planted himself the way you do when you're alone in a place you're responsible for. "If you're from the county, everything's documented. Every colony, every date. I've got copies."

"We're not from the county," Mel said. "I'm Mel Hunter. I run The Giving Spoon, in town. This is Noreen Siegel."

The change in him was a window opening. "The pantry." He lowered the pail. "Arthur talks about you. The honey-jar lady. He says you move more of his jars than the farm stand does." He wiped his palm on his jacket and offered his hand. "Derek. I help out here. Helped." The correction cost him something. "I'm keeping them fed while he's away."

He'd been at it since dawn, by the look of the row behind him, feeder tops off and squared in a line on the grass. He walked them up between the hives, talking the way lonely people talk when the right listener finally arrives. Two years he'd been coming out here. Arthur had taught him smoke and patience and the manners of the yard, never to stand in the flight path, never to hurry. His father played chess, had wanted him at the boards every weekend of his childhood. The apiary was the one place the game had never followed him. He said that last part with his back half-turned, putting a feeder top to rights, and Mel let it lie where he'd set it.

"Derek, I need to ask you about Saturday," she said. "Not where you were. What the bees are."

"They're gentle stock." He said it before she'd finished. "The state apiarist was out here in September. Walked every colony. Rated the whole yard healthy, good temperament, low defensiveness. It's in the file, I'll show you the carbon. Arthur's kept this yard eleven years and there's never been an aggression complaint. Not one. No unprovoked swarming, ever. These bees winter calm and they fly calm." He looked down the row toward the cedar screen, and his jaw set like a much older man's. "What they're saying these bees did, crossing that screen, going through a hundred people to get at one man. Ask anybody who's actually worked this yard. They don't do that. They wouldn't know how to want to."

"Unless something taught them to want it," Noreen said.

"Yes, ma'am. Unless that."

Mel had used the word 'evidence' at the council session about these hives. Standing in the yard itself she understood she'd been arguing better than she knew. A hundred thousand witnesses, and here was their keeper's apprentice, feeding them through an autumn none of them would see the far side of unless somebody pried the truth loose in twenty-one days.

They left him working. At the gap Mel looked back once. Derek had a hive open and was lifting a frame to the light, holding it at the exact angle Arthur held them, tilted out of the sun's glare, and for a moment the yard had its keeper in it again, thirty pounds lighter and fifty years younger. She carried that the whole way back through the cedars, and didn't try to put it down.

Silver Oak Hospital kept its fourth-floor hallway dim at the patient end, and a sheriff's deputy kept a chair outside the last door on the left, a paperback folded over his knee. The county had moved Arthur up here Tuesday, when the cough turned into something the lockup nurse declined to sign her name under, and the deputy was the cost of the better bed. He knew Mel by now. Second day running. He nodded her past without getting up.

The nurse caught her at the supply alcove, the one with the kind eyes who'd taken the soup container off her hands yesterday and pretended she could allow that.

"He didn't eat this morning," the nurse said. "He'll tell you he did."

Mel shifted the bag on her arm. Two library westerns and a wedge of cornbread wrapped in wax paper. The contraband of caring for someone past the reach of casseroles. "I keep waiting for somebody to tell me he's turning a corner," she said. "Nobody's said it. Two days of nobody saying it." She made herself ask the thing flat out. "There's no corner, is there."

The nurse looked at her a moment, her face worn smooth by years of exactly this hallway. "He's comfortable," she said. "Visits help more than the food does. Go on in."

Arthur was propped against two pillows with the window light on him, and the bed shrank him further than the plastic chair at the county lockup had managed. The tremor in his right hand kept its slow time on the blanket. He read her face from the doorway with no trouble at all.

"They sent the nurse to head you off," he said. "Didn't work, I see."

"I asked her a question. She didn't answer it." Mel set the books on the nightstand and sat in the chair angled toward his good side. "That was the answer."

"It generally is." No apology in it, no bid for softness. The energy a man spends managing other people's grief was gone out of him, spent somewhere back down the hallway of the last year, and what remained was plain as the blanket. "Cancer's had the run of me since spring, Mel. They say months. They get shy about how many." His thumb moved against his fingers, the old wax-smoothing motion, around and around. "I'd as soon you knew. I'm tired of being the only one carrying it, excepting the doctors, and they bill for it."

The cornbread sat on her knee in its wax paper. She did not cry, the same way she didn't cry the morning the dairy delivery failed, by finding the next thing that needed two hands. She unwrapped the cornbread and set it where he could reach it.

"Derek's keeping the yard," she said. "He had the feeders squared away by nine this morning. He holds the frames the way you do. And he said he never gets stung."

That landed deeper than any word she might have picked. He looked at the window awhile, working his jaw.

"I've been hanging on by the bees," he said finally. "That's not a figure of speech. A man can set his feet against a thing left undone. Forty harvests and I've nothing else unfinished worth the name. No wife to leave, no children waiting on me. Just sixty colonies that the county's fixing to kill for a crime somebody borrowed them for." He turned from the window then and looked at her straight, and his hand quit its circling. "So I'll ask you the one thing I've got the standing to ask. Don't you spend your strength trying to save me. That job's filled. Save the bees, Mel. Get them to the other side of November with the truth attached. After that I can turn loose of all of it in good order."

"Arthur."

"In good order," he said again, gently, like a man closing a hive for winter. "It's all I want. It's the whole of it."

She drove home with the radio off. Dusk came down over the stripped corn the way it does in the first week of November, fast and without ceremony, and the white lines fed under the headlights one at a time. Twenty-one days on the county's clock, and no number at all on his, and both of those clocks now hung from her neck on the same string. She had told a dying man she didn't argue with that she would save what he loved. The road hummed. Her hands stayed at ten and two the whole way, as if the car required holding together too.

The Spoon was dark when she let herself in the back. She didn't bother with the kitchen lights, just the office lamp, and stood in its circle going through the day's mail because the mail was a thing with edges and her head wanted edges. Supplier bill. A donor's thank-you card with a kitten on it. A county envelope, stiff and official, her name showing through the window.

She opened it expecting compliance paperwork. The words NOTICE OF AUDIT sat at the top of the page in bold, and the lamplight seemed to swell and right itself.

The County would conduct a full financial audit of The Giving Spoon. Concerns regarding irregular bookkeeping practices and potential mismanagement of grant funds. To commence December 1. All financial records, donor lists, and operational documents must be available. Failure to cooperate would trigger review of nonprofit status.

Mel read it twice, standing very still. Quarterly summaries instead of monthly spreadsheets. Photographs of fed families instead of line items. Four years of feeding a town, recast by a form letter as concerns. Then her eye reached the filing block at the bottom of the page and stopped going forward at all.

Dated the seventh of October. Three weeks to the day before the festival.

Below the date, a signature in cramped, angular script she'd seen on tournament flyers tacked to the co-op board.

Bernard A. Travers, County Oversight Board Member.

She sat down in the desk chair with the page in both hands. Bernie. Bernie had read her flexible bookkeeping the way he'd read a sloppy opening, as disorder wanting correction, and he'd filed the correction with the county the way he did everything, formally, thoroughly, and signed. It wasn't even malice. That was the worst of it. He'd probably thought he was helping.

The other thing arrived a breath later, cold and complete. Her life's work threatened by Bernie Travers, three weeks before somebody killed him. Motive, documented, in county records, wearing her name. If Corbin came across this letter he wouldn't even be wrong to look at her the way he'd look at her. She'd taught him to respect facts, and this was a fact.

Mel opened the bottom drawer, lifted the grant files, and slid the notice flat beneath them. The drawer ran shut on its rails with a small, well-oiled click, the sound of a thing done that she could never explain later in any words that would help.

She sat a minute longer in the lamp's small circle of light, in the cardboard-and-disinfectant smell of the only thing she'd ever built.

Then she locked up and went home, carrying her guilt.

The Living and the Dead

Christ Lutheran could seat a hundred and forty. By ten past the hour it held perhaps two dozen, and the two dozen had spread themselves through the sanctuary as if grief required elbow room.

Mel sat with Noreen a third of the way back and did not remark on the empty pews, and neither did anyone else, which was its own kind of remark. The radiators ticked under the stained glass. Candle wax and old hymnals and somebody's drugstore perfume, and over all of it the organ working through a prelude that had too much room to die in. When the pastor welcomed them, his voice came back off the rear wall a half-second late, the building answering for the people who hadn't.

Bernie Travers had lived in Possum Gap for forty years, and this was the size of the hole he left.

The chess club had set a table at the head of the aisle, beside the casket. A folding board stood open on it, mid-game, the pieces fixed in some position that meant a great deal to eleven people in the room and nothing to the rest, and beside the board a photograph of a young Bernie in heavy-rimmed glasses, shaking hands across a table with somebody important, his grin wide and his tie too narrow, a Bernie from before any of his folders got thick. Mel looked at the grin longer than she meant to. The young man in the photograph had not yet ruined anyone.

She had dressed for it the way she dressed for board meetings, and she had come with two jobs, and the second job sat in her chest like a swallowed stone. Mourn with your neighbors. Watch your neighbors mourn. The pastor said *community* twice in his opening and Mel looked at her hands. A pantry teaches you to feed people without judging the line, and here she sat, judging the line. If anyone in these pews could read her, they'd be right to move away from her, and the worst of it was that she still intended to do the work.

The chess people had come, nearly all of them. The tournament committee filled the third pew, Eleanor's banner crew, the woman who ran the brackets with a clipboard and now held a hymnal the same way. Behind them the players sat as they sat at the boards, upright and contained, a congregation within the congregation. The rest were neighbors doing what neighbors do. Women from the church circle who would have baked for the reception regardless of the name in the program. Two men from the co-op board with their hats on their knees. Mayor Coldwell, third row, dressed for a photograph nobody would take.

Her eye moved, one face at a time.

Eleanor Vance sat near the front, alone in her pew, in the good gray coat she wore for Historical Society lectures. She held her program with both hands and looked at the casket the way she looked at a document she wasn't permitted to copy. Whatever Eleanor was burying today, it had footnotes.

Two rows behind her, Agnes Moskov sat straight-backed between her husband and her son. As Mel watched, Agnes reached over without turning her head and smoothed the lie of Derek's tie, flattening it against his shirt with two fingers, and left her hand on his arm a moment after. Derek bore it. He was here for his father's world, not for Bernie, and his face said he was counting the hymns. Kristian Moskov watched the casket and nothing else.

And across the aisle, alone at the end of a pew, the still man.

Mel knew him from the festival, the way you know a face you've stood in a crowd with. He'd spent Saturday on the east bench with a book, one of the out-of-town chess followers, the kind of man tournaments collect and nobody introduces. He sat now with his hands folded and his back not touching the pew, and he did not fidget, and he did not look around, and in a room where everyone was managing themselves in some visible fashion, he alone required no management. A gray man, gray-suited, his age hard to fix. He'd brought no one.

She put her eyes back on the program.

A young man who'd driven down from Knoxville gave the eulogy. He had introduced himself as one of Bernie's students from his university years and stood at the lectern without notes for a moment, deciding something, before he took the notes out anyway.

"People will tell you he was hard to like," he said. "He was. He was also the first person who treated my mind like it deserved discipline. I was fourteen and bad at losing. Bernie sat me down across a board and beat me nine games in a row, and after the ninth one he said, a lost position is information. Stop moaning and read it." He looked up from the notes. "I've been reading losses for him for thirty years now. In my work, in my marriage, the year my daughter was sick. A lost position is information. It's the most useful thing anybody ever taught me, and I wanted to come say so while it could still be said in front of him."

He sat down to the kind of quiet a small crowd makes when it has been handed a bigger man than it came to bury.

Mel watched it land. Some of the faces around her were moved. Some were arranging themselves to look moved, and you could tell those by the speed of it. And some, the chess faces mostly, just waited, holding whatever they held, men and women who had sat across a board from Bernie Travers and were filing the eulogy against their own ninth games.

Bernie the tormentor, Bernie the teacher. Both true. The room had to hold them together for an hour, and so did she, and it cost more than she'd budgeted. It is one thing to clear an innocent man. It is another to learn the dead man was somebody's lost position, read and kept for thirty years.

Near the back, in the last occupied pew, Tim Renshaw sat with his head slightly bowed. He caught her looking on her way to not looking. He nodded, small, the nod you give across a church. Mel felt it somewhere unhelpful and looked away first, and spent the better part of a hymn getting the heat out of her ears.

The organ took up the closing with too few voices under it. Somewhere in the rows of chess people there was a gap where an argument used to stand, a missing man whose empty chair had already rearranged one Saturday this month. He hadn't come to the tournament he'd fought to play in. He hadn't come to this either, and nobody seemed to find that strange, and Mel found that strange all by itself.

The fellowship hall smelled like a county's worth of casseroles.

Mel catalogued them without meaning to. Broccoli-rice from Mrs. Abernathy. The Second Baptist green beans that always traveled in the speckled roaster. Three plates of funeral potatoes from three kitchens that did not consult each other, and a sheet cake with PEACE piped on it by someone whose icing was better than their planning. The community said with food what it had not managed to say in the pews, and what it said was complicated, and generous, and a little guilty.

She kept to the edge of the room with a coffee she didn't want, and she watched the still man.

He moved through the reception like a man discharging an obligation, with an economy that wasted nothing. When spoken to he spoke, and the speaking ended when the other person stopped, every time; he left no conversational tails. He signed the condolence book, waiting his turn behind two church women, and wrote a single line without bending to compose it, the pen on its ribbon barely pausing. The plate he accepted, because refusing would have drawn the eye in the wrong direction, and then he held it, squarely, in front of him, and ate none of it. He stood near the coffee urn for some minutes and drank no coffee.

Reserved grief, she tried. Some men locked down at funerals. Her own father had stood at gravesides like a fence post, and it hadn't meant he felt nothing; it had meant the feeling had no door. Or guilt, the word arriving on its own, uninvited, the investigator's word, and she made herself hold it at arm's length because it fit too easily. Or nothing at all. An introvert in a county of huggers, a man waiting out social weather he hadn't dressed for, who would drive home tonight and be glad it was over the way half the room would. Each label fit. None fit better than the others, and that was the thing she couldn't put down. The man was data that refused to sort.

She drifted two tables closer with the vague idea of listening, close to him as a woman refilling her coffee, and got as far as the urn before her nerve went. What would she even say. *Lovely service. Did you kill him?* She topped off the coffee she didn't want and retreated, and felt fourteen years old and scolded.

She was still working on the labels when he turned and looked at her.

Not a glance. He turned his head the way a man turns to a sound he expected, and he found her eyes across the fellowship hall and held them, and there was nothing in his face at all. No challenge, no alarm, no social smile. He nodded. Once, exactly, the depth of a period at the end of a sentence. Then he turned back to the committee woman at his elbow and said something that made her touch her collarbone and laugh sadly.

Mel stood at the edge of the room with her coffee going cold against her fingers, feeling like a window someone had looked through and accurately priced.

Around her the reception ran its course. She heard, without hunting for it, the talk a small town makes over funeral potatoes. Poor Arthur, and can you believe, and the hives, and my sister won't let her kids play outside till it's settled. Twice she heard the out-of-town mourner discussed in the kind tones reserved for strangers who show up properly dressed. The committee ladies had decided he was respectful. Noreen was over there among them with a paper cup, not taking notes, which Mel understood by now meant she was taking notes.

The Moskov family left early. Mel saw it happen by the door: Agnes gathering coats while her husband worked the room toward the exit one handshake at a time, and Derek already half outside, escaped, a boy with somewhere true to be. The light would be gone by five thirty and there were feeders to check east of town. Agnes paused at the door to look back once, at the room or at the casket table or at nothing, her face doing none of the things faces do, and then she put her hand between

Derek's shoulders and steered him out, and the door swung the November in and shut it out again.

They left together, shrugging into November at the coat rack.

"The man with the plate," Mel said. "He knew I was watching him."

"He knew you were watching him," Noreen said, "the way you'd know it was raining."

Neither of them said what that meant. They carried it out into the parking lot like a dish someone would want returned.

*

Eleanor caught up with her on the gravel, the wind off the ridge taking the funeral smell out of their coats.

"Mel." Her voice had the scraped-flat sound of a person who has been polite for two hours straight. "I keep thinking I should go see Arthur. And then I keep not going."

"He'd be glad of it. He's at Silver Oak now. The visiting's easier than the county was."

"I heard." Eleanor looked at her keys. "It's a terrible thing to say at a man's funeral, but I sat in there thinking, this is going to kill Arthur too, and nobody in this church would call it murder."

"How is he," Eleanor said. "The unabridged version."

"Tired. Worried for the bees more than for himself." Both true. Mel left the rest where it lived, under its own grant files; it was Arthur's to tell. She was getting practiced at drawers. "Visit him, Mazie. He counts callers the way other men count money."

"I will." Eleanor said it like a debt she meant to pay.

"You knew Bernie longer than most," Mel said. "Today can't have been simple."

"Nothing about Bernie was simple. I've spent a career filing this town's quarrels, and his are the thickest folders in the building." It came out closer to tired than bitter. "That boy from Knoxville told the truth. So would half the people Bernie ruined, if you asked them under oath.

Both sets of folders are real. That's what nobody tells you about archives. They don't resolve anything. They just keep it."

Gravel went under their shoes. Eleanor's car sat at the far edge of the lot, under the bare maple, and Eleanor slowed as they came to it instead of finishing the conversation at speed, which Mel noticed, and understood properly only later. Some things need the whole length of a parking lot to come out.

Eleanor touched Mel's arm lightly. "Do you know Gregory Dowen? The chess player?"

"From the tournament," Mel said.

"He spent… Oh, I don't know, maybe ten years trying to correct a record that Bernie had made wrong." A pause. Not quite a look at Mel. More at the middle distance. "My family was involved, in a peripheral way. I won't go into that." She said it with the quiet of someone managing a guilt that belongs to a person who is no longer alive to carry it. "He couldn't get anyone to listen. Bernie had too many connections. Important connections."

"What kind of record?" Mel asked.

"A patent." Eleanor got in the car. She didn't say more. Through the window, she looked older than she did inside the church.

The maple let go of a leaf onto the windshield. The car backed out and carried Eleanor away, and left the name standing in the gravel lot with Mel, where it stayed.

By eight that evening the Spoon was theirs, the front dark, the office lamp on, and Leo had brought his binder.

He'd missed the memorial for a chemistry test, a sentence that would have been funny in any other month. Now he stood at the desk with printouts of supplier forums fanned out like a losing hand. Noreen had claimed the desk chair and her notebook. Mel took the order pad off its nail, turned it over to the blank cardboard back, and wrote at the top: WHO.

"Say them," Noreen said. "I'll keep us honest."

"Arthur." Mel wrote it and made herself look at it. "Charged. Corbin's case is motive, method, opportunity, and I can't argue with any one of those words except all of them together. The method is the problem. Whoever did this ordered compounds from a research supplier and aimed a colony like a garden hose. Arthur keeps bees the way Eleanor keeps documents. He'd no more brew a queen in a jar than she'd forge a deed."

"Could he have bought it, though." Leo said it to the desk, apologizing for it as he went. "That's what Corbin will say. You don't have to be a chemist to have a credit card. I checked anyway." He pulled a sheet from the binder. "Arthur's never owned a computer. He does his ordering through the co-op on paper, Papá-style. The co-op manager would remember a research-supply order the way he'd remember a giraffe."

"Write that down somewhere we won't lose it," Noreen said. "On the record, the State of Tennessee disagrees with all three of us. Noted and continuing."

"Cheswick." The pen waited. "David Cheswick. Due at that tournament, never came, and nobody's seen him since before Saturday. The whole bracket changed because of his empty chair. A man with a public history with Bernie goes missing the same weekend Bernie dies, and the chess people are so used to his feuds that the missing part hasn't struck them as the headline." Mel wrote MISSING and underlined it once. "That's either the best alibi I ever heard of or the worst."

"I'll find out where his mail is going," Noreen said, as though announcing she'd water someone's plants.

"Third." Leo slid a printout across the desk, a forum thread with a username circled in pencil. "I wasn't looking for this. I was reading swarm-lure threads for Papá, and there's a buyer in this county asking about citrus-type attractants last spring. The shipping town is Possum Gap. The handle is AMoskov." He handed it over the way you hand someone a fragile thing. "It's probably beekeeping. People buy lures for swarm traps all the time, it's geraniol-and-citral stuff, the legal kind, it wouldn't move a colony across a road. It's just. The name."

Mel thought about a straight-backed woman smoothing a boy's tie flat, and wrote AGNES, and after it a question mark, and felt like an informer doing it.

"Thin," she said.

"Tissue," Noreen agreed. "Keep it anyway. Lists don't convict people. They keep us from forgetting what we haven't asked yet."

"Fourth." Mel looked at the cardboard. "Gregory Dowen."

She gave them the parking lot. Eleanor's hand on her arm, ten years, a record made wrong, a patent, a family involved in a peripheral way that would not be gone into. The older face through the window, and the car carrying it off before Mel had known what to ask.

Noreen was quiet a moment, and when she spoke it was in her cataloging voice, the unhurried one that set each fact on its shelf.

"Now, there's a thing I collected at the reception and didn't have a place for," she said. "The committee ladies were being kind about the out-of-town mourner. The quiet one with the plate. He's not visiting. He didn't show up for the tournament weekend like the rest of the chess crowd. He rented at Haven Terrace, three weeks back, by the month. Doris's cousin cleans out there, and a cleaner knows a lease from a layover better than any leasing agent alive." She let that sit on the desk with the printouts. "A visit is a tank of gas. A lease is intent."

The lamp hummed. Leo looked from one of them to the other, doing the arithmetic young, the way he did everything.

"The man at the reception," Mel said. "The still one."

"The chess player," Noreen said. "It's the same man, Mel. Eleanor handed you his name in the parking lot an hour after he nodded at you across the hall."

Leo straightened his printouts to have something to square. "So what do we do with him?"

"What we'd do with any of them." Mel heard how steady it came out, and was glad nobody could check the inside against it. "We ask. People who've waited ten years to be listened to generally want to talk. I'll go see him myself." The words were out before she had inspected them, and she found she meant them. Forty feet of fellowship hall had told her nothing. A doorway might.

Mel looked down at the cardboard. Four names. One of them a friend, one of them a ghost, one of them a tissue, and the last one written in her own hand on the same afternoon the man himself had measured her across a church hall, once, like a period.

GREGORY DOWEN, the cardboard said, in her own block capitals. East bench. Ten years. A patent. Three weeks at the Terrace.

The drawer beside her knee held its own paper under the grant files, and she did not open it, and she knew it was there the whole time, which she was learning was how hidden things worked.

Twenty days to the twenty-second. She squared the order pad against the desk edge and looked at the fourth name, and the fourth name sat on its shelf with the patience of an old wound, history folded shut, the way the still man had held his plate all afternoon and never eaten. Whatever was under that name had been under it a long time. Long enough to learn stillness. She'd met patience like that exactly nowhere in her life, and she'd just put it on a list in a food pantry, between a question mark and a missing man.

She turned off the lamp. In the dark the names kept their order, and the last one kept it longest.

Interview and Caution

Haven Terrace kept its stairs waxed and its brass numbers polished, and the second-floor hall smelled of floor polish and somebody's toast. Mel had climbed it rehearsing an opening line, something neighborly with a spine in it, and Noreen had climbed it behind her saying nothing at all, which from Noreen was a form of coaching.

The door opened before Mel's knuckles reached it a second time.

"Ms. Hunter. Ms. Siegel." Gregory Dowen stood back to let them in, and the standing back had no surprise in it anywhere. He wore a cardigan the color of wet slate over a collared shirt, not formal, not casual, ironed. Behind him, somewhere in the apartment, a coffee maker finished its work with a sigh, and the smell of a fresh pot came down the hall to meet them like a butler. "I wondered which morning it would be."

Mel lost the rehearsed line in the surrender of the door and stood there holding her own name. Being expected, she found, was its own kind of answer, and she didn't know yet what the question had been. Behind her, Noreen said good morning in the pleasant, unhurried voice she used on reference patrons who were about to be told the book was non-circulating.

The dog appeared.

She came around Dowen's leg at a trot, a little Cavalier King Charles Spaniel, black and white with bright copper points at the eyebrows and ears. Her ears swung like a girl's braids, and her whole rear half wagged because the tail alone couldn't carry the freight of her feelings about company. She went to Noreen first, reconsidered, and presented herself to Mel.

Mel crouched. Thirty years of food lines taught a body to get down to the level of whatever came to it gladly. The dog pushed her head into Mel's palm, then sat and offered one paw with the practiced manners of a creature who had spent her life enjoying formal appreciation.

Mel took the paw, small and warm in her hand. Left front. Her thumb lay across the pads a moment.

Five. Four in their neat arc and a fifth set in, riding low where no toe belonged, with its own small nail.

"She's got an extra toe," Mel said.

"Yes. Left front. The disqualified her from showing because of it. She had seven Best in Show titles before the judges noticed." A pause. "She and I have a great deal in common."

Mel looked up. Dowen was watching her with an expression she could not read, which by now she understood was the only kind he kept. The line had sounded like a small joke and had not been one, or had been one and also the truest thing in the hallway, and he gave her no help deciding.

"Trixie," he said to the dog, "let them through the door at least."

The dog returned to him with her ears swinging and took up station at his heel. They had the look of long agreement between them, two creatures who had settled their treaty years ago and kept its terms without thinking.

He invited them in.

The sitting room was an argument for the man. Books shelved by author, a chess library two cases deep. A board on a side table held a position mid-study, pieces stopped in their tracks like a photograph of an accident. Two chairs and a sofa arranged for conversation that expected no crowd. Nothing on the walls but a county map, old, framed, and one photograph too small to read from where Mel sat, a younger man and a machine of some kind, the man's hand resting on it the way you rest a hand on a dog. It was the most permanent-looking room she'd ever stood in, and the man was renting it by the month, and the wrongness of that hummed under everything like a wire.

He brought the coffee unasked, remembered that Noreen took hers black, and sat.

"You're asking about Saturday," he said. "Ask."

"You were there early," Mel said.

"I'm everywhere early. Trixie wakes at five whether I vote or not, and we walk. We walked the festival grounds at first light, before the crowds, the same route we'd walk any morning. Habit is most of what I have, Ms. Hunter. Then I took her home, and I came back, and I spent the day on the east bench, and I left at half past four, after the ambulance had gone and they suspended the tournament. You may have seen me there. Most people did, without noticing."

It had the sound of a thing already composed, every clause load-bearing, and none of it disagreed with anything Mel knew. That was what unsettled her about it. People remembered Saturdays in fragments and apologies. He had his in paragraphs.

"You came to town three weeks before the tournament," Mel said. "That's a long run-up for one Saturday of chess."

"It is. I'm between obligations, and Hickory Valley has gotten loud in the way small places do when the highway finds them. I wanted somewhere with a library that opens on time and streets a dog can think on." He said it without defending it, which defended it. "I looked at three towns. This one had the festival coming, which decided me. I don't expect you to find that persuasive. It happens to be true."

Noreen tilted her head a degree, the way she did when a fact went onto a shelf next to another fact and the two of them looked at each other.

On the side table the abandoned game sat in its photograph stillness, and Mel, buying a moment, asked what it was.

"A famous loss." He didn't look at it. "I set out positions the way other men do crosswords. The interesting ones are never the wins. A win tells you what worked. A loss tells you what you believed that wasn't so." He turned his cup again, the small quarter-turn, his one tic. "It's a more useful education, if you have the stomach for it."

The room's faint sweetness reached her then, under the coffee. Floral, and under the floral something with an edge on it, like fruit going to chemistry. Her body knew it before she did. She was kneeling again by a chess table in October with her face close to a white queen, and her stomach dropped an inch before her mind caught up and asked it why.

Her eyes must have gone looking, because they found the utility nook off the kitchen. A careful stack: garden gloves, a pump sprayer, boxes with the plain look of mail-order.

"I keep a hive," Dowen said, following her glance without hurry. "A single box, behind the building. The landlord finds it eccentric and the honey persuades him. I bait swarm lures in the spring, for wild colonies. The smell gets into everything, I'm told. I've stopped being able to smell it myself." He turned his cup a quarter-turn on its saucer. "You develop a nose for what you live with, and go blind to it. True of more than bees."

A reasonable explanation, delivered reasonably. It was the volunteering she filed, not the facts. He had answered a question she hadn't asked yet.

"What was Bernie to you?" she asked.

"A colleague. The chess community is small and long. We were in it together for many years."

"That's a long way from an answer."

Noreen had gone very still across the room, the stillness she did when she wanted the furniture to forget her.

Dowen looked into his coffee, and for the first time since the door, he took a moment he hadn't already budgeted. When he spoke, the voice was the same and the floor under it was not.

"Bernie was a man who took what didn't belong to him and called it discovery. He did it in chess, and he did it once in a much more consequential way. He spent twenty-four years profiting from work that was not his."

The clock in the kitchen kept going. Trixie, asleep on her cushion, sighed for the whole room.

Then his face arranged itself again, a man stepping back behind his own counter. "Professionally speaking, I found him difficult."

"You'll appreciate that people are going to wonder," Mel said, gently, "where a sentence like the first one goes when it grows up."

"They may wonder." He set the cup down. "If you're cataloguing the people Bernard wronged, the list is long, and I'll save you some shoe leather. Mr. Cheswick's feud was the loud one. Mine was merely the old one. Loud is generally more recent than old, and recent is generally what matters in these things. Although you'd know better than I would. You're the one the town talks to."

He stood, which meant the visit had its length, the way Corbin's hat did. At the door Trixie woke and performed her goodbyes for both of them as though they'd been gone a year, and Dowen thanked them for coming with the courtesy of a man thanking a delivery service. The door clicked shut on a well-oiled latch.

In the car Noreen looked at her notebook without opening it.

"Five years in the reference section teaches you the sound of a rehearsed answer," she said.

"All of it?"

"Every word he planned. That's not the same as every word being false." She put the notebook away. "The dog's lovely."

"The dog's lovely," Mel agreed, and they drove back to town with the smell of someone else's spring still in her coat.

Saturday at the apiary, the November light came in flat and the yard had gone quiet enough to hear the creek.

Derek had the smoker cold on its hook and the last feeders out, and on the work table under the lean-to lay a three-ring binder, hand-tabbed, the tabs lettered in a print Mel knew from eleven years of honey-jar price cards.

"He sends instructions," Derek said, half embarrassed, wholly proud. "Through his lawyer, with the visiting nurse's help. Feeding schedules. Which colonies to double up if it turns cold early. Mrs. Gaskins drove it out Tuesday." He touched the binder's edge square to the table. "He puts the date on every page like I might shuffle them."

They walked the rows. Derek talked, and Mel let him, because the boy had a week of unsaid things stacked up and no one out here but bees to say them to. His father had wanted tournaments. Saturdays in church basements, notation to study like scripture, a boy's losses gone over at the dinner table move by move. "The yard doesn't keep score," he said, with one shoulder up, and that was the whole speech, and Mel asked nothing further, and he loved her visibly for it.

He knew the colonies apart by temper. This one ran calm as a draft horse. That one took offense at thunder. The one in the third row had requeened itself in August and was still deciding who it was now, which he said the way you'd describe a cousin in a difficult year.

He showed her the rows like a foreman with a good crew. The fourth colony was the strongest going into winter, he said, heavy as a safe when you lifted the back. A young one from the August split would need feeding into December. The yard had its politics, its steady citizens and its one difficult neighbor, and he spoke of all of it in the present tense, eighteen days from the county's date, and Mel did not correct the tense, and would not have for money.

She'd sit with Arthur tomorrow and bring him this: the rows fed, the binder followed, the boy talking about December. Some medicine the hospital didn't stock.

She told him, finally, what she needed told. The cedar screen. That long, wrong crossing. The way the swarm had moved through a hundred people as though they were furniture, to one man.

Derek shook his head before she finished. Not denial. Recognition.

"That colony has never once cleared the cedars. Not in the two years I've been here. They have no reason to. Everything they need is on this side." He looked down the rows toward the dark line of the screen, and the creek going on behind it. "Something pulled them. Bees don't cross open ground toward people, it's backwards, it costs them everything. Something at that table was shouting in the only language they hear, and it was shouting at three hundred meters, and it was shouting that one spot." He wiped his palms on his jacket, fifteen seconds of being a scientist done, a boy again. "Whoever says Arthur did that doesn't know one thing about the man and less about the bees."

Mel watched him set a feeder top to rights on his way past the row's end, not breaking stride to do it, an Arthur motion if she'd ever seen one, and she thought: eighteen days. The county had given the yard eighteen more days, and the boy was keeping its calendar in another man's handwriting.

He looked at the empty frames stacked by the lean-to the way you look at someone you've been taking care of. Nobody had told him he was the successor. Nobody was going to have to.

Sunday evening, the Spoon's office lamp came on again, and Leo laid it out like a dinner service.

"I went at it backwards," he said. "Stop looking for who's mad at Bernie. Look for who in this county could lay hands on lure-class compounds at all. It's a short list. Shorter than the suspect list." He set down a printout, then a second under it, edges squared. "Then it got shorter in the wrong direction."

The order was real. A beekeeping supplier out of Nashville, an account opened in the spring, one sizeable order shipped to Possum Gap several weeks before the festival. Citrus-family attractant blend among the line items, the lemongrass class. Geraniol and citral, the come-here notes.

The account name was Agnes Moskov.

"It's the same family of smell," Leo said, careful as a man carrying a full pot. "It is not the same product as what I think was on that queen, and before anybody stands up, I'd want to know exactly what was in the bottle. Exactly. The family is cheap and legal and people bait swarm traps with it every spring." He pushed his glasses up. "But she doesn't keep bees, Mel. Derek's the bee one, and his hives are Arthur's. What's a sizeable order of swarm bait doing in a house with no hives?"

"And there's the other thing," Noreen said, from the desk chair, unhurried. "The expansion."

Mel knew the bones of it the way the whole town did. Agnes had filed to expand her shop into the vacant half of her building, two years of savings drawn up into a planning application, and Bernie Travers had stood up at the county meeting with a folder under his arm and objected it to death. Heritage setbacks, parking variances, the works. The application died in committee. Agnes had stood in the lot afterward, one of the co-op men liked to tell it, and said nothing at all in two languages.

Motive, in a folder. A festival she'd attended. An order with the right smell and the wrong everything else, maybe, if Leo's caution held.

"The meeting's in the county minutes," Noreen said. "I pulled them Friday for another reason and read them twice for this one. Bernie spoke for eleven minutes. He'd brought photographs of the building from 1958. He used the word stewardship four times." She let the minutes speak for themselves, which they did, in Bernie's voice. "The committee thanked Mrs. Moskov for her investment in the community and declined the application without recording a vote against any one name. That's the genius of committees. Nobody, by name, says no."

"And nobody, by name, gets forgiven for it," Mel said. "So it all lands on the man with the folder."

The rest of the table got its lines too, because a list was only honest if every name moved. Cheswick: the mail inquiry still out, an answer promised by midweek from a cousin of a cousin at the regional sorting center, Noreen's network grinding slow and exceedingly fine. Arthur: visited Sunday afternoon, sitting up, demanding apiary news before hello, sending Derek a message about mouse guards that ran to a paragraph. Dowen: interviewed, filed, his Saturday too clean to grip.

Mel got the cardboard list out of the drawer above the one she didn't open, and rewrote it, and when she finished, the order of names had changed. AGNES, at the top now, with the question mark gone hard at the end of her line like a fist on a table. Then CHESWICK, still MISSING, Noreen's mail inquiry still unanswered. DOWEN came third, the old wound, the rehearsed Saturday. And ARTHUR last, where she meant to keep him.

"Before we hang a neighbor," Noreen said, watching her write, "we find out where she stood Saturday, and when, and what was actually in the bottle. Both pieces, or neither."

"Both pieces," Mel said. "But it's hers. The motive's better than Dowen's. Dowen's is twenty-four years cold. Hers is two years hot, and her boy's out there feeding the evidence."

Leo flinched at that, and she was sorry for it and didn't take it back, because it was true, and the list existed to hold true things up to the lamp.

She drove home at nine with the list in her coat pocket and the day stacked in her like dishes, and her headlights, swinging into the driveway, found a man standing at the bottom of her porch steps with a small dog sitting on his shoe.

Her foot held the brake a beat longer than the stop needed. Then she shut the engine off, because whatever this was, idling at her own house wasn't going to improve it, and got out into the cold.

"Ms. Hunter. Forgive the hour. We walk this way on Sundays." Dowen held the leash loose, coiled once around his hand. Under her porch light the cardigan was charcoal and the dog's copper points had gone amber. "I won't keep you in the cold. I wanted to say something I didn't say Friday, and didn't want to owe it."

Mel stood with her keys in her fist and the porch boards complaining under her and waited.

"You'll keep asking questions. I'd do the same, for a friend in a cell. I'd only ask you to remember that some of the people you'll be asking about have already paid for the privilege of coming under suspicion once." The light caught his glasses. "I spent ten years asking a town like this one to believe me about a thing that mattered, and I'll tell you what I learned. The past stays buried because the ground over it has settled. Dig, and the footing goes uneven for everyone walking above. Most of all for the man it nearly buried the first time."

Trixie stood, shook herself ears to tail, and looked up at him with her whole undivided heart.

"That's all," he said. "Good night, Ms. Hunter. She'll want her biscuit."

She watched them go up the dark street, the little dog's white parts moving like a lantern carried low, and stood there longer than the cold called for, sorting it. A threatened man closing a door before a draft got in. That was the likeliest reading, and it held, mostly, the way a chair with three legs holds if you sit it gently: an old humiliation asking, with some dignity, not to be dug back up.

Inside, she hung her coat and stood in her own kitchen without turning the light on, the house ticking around her the way houses do when you bring a question home with you. A courteous man. A friendly dog. A request any wounded neighbor might make, and gently made at that.

It was only later, locking up, that she heard the other thing in it, small and far off, like a clock in another room. He had not asked her to stop.

He had told her where not to dig.

Obsession

"The favor I'm about to ask isn't small," Mel said, "and I can't tell you all of my reasons for asking it."

Tim Renshaw's office smelled of paper and burnt coffee, the smell of a business that ran on filing and made no apologies for it. The gold lettering on the front glass said RENSHAW INSURANCE AND FINANCIAL SERVICES in letters his father had paid for, and the desk held three squared stacks and a mug with a faded church-league logo, and Tim sat behind all of it looking at her the way he had looked at her across twenty feet of festival crowd. Warm, brief, and careful not to make it anything.

"All right," he said.

"David Cheswick. You know him."

"I know him the way the circuit knows him." Tim leaned back, and the chair received him with the creak of long acquaintance. "I followed tournament chess in college the way some men follow a band. Never any good at it myself, which is freeing. You can love a thing properly when it's never going to love you back." He smiled at his own expense and let it go. "David. I've known since he was a teenager on this circuit. He's better company than his reputation."

"Nobody's seen him since before the festival," Mel said. "Not at the tournament he spent two years insisting on. Not at the funeral. His rent's paid and his mail is all sealed, and I would like to know he isn't lying on a floor somewhere while the whole county talks about him over pie."

She had thought about how much of that to say, on the walk over. All of it was true. It just wasn't all of it.

Tim looked at her for a moment, and she watched him decide not to ask for the rest. It was a generous piece of arithmetic, done quickly, and it left a small warmth in the room that neither of them stopped to examine.

"Martin Kenlee owns Pinewoods," he said, reaching for the phone. "I do his taxes. Martin worries about his tenants roughly in the order their rent arrives, but he does worry." He dialed from memory, said his own name, said hers, and said the words welfare check twice, the second time more slowly, for the benefit of a man who was already agreeing with him. When he hung up he wrote nothing down, which told her the favor had ended. "He'll meet you there at ten. Mel." He said her name like the start of a sentence he had decided against. What arrived instead was, "Tell Dave the circuit misses him. If you find him."

"I will."

Pinewoods Apartments stood off Magnolia Street in two long brick buildings the color of dried beans, facing each other across a parking lot seal-coated in patches, so that the asphalt read like a map of what Martin Kenlee could afford and when. Noreen was waiting at the foot of the building-two stairs with her notebook in her coat pocket and her hands around a travel mug.

"Top floor, corner unit," she said. "Doris's nephew carries mail up here. He's been leaving Cheswick's with the office since the box quit shutting."

Kenlee came across the lot sorting through a ring of keys, a slightly built man going stoop-shouldered, in an Atlanta Braves cap that had faded to the pink of an old scar. He stood for a moment the way a man stands when he's been told at length how to stand and has been letting it go ever since, and he squinted at the two of them, the squint of a man whose glasses were in a drawer somewhere, kept shut against a vanity nobody would have begrudged him.

"Renshaw says you're worried about Dave."

“Aren’t you?”

“Mail’s what done it.” He found the key he wanted and held it apart from the others. “Box filled the first week. I been bringing it in so the lid would shut. Rent’s paid through the end of the month, first-of-the-month money, never one day’s trouble out of Dave, but a man’s mail tells you things his rent don’t.” He started up the stairs, talking to the steps. “Two weeks and better since anybody’s laid eyes on him. I’d have called somebody my own self by Friday.”

Maybe he wanted credit for the worry. Mel listened to him climb, heard the catch in his breathing on the landing, and decided he had earned it either way.

“What kind of tenant is he,” Mel asked, “when he’s here?”

“Quiet. Polite when you catch him, which you mostly don’t.” Kenlee gave it the consideration he would give a unit inventory. “Keeps his own counsel. Soda cans and chess magazines in the recycling, regular as church. Once a year he asks after the hot water and apologizes for the asking.” He shook his head at the stairs. “You rent to enough people, you learn the difference between a man hiding from you and a man hiding from everything. Dave never hid from me.”

At the corner unit Kenlee knocked, called the name twice with his face close to the door, and waited longer than he needed to. Then he used the key.

The smell came out to meet them first.

It was not the smell either of them had braced for on the stairs, and the relief of that arrived before the sense of it. Old take-out. Dishes gone sour in a sink. Air once circulated, long ago, the closed off and gone stale. Under all of it a thin chemical edge that resolved, once Mel stood in it, into pine cleaner. The cheap kind. Used a long time ago, and losing.

Drawn curtains, blocking two weeks of daylight. Kenlee reached past the frame and turned on the overhead light, and then he stayed where he was, one shoulder against the doorjamb, his cap brim down.

"I rent to the man," he said, to nobody at all, as if stating the exact boundary of what he could do without overstepping a boundary.

The apartment was small, lived in hard. Clothes draped a chair, landed there by a man who meant to deal with them tomorrow. A jacket hung on its hook by the door. Three mugs stood on the counter in a week's worth of rings, and a paperback lay split open over the arm of the couch, twenty pages from its end. Nobody had cleared out of this place. This was a room somebody had walked out of, meaning to come back, and then had not come back to.

On the bookshelf, between a chess clock and a row of paperbacks broken to the same curve, a small brass trophy stood turned to face the wall. Mel did not touch it. Whatever the engraved year was, the man had wanted it where he couldn't read it.

Then Mel turned, and the wall took the rest of her attention away from her.

One wall of the living room was working for its living. Corner to corner, floor to eye height, paper lapped over paper like shingles. Tournament crosstables, photocopied and original. Notation sheets in a cramped, spiky hand, whole games rendered in a code of letters and numbers, with single moves circled in red and pressed hard enough to tear. Newspaper chess columns gone amber at the folds, some of them older than Leo. Names. Dates. Scores. A line of years ran along the top of it like a frieze, and under each year hung its evidence, and through all of it, left to right, one name rose and kept rising while a handful of other names appeared, thinned, and dropped away.

It was Bernie Travers's career, laid out the way a man lays out a proof.

Noreen had come to stand beside her. For a while neither of them said anything, and the refrigerator hummed on into the quiet, the only thing in the room still doing its job.

"He's been at this for a while," Noreen said, quietly.

Years, by the paper alone. On the desk beneath the wall sat the drafts. Letters to the Hickory County Historical Society, the earliest of them typed, courteous, footnoted like a term paper, requesting access to tournament records of the county chess association for the years listed below. The dates on them walked forward through a decade. So did the handwriting that took over from the typing, and the courtesy wore through it as it went, the requests becoming demands, the footnotes becoming underlines, three drafts of the same letter abandoned in a row because the sentences kept standing up and shouting.

Propped against the lamp was an index card, in the spiky hand, pressed hard.

PROOF OF CHEATING.

And beneath it, smaller: Eleanor's father knew.

Mel read the card twice, and put it away whole, the way you pocket a key you don't have the lock for. It went somewhere in her and sat down next to a church parking lot, and she did not introduce the two of them. Not here, standing in another man's grief with his landlord at the door.

She walked the wall a second time, slower, making herself read it as inventory. Crosstables. Notation. Clippings. Letters. Red ink in a code of grievance she couldn't fully parse, circles and crosses and one word, RIGGED, printed sideways in a margin in letters gone through the paper.

And that was all of it. That was everything.

No bees. Not a clipping, not a diagram, not a line. No chemistry beyond pine cleaner losing its argument with the dishes. Nothing about the festival but a single flyer for the tournament itself, dated and squared and thumbtacked at eye height like an appointment kept faithfully for months. The wall did not know how Bernie Travers died. It only knew how he had lived, and what he had taken, and from whom. Built by a man who needed that known in the record by somebody besides himself.

The understanding arrived in her quietly, the way the true shape of a thing does. This was not a murder wall. It was a case. A brief for a prosecution no court was ever going to convene, assembled over ten years by a man who wanted one thing, and the one thing was not Bernie dead. It was Bernie wrong. Publicly, provably, in-the-record wrong, with the record corrected and the name Cheswick restored to wherever it should have stood. You did not spend a decade building a courtroom for a man you meant to bury. The wall needed Bernie alive. Alive to be wrong, alive for him to feel the shame; alive to sit in the front row while the proof was read out.

Somebody had taken that from David Cheswick three days before his tournament, and whatever else his vanishing meant, Mel understood, standing in the smell of his unwashed dishes, that the dead man had ruined him one last time on the way down.

"He didn't run from what he did," she said. "There's nothing here that did anything."

"No," Noreen said. She was looking at the split-open paperback, twenty pages from its end. "There is not."

Mel took a pantry card from her coat, wrote her name and the Spoon's number on the back, and handed it to Kenlee at the door. "If the mail changes. If anything changes. Or if he just comes home."

Kenlee studied the card with his arms straight down, then put it in his shirt pocket behind a folded receipt. "I'll know it from the box before I know it from the man," he said, which from him was a promise, and Mel took it as one.

Going down the stairs she carried the lightness of the wrong answer subtracted, and it weighed more than the question had. They had come looking for a suspect. They were leaving with a man you could only be sorry for, and that was worse than leaving with nothing. The list was shorter now, and the day was older, and she had not added a single thing.

By evening the Spoon had given the day its ordinary shape back. Mel worked the close as she always did, crates broken down and the floor mopped to the door, and the kitchen settled into its after-hours self, furnace ticking somewhere under the floor, the steel counter giving back the lamp. The calendar by the desk had a circle around the twenty-second that she had stopped pretending not to look at. Sixteen days. And east of town, in a binder with the date written on every page in another man's careful print, a boy was keeping a second calendar nobody talked about. On her way past the desk her eye crossed the drawer she didn't open, and kept going.

Mozart was on the phone on the shelf, down low.

Noreen tipped her head at it. "Mozart."

"It helps me think."

"That's what concerns me."

Leo came in at half past eight with his chemistry folder under his arm, smelling faintly of the Sunflower's fryer, and when Mel told him where they had spent their morning he stopped with one arm out of his jacket.

"Building two," he said, and looked personally affronted. "I am in building one. Two years, Mel. I have never once seen that man."

"You work nights and he grieved days," Noreen said. "Sit."

The week went out on the steel counter, all of it. The county minutes and Noreen's notebook. Leo's printouts, squared. The cardboard list with AGNES at the top of it in Mel's own handwriting, the question mark pressed hard. What they had, when you stood back from it, was motive. Arthur's, in a folder Corbin kept. Cheswick's, on a wall ten years deep. Agnes's, two years hot, with an order sheet behind it. Dowen's, twenty-four years cold and rehearsed smooth. Eleanor's father's, even, if you wanted to walk that road. It was a county of motive. The pile on the counter proved nothing except that Bernie Travers had spent forty years with the town owing him, and that everyone in Possum Gap had a reason to dislike or hate him.

Mel had stopped listening to herself shuffle paper. Her eye had gone to the paper bag.

Leo had kept it, folded along its creases in the chemistry folder the way other men keep photographs. The diagram from that first Tuesday evening, drawn in pencil while the kettle cooled: the cedar line, the creek behind it, the little squares of the hives in their rows, the pavilion tent on the far side, and the long arrow crossing all of it, three hundred meters with a favorable breeze.

"This isn't a question of who," Mel said. "Everyone wanted Bernie gone. The question is who could have done this."

She tapped the diagram.

Leo straightened. He had been waiting for her to get there, she saw that now. It was why he'd kept the bag.

"Walk it back to Saturday," she said, and her voice had gone quiet, as it always did when the thing was finally in front of her. "I was twenty feet away. I watched the whole match, same as a hundred other people. Bernie sat down at half past two and from the first move to the moment the air went wrong he never left that chair. Nobody touched him. Nobody handed him so much as a cup of water. Nothing reached that table all afternoon."

"So it couldn't have happened during the game," Leo said.

"It didn't need to." She could see it as she said it, the pavilion light, the felt-lined box. "He opened the box. He took out the white queen and cupped her in both hands and breathed on her, and polished her with that cloth out of his jacket, slow circles, held her up to the light and polished her again. And then he wiped the cloth across his palms." Her own hands had gone still on the counter. "He did it the way he'd done it before every match for as long as Possum Gap had watched him play. The way anybody who had ever once watched Bernie Travers play knew for certain he would do it."

The furnace ticked. Leo had gone very still, the way he did when a mechanism assembled itself in front of him and he didn't want to scare it.

"It was already there," Mel said. "On the queen, before play ever started. Whoever did this never had to come near him. They put it where his own ritual would pick it up, and he lifted it and shined it and rubbed it into his own skin in front of the whole county. He carried it himself."

"Skin's better than wood for it, too," Leo said quietly. "Warm. Moving. A mark on skin doesn't sit still. It rides the man." He looked a little sick saying it, and said it anyway. "His rite did the delivering."

Noreen had not moved from the desk chair, and her stillness had the quality of a court reporter's. Get it all. Sort it later.

"So walk the rest with me," Mel said. "Forget who hated him. Everybody hated him. To do this, this exact thing, you needed three doors to be open to you. You needed the compound, the real one, the one that works, and the knowledge to choose it. You needed the master's table before the grounds filled, when a minute alone at that pavilion belonged to nobody. And then you needed the nerve to stay. All day. To sit in a crowd at a festival and wait for it, and watch it land, and walk out at the end of the afternoon the same color you walked in."

"Three doors," Noreen said, "and every name on that cardboard has to pass all three."

They walked the names through. Arthur, who knew bees better than any man in the county and ordered his supplies on paper through the co-op, who had no catalog account and no card and no use for a synthetic anything, and whose three doors led, every one, to the destruction of the only thing he was staying alive for. Cheswick, who had built a courtroom, not a funeral, and whose entire apartment did not know one thing about bees. The mail answer Noreen's cousin-of-a-cousin had promised was still due midweek, and it mattered differently now. You traced a suspect to catch him. You traced this man to tell him you were sorry, and that he had twenty pages left in his book. And Agnes.

Leo pulled his printout to the front and squared it on the counter, scruple sitting on him like a coat two sizes heavy.

"I got the supplier to confirm the line item this afternoon," he said. "It's what I thought it might be. What Agnes ordered was lemongrass extract, essentially. Geraniol and citral. No 9-ODA. Without the queen compound, you can attract scouts. You cannot direct a swarm." He laid his finger on the chemical names like a man closing a door gently. "What crossed those cedars was directed."

"So not Agnes," Mel said, and was surprised at how much of her wanted it said twice.

"Not with that bottle," Noreen said, in the unhurried way that put each word away clean. "Where she stood Saturday morning is still an open entry, and I will close it properly before anybody strikes her through. But no. Not with that bottle."

The kitchen sat with it. The phone had gone quiet on the shelf without anyone noticing the music end. On the counter the cardboard list lay where Mel had left it, AGNES at the top with the question mark pressed hard, and it looked, suddenly, like a document from an earlier century, a map drawn by people who thought the world was flat. Wrong question, all of it. A week of the wrong question, asked in good faith, of everyone.

Noreen said it from across the room, not loudly.

"Who's left?"

Nobody answered her. Leo looked at his diagram. Mel looked at the penciled cedar line, the little squares in their rows, the long patient arrow crossing three hundred meters to one man, and the answer stood up at the back of her mind and waited there, patient as a man at a door she had not yet opened.

She didn't say it. Not yet. Saying a name out loud was a move, and she had spent enough of this October around chess players to know better than to move before she could see the whole board.

She folded the paper bag along its old creases and handed it back to Leo.

"Keep that safe," she said. "We're going to need it."

More Bad News

The knock came; once, twice, on a cold Tuesday evening. Mel opened the door.

Leo said, "He did it."

Noreen was looking at her notebook, hands flat on the cover, closed. "Knowing and proving are different things."

The furnace ticked under the floor. The calendar by the desk had a circle around the twenty-second that Mel had drawn with a red marker six days ago and had been looking at every evening since without letting herself really look at it. Now she really looked at it. Sixteen days. The circle didn't care.

"It's not a confession either," she said.

Nobody disagreed. The paper bag was in Leo's folder and the cardboard list was on the counter where she'd left it, and neither of them had any use left in them tonight. Outside, the November dark had come in under a clear sky, the kind that meant frost before morning, and the Spoon's front windows had gone black and reflective, nothing beyond them but the shape of the town that would be there again in the morning.

Leo pulled his jacket on. Noreen collected her things with the efficiency of a person who had already decided what came next and needed no time to decide it. Mel walked them out and locked the door and stood on the step a minute in the cold, breathing air that smelled of dead leaves and chimney smoke and the particular silence of a November evening in Possum Gap, and then she went to her car and drove home and did not think about the name, which meant she thought about it the whole way there.

She opened the Giving Spoon at seven as usual, and it looked and smelled the same as it always did in the early hour: coffee and the ghost of yesterday's bread and the particular cold of a closed-off space that waited all night and is only beginning to remember how to be warm. The light came in low and amber through the east window and laid itself across the counter in a long bar that moved slowly, the way autumn light moves when the angle is already everything it's going to be.

Noreen arrived at quarter past and came in through the back, and they worked the open together, Leo coming in at half past with the dairy delivery because the usual driver had called out and Leo had offered because that was the kind of person he was, and by eight the Spoon had its people in it and the morning was doing what mornings do. Mrs. Lund had her usual table. The Mercer brothers came in together for the first time in three weeks and sat without looking at each other, which meant they had made up about something but were not yet ready to say so. The coffee ran out and Leo made more and the smell of it filled the room the way it always did, simple and reliable, and for a while the morning let Mel be someone who just ran a food pantry in a small Tennessee town in November and was mostly glad of it.

It was Sheila Baxter who brought it in. Sheila drove a county school bus route and came in every Tuesday for a coffee and a biscuit before her first run. She set her cup on the counter and said, "Did you all hear what the council did?"

Mel had not heard. She leaned on the counter.

The council had voted Monday morning. Not their regular evening session, but a special meeting called on short notice. Unknown to all until the they had recorded the vote. The item on the agenda: the eradication timeline for the Pumble apiary, given the ongoing burden on county resources and public health concerns, given the petition filed on behalf of concerned citizens. The vote had been four to one to move the date. The new deadline was November fourteenth. Next Tuesday.

The county would move on the apiary unless the police resolved the situation quickly. The petition, Sheila said, had something like fifty names on it.

Sheila said she thought it was a shame, and she did think so, and then her bus route called and she left.

At the far table the Mercer brothers had gone quiet. Mrs. Lund was looking at her coffee cup with the careful attention of a woman who has heard everything and is deciding what to do with it. The morning had not changed. The light still came in at the same angle, the coffee still smelled right, Leo was still in the kitchen. But there was a quality to the room now that had not been there thirty seconds ago, a collective stillness, the way a space changes when everyone in it has heard the same bad news and is waiting to see who will speak first.

Nobody spoke first. Mel stood behind the counter with a coffee going cold in her hand and did the arithmetic.

November seventh. November fourteenth. Seven days. And six of them were actually useful, because the council would meet the day before: Monday the thirteenth, their regular evening time, to confirm the eradication arrangements, which meant Monday the thirteenth was the real door. No matter what should found after that, the bees would be gone. And with them, a significant part of the local color and economy.

Six days.

Noreen was at the back table with her notebook already open, pen uncapped, running some inner calculation that had gotten further than Mel's.

"Then we have a week," Noreen said.

It was not resignation and it was not panic. It was the voice of someone who had already converted catastrophe into a schedule, and it was one of the most useful sounds Mel had ever heard.

"A petition with fifty names," Mel said.

"I heard that part."

"I want to know whose names are on it."

Noreen was already reaching for her phone. "Public record," she said. "Give me until mid-morning."

Mel went back to the kitchen and stood at the sink and did the arithmetic a second time, to see if it came out different. It didn't. Six days, and the last of them was a Monday evening when the council would be meeting, and she would need to be standing in that room with something solid enough that four people who had already voted once would vote the other way. The forged petition, if truly forged, if Noreen found what Mel suspected was there, was only a tool, not a case. It might buy an argument. It would not buy an acquittal. It wouldn't spare the honeybees.

She washed the cup she'd been holding and set it on the rack and went back out.

Noreen had her notebook flat and her phone cradled between ear and shoulder, and she gave Mel a look over the rims of her glasses that meant: *I'm working, don't hover.* Mel didn't hover. She went to work on the mid-morning pantry run, and the Spoon did what the Spoon did, and at nine-fifteen Noreen said "thank you, Denise" into her phone and uncapped her pen, and Mel knew they had the petition.

It was eleven pages. Noreen had it from a woman at Town Hall she'd known since high school, who understood that public records were public and that the quickest way to get Noreen off the phone was to give her what she'd asked for.

Noreen worked from the back table, phone and notebook and printed pages before her, with the steady industry of someone doing a job they know how to do, and she did not rush, and she did not perform. Around her the Spoon did its business. She was not conspicuous about it.

The first problem she found was a man named Russell Tate, page three, who had not signed anything. He told her in some detail that nobody had asked him, that he had no opinion on the subject, and he was fairly certain his name had appeared on a neighborhood feedback form about the sidewalk repair on Magnolia Street, which was a different matter entirely.

The second was Cynthia Pruett, page six, who had moved to Knoxville in September. Noreen confirmed this through the address listed on the petition, still Cochran Street, where a retired schoolteacher named Warren Swan had been renting since October first. Warren Pruett confirmed that Cynthia had given up the lease in late September.

The third she brought to Mel.

"Harold Pickett," Noreen said. She set the page on the counter and put her finger on the line. "Signed October the fourteenth."

Mel read it. Then she read the filing date on the cover page, which Noreen had brought along. The petition had an official stamp showing when it arrived at City Hall: September nineteenth.

Harold Pickett had died August fourteenth.

She had known him. He had been a Giving Spoon regular for as long as she had run the Spoon, a quiet man in his eighties with enormous hands and a brown cardigan he wore from October through April, and a slow particular way of sitting at the counter that said he was in no hurry, had never been in a hurry, considered hurry to be a different person's problem. Every October, without fail, he brought in four jars of crabapple preserves his wife Miriam had put up before she died, working through the last of the supply one jar at a time for the pantry shelf. *She made forty-something years' worth*, he had told Mel once, in the way someone tells you a thing they have decided to find funny because the alternative is worse. He had died in August, cancer and quick, and he had been eighty-one years old, and he had opposed every development proposal that had come before the county commission in the last decade, on grounds he was always prepared to articulate clearly and defend at length, and he would have opposed this one.

His name was on it. Signed two months after he died, and filed the month before.

"He signed this on October the fourteenth," Mel said.

"Two months and some days after he died," Noreen said. "Yes."

Leo had come out of the kitchen, dish towel in his hands, and he read the page over Mel's shoulder and stood there a moment.

"Harold Pickett has been signing things from beyond the grave," he said. "Bernie Travers is not a man who improved in death."

It was exactly the right way to put it.

Mel took the three flagged pages, Tate, Pruett, and Pickett, and the cover page with the petition number and the filing date. The filing date was September nineteenth, three weeks after Harold Pickett had been in the ground and eighteen days after Cynthia Pruett had vacated her lease. The petition had been assembled in advance and padded, and whoever had padded it had not been careful, or had not cared, or had expected the names to pass without anyone looking at them. Bernie's name was not on the filing. His was the kind of operation that left other people's names on the paperwork.

"I'll bring this to Corbin," Mel said.

"It won't close the murder case," Noreen said. She was not discouraging. She was being accurate, which was different. "But it's grounds to challenge the shortened deadline. The council voted on a petition they didn't verify. If you put this in front of Corbin and he puts it in front of the county attorney, Monday the thirteenth becomes a real conversation instead of a formality." She tapped her pen once on the table. "That's what it's worth."

"That's enough," Mel said.

She folded the pages into her coat pocket. It was something solid. In six days with nothing solid, a forged signature in a dead man's name was something she could hold on to.

She stood at the counter a moment and looked at the morning coming through the east window, lower now than it had been an hour ago, the amber bar on the counter gone. Noreen had gone back to her notebook. Leo had gone back to the kitchen. The Spoon was doing its work.

"He had a hobby hive," Mel said.

Noreen did not look up. "Who did."

"Dowen." She hadn't planned to say it aloud. "He mentioned it weeks ago — he uses a swarm lure to attract colonies. I've been thinking about what Leo found last night. About who knew the chemistry well enough to plan for it. Not just guess at it. Plan precisely." She left it there.

Noreen looked up and gave her the look she reserved for sentences that were still missing their last few words.

"I want to go back and talk to him," Mel said.

"Then go talk to him," Noreen said. "I'll be here."

Haven Terrace on a Tuesday afternoon had the quiet of a building going about its own business. The waxed wood of the stairs held the cold of autumn coming in through the weather-stripping, and the brass numbers on the doors caught the corridor window-light and gave it back in a long smear.

Dowen answered at the first knock. He had the manner of a man who did not leave things pending. If there was a knock at his door, he answered it, and he stepped back to let her in without making a production of it. She had not called ahead. He did not seem surprised.

The apartment was as it had been in October: an economy of objects, nothing out of place, the chess board on the side table with a game in progress and no opponent visible. The afternoon light came in from the south window and lay across the floor in a long bar. After a moment Trixie came around the corner from the back hallway at her rolling trot, investigated Mel's coat with professional thoroughness, and went to her bed under the window and turned twice and settled.

Dowen had taken the chair across from hers, unhurried, with the particular stillness of a man who has already decided what kind of conversation this is going to be and does not need it to be anything else.

"I've been doing some research into Bernard Travers's background," Mel said. "Some things came up that I wanted to ask you about."

"All right," he said.

She laid it out simply. The startup, 1998. The algorithm patents filed in 1999, sole inventor named. The attorney. She had documentation, and she did not wave it around. She told him she had it, and she watched him receive that information. He received it with no change in expression. It was not news to him. It had always been documentable. It simply had not, for twenty-four years. Not by anyone with reason to act on it.

"We met at a regional tournament in 1996," he said. His voice had the flat precision of a man reading from a document he has rehearsed enough times that the words have gone smooth, not cold but smooth, with all the inflection worn off. "He had a facility with the endgame I hadn't seen in a non-professional player. When the chess software market opened up after Kasparov and Deep Blue, it seemed like the appropriate moment to put something serious behind a serious idea." A brief pause. "The core algorithm was joint work. There is no version of that work that is not joint work. The patent filing in 1999 named one inventor. Duncan Vance prepared the paperwork."

"And the company."

"Collapsed in 2001 along with everything else in that market. Except that when it collapsed, he had the patents and I had the experience of watching a man I had trusted take the most valuable thing I had built and walk out with it in his briefcase." He looked at the chess board. "Twenty-four years."

No rounding. No *almost a quarter century*. The precision was just how he counted.

"I appreciate you explaining it," Mel said. She let the sentence settle before she went on. "I've also been trying to understand the mechanism of what happened at the festival. The pheromone chemistry. I've talked to someone with a background in it, but I wanted to ask you, since you've been in Possum Gap and following the situation, whether you'd come across anything in your reading about how synthetic bee lure compounds work. The science of it."

He looked at her with the hazel eyes that gave the impression of focused calm.

"A bit," he said.

"The theory I've been given involves a Nasonov component," she said. "Lemon-scented. I wondered if you'd come across anything along those lines."

He turned the question over for a moment the way he might consider a board position, not stalling but actually looking at it.

"The Nasonov pheromone is a recruitment signal," he said. "Geraniol, citral, that whole family. It's what you'll find in most commercial swarm lures. Beekeepers use it to encourage swarms into hive boxes." He paused. "But it isn't the relevant component for what you're describing. Not for direction."

She waited.

"The compound that matters isn't the Nasonov component," he said. "It's the queen mandibular element. Without that, you attract scouts. You don't move a colony."

The afternoon light lay across the floor and the apartment was very quiet. Trixie's ear twitched once and settled.

He seemed to hear what he'd said. Not a falter. Nothing in his face moved. A recalibration, nearly invisible, the adjustment of a man who has said one sentence past where he intended to stop.

"I did some reading," he said. "After what happened at the festival. I imagine a lot of people connected to the chess community did."

"Of course," Mel said.

She asked him two more questions, about the tournament circuit and about Bernie's standing in the local chess community in the years before the dispute went public, and he answered both of them completely and without hesitation, and the answers told her nothing she hadn't already had from other sources, which was exactly what she'd expected.

Then she thanked him and collected her coat from the arm of the chair and stood.

Trixie raised her head from the bed under the window. Then put it back down.

At the door Dowen said, "I hope the situation with Arthur Pumble resolves before the council moves."

"So do I," Mel said.

She went down the waxed stairs, past the brass numbers, and out of the building into the cold of the Tuesday afternoon. She stood on the sidewalk. She let the conversation sit. She was not sure yet what it was or where to put it.

He had corrected her. She had given him a loose description of the chemistry on purpose, the way you give a test something you know the right answer to, to see if it knows the answer back. And he had corrected her without being able to stop himself. *You attract scouts, you don't move a colony*. Then he had heard himself and covered it, and the cover was plausible. Plausible was not the same as true.

She was not going to say so to anyone yet. She had nothing that amounted to anything. She had the chemistry of a man who had done some reading, according to himself, and who could not let an imprecision stand.

She had six days. She had a forged signature in her coat pocket that might buy one more conversation with the council. She had a list with Agnes at the top of it, Agnes whose timing on Saturday morning was still an open question, whose lemon-myrtle order still sat in a supplier's records regardless of what Leo had said about the chemistry, and she had Leo still running his numbers, and she had November fourteenth waiting at the end of the week the way a door waits at the end of a corridor, and behind that door the council and Arthur's bees and a verdict that could not be undone once it was done.

She walked to her car and got in and sat without starting it for a moment, the way she sometimes needed to.

You attract scouts. You don't move a colony.

She started the car. She had work to do.

Thieves and Vandals

The back door was open.

Not all the way. Just a few inches, the way a door stands when someone has pulled it not quite shut on the way out and the latch hasn't caught and the November air has been pushing it open by degrees through the night. The cold came in through the gap and met the residual warmth of the kitchen and made something that was neither, and Mel stood in the alley with her key still in her hand, looking at the gap of darkness between the door and the frame.

She had locked this door. She had locked it at ten Monday evening and tested the knob the way she always did, habit older than the investigation. She had locked it.

She went in.

The kitchen was wrong before she could name any specific thing. The overhead light showed her touches in a room where it had no business being touched: a cabinet not quite closed, a rack of pans shifted half an inch, something on the prep counter moved from where she kept it. The Giving Spoon had a particular grammar of placement, objects in their positions the same way every morning, and what she was looking at was a sentence with the words in the wrong order. She moved through to the office area behind the counter and found what she had already been afraid to find.

The folder was gone.

The cabinet under the register, the one she'd bought specifically because it locked though she hadn't bothered to lock it, was closed but not latched. The folder that had lived in it was not there. The one with her handwritten case notes. The chemistry summary Leo had printed and annotated for her. The cardboard suspect list she had rewritten twice, AGNES at the top each time, the question mark pressed hard. The timeline, the supplier printout, the stack of notes from six days of trying to understand what had happened at the festival. Gone.

The petty cash tin was on its shelf. She opened it. Untouched.

She stood in the quiet of the Giving Spoon in the early morning and looked at the space where the folder had been and let the message land.

Leo arrived eleven minutes later, before she had called him. He had come for the early prep as usual and found her standing in the office with the cabinet open. He looked at it. He looked at her. He put the kettle on and while it heated he walked the room with her: the kitchen, the pantry shelves, the two back tables with their chairs turned at odd angles, the half-open drawer of vendor invoices that had been gone through and left that way.

It was Leo who noticed the granola bars.

He stopped at the end of the pantry shelf and looked at the gap between the trail mix and the protein bars, a space that had held a small orange box of oats-and-honey granola bars since Monday. He stood there with the expression of a man who has found himself unexpectedly offended.

"They took the granola bars," he said.

"I see that."

"They broke into the Giving Spoon, went through your investigation files, and took a box of granola bars."

"It appears so."

He looked at the gap a moment longer. "I find that both reassuring and deeply irritating," he said, and went to finish making coffee.

She called Corbin while the coffee brewed. He arrived in twenty-five minutes, which told her he had not been entirely surprised by the call. He moved through the space with the economy of motion of someone who knew what he could document and what he couldn't. He wrote down the missing folder and the open cabinet and the forced latch, near-forced enough to count, and examined the back door without touching it and asked her in a neutral tone whether she had any sense of who might have been interested in those files. She told him she had no specific person to name. He wrote something in his notebook and did not share it.

"You want to file a report," he said. It was not quite a question.

"Yes," she said.

He filed it. He was thorough and professional and offered nothing that would have been useful to her. He asked her, as he was putting his notebook away, whether she had been in contact with any individuals who might have reason to interfere with an informal investigation. She said she had spoken with several people in the course of asking about the festival. He nodded as if this confirmed a working theory he was keeping to himself, and she did not ask what the theory was because she knew he would not tell her.

He stayed twenty minutes and left. She walked him to the back door and stood in the open frame after his car pulled out of the alley, the cold coming in around her.

She did not tell him about the petition pages. They were at home, in her coat pocket, exactly where she had put them Tuesday afternoon. Whoever had come through her kitchen the night before had not gotten them. She turned this over once: the folder had been taken, and the petition had not, because the petition had been with her. The investigation had been visible enough to target but not complete enough to stop. She put it away.

Noreen arrived at quarter to eight and asked her first question before she had taken off her coat.

"Is anything actually irreplaceable?"

Mel considered it the way the question deserved. The chemistry notes were Leo's, generated from his own research and living in his head with more precision than she had written down. The suspect timeline she could reconstruct in an hour. The cardboard list was in her memory better than it had ever been on paper.

"No," she said.

"Then they've inconvenienced us." Noreen hung her coat, took out her notebook, uncapped her pen. "That's all."

Mel wanted to believe the first part. The second part she had already been sitting with for an hour.

"What they've told us by doing this," Noreen said, as if she had been continuing a thought rather than starting one, "is considerably more useful than anything that was in that folder." She looked at the cabinet. "They knew which one. They came here knowing where to look."

She said it the way she said things she had already worked out, clearly and without drama, and went to put the coffee on for the regulars.

Mel stood at the counter and looked at the Spoon, her kitchen, her tables, the window with the early-morning light coming through it low and amber. She held onto thoughts of what she couldn't say in any way that was useful: that the injury was not the notes. Someone had been in here in the dark. Had stood where she stood, gone through what she kept. Had walked out with her work and a box of granola bars, and the particular violation was not the theft but the visibility. Someone knew what she had been doing. Someone had come to look at it.

She opened the Giving Spoon an hour late and let the morning do what mornings do. The regulars came in and did not ask about the hour, which was its own sort of kindness: Mrs. Lund with her usual order, two men from the electricians' shop who always took the far table, a woman Mel did not know by name but recognized by the order she never changed. The Giving Spoon has always been a place where people come to be ordinary when ordinary is what they need, and that morning the ordinary held, and Mel was grateful for it the way you are grateful for things you have taken for granted until the day you needed them.

Derek called at half past nine. His voice had the tight flatness of a man managing something he had not yet had time to feel. She drove out to Mashburn Creek without telling anyone where she was going.

She found him already working in the hive rows.

Two hives lay on their sides, their frames knocked loose, the inner covers scattered in the frost-bitten grass. Three more had their entrances blocked with bunched rags, the cloth gray from having been there a few hours in the cold. Derek had cleared the entrances before she arrived and was resettling the frames in the first tipped hive now, his movements precise and careful in a way that cost him something to maintain. The smoker sat lit beside him on the upturned crate he used for a work table, and the smell of it met her halfway down the row: cool and woody, the sweet-ferment scent of disturbed colonies underneath, smoke and cold and the smell of November at a working apiary.

She pulled her collar up and came alongside him.

"Queens are intact," he said without looking up. "Both. I checked before I called you." Meaning: this was my first concern and I addressed it before I did anything else. "The colonies are stressed but they're not broken. Blocked entrances in warm weather would have overheated the little workers. We're lucky it isn't warm."

"Lucky."

"Not luck, I think. They did it when they knew it would be cold." He worked a damaged frame back into its slot with careful even pressure. "Planned."

Mel looked at the blocked entrances Derek had cleared. Cut or torn rags, in rough strips rather than whole-cloth; the kind of preparation that suggested they weren't from a rag bag but something brought specifically for this purpose. She said nothing about this. Derek would have noticed it too, and noticed her noticing it, and neither of them needed to say the obvious thing aloud.

Mel helped where she could. Hold this. Pass that. Stand here so the entrance is clear while I work. She had no real bee skills and Derek did not waste time pretending she did; he gave her the simple tasks and did the rest himself, and she followed his lead and watched his hands. He knew these colonies. She could see it in how he moved between them, the small adjustments he made, the things he checked that she would not have known to check.

They worked through the cold in a rhythm that did not require much conversation. The hive rows stretched south toward Mashburn Creek, and the cedar line to the west stood dark against the gray November sky, and through the gap where the windbreak had a thinning she could see, at a distance, the pale shape of the festival tent still standing at the park's eastern edge. She did not look at it long.

After a while Derek said, "I've been through every hive in the row. The other seven are untouched. Whatever they wanted, they got enough of it." He said this with the same dispassion he had used for everything else, a man reading a damage report.

Mel pulled a frame steady while he examined it. "The colonies. Can they recover before the deadline?"

"If they're left alone from here out? Yes." He didn't say what they both understood: There were no guarantees.

They resettled the second colony and Derek fitted the inner cover and stood back to look at the row. He stripped his outer gloves and the cold took his hands immediately.

"Arthur is going to hear about this," he said.

"I know."

"He can't. Not yet."

They both understood this was not a decision they could hold for long. The hospital had visitors. People from the chess club had already been out twice. The information would find its own way there, and the only question was when and from what direction.

"I know," Mel said.

He nodded once, as if that settled what it could settle. He put his gloves back on and moved to the next hive in the row, beginning the systematic check he had already planned for himself, working from south to north. He had a notebook in his jacket pocket. He had already called two experienced keepers he'd gotten from the contact list in Arthur's binder; they were coming Friday.

Mel stayed until the third hive stood where it belonged. The hive rows looked, from the far end of the line, as they always did: white boxes in their south-facing run, the creek behind them, the cedar windbreak to the west blocking the view of the park. Normal. Only the flattened grass near the two tipped hives and the faint sweet smell of disturbed wax said otherwise. She stood there a moment with that contrast, the ordinary view and the ordinary broken inside it, and then she filed it where she filed things she could not act on yet.

Then she said she needed to get back, and he said he knew, and she walked up through the meadow without looking at the festival tent again. The cold was in her hands by the time she reached her car, and she sat a moment with the heater running before she pulled out, her breath making a small cloud in the front seat. Ahead of her the road ran back toward town, and behind her the apiary was quiet in the November air, and Derek was still in it, working.

Silver Oak in the afternoon had a different quality than Silver Oak in the morning. The overhead lights ran at a steadier pitch, the nursing staff moved with the particular unhurried competence of people who have been at this for hours and have hours still to go, and the smell of the place had become, after six weeks of visits, a smell she knew: antiseptic braided with something staler and more human, the layered smell of a building where people spent long days in small rooms.

Arthur's room was on the second floor. The window looked out over the parking structure and, above it, a narrow band of sky. The fluorescent light kept an even white that had nothing to do with the time of day or the weather outside. On the bedside table: a plastic cup with a flexible straw, a small bottle of hand lotion, the laminated chess problem card face-down. The chair that she'd placed close to the bed on her first visit had never been moved back to its original position. Someone was always coming to see Arthur, and the nurses had stopped moving it.

He was awake. His eyes tracked her from the door and he said "Mel" in the voice that was all he had to spare now: even, unhurried, a voice that had stopped performing. She came in and sat in the chair.

He asked about the hives before he asked about anything else. She had expected this and had decided on the drive over to tell him plainly, because he would know if she softened it. She told him: two tipped, three blocked, both queens intact, Derek managing, keepers coming Friday.

He looked at the sky above the parking structure while she said it. When she finished he was quiet for a moment.

"How bad is the frame damage," he said.

"Derek says repairable."

"He would know."

"Yes."

He closed his eyes.

"Derek's a good boy," he said.

He said it the way someone says a thing they have been hoping was true and now know is, the settling of an account that had been open without either party naming it. Eyes closed, voice level, no inflection except the one that meant: this is not a compliment, this is a conclusion. There was a quality to his stillness afterward, a loosening. Some tension he had held tight to for a long time. He had given it leave to stop.

Mel sat with him as the strain slipped away.

They talked for a while after that. He asked about the pantry and she told him they were managing, which was true, and he said that was good and didn't press it. A woman from the chess club had brought him a chess problem on a laminated card. He showed it to her from the bedside table, a middlegame position printed in black and white. *Take as long as you need* showed on the back in a careful hand. She said it looked hard. He said most of the interesting ones were. His hands lay on the blanket above the covers, and she noticed, as she always did now, how different they looked from the hands that had delivered honey to the Giving Spoon for four years, still large, still the right shape, but with some quality of lightness they had not always had, the weight migrated somewhere he had not needed it.

He asked about Noreen. She told him Noreen had been essential, the way Noreen always was when things were serious. He smiled. He asked about Leo. She told him Leo was still running down the chemistry. He nodded as if he had known this would be the case.

"You're going to clear this," he said. He said it the way he said things he had decided: not a wish, not a question, not encouragement. A conclusion drawn from evidence.

"That's the plan," she said.

He looked at her for a moment. "You've been a good neighbor to me, Mel."

She didn't know what to say to that, so she said thank you and he nodded and they sat quietly for a while, and then his breathing changed as it does when the effort of being awake has tipped past what the body will sustain, and his eyes closed, and he was asleep.

The doctor caught her in the corridor. Young and practical, possessed of the skill of reading what kind of information a person could receive without a cushion. He saw quickly that Mel was the plainspoken kind.

"The stress has accelerated things," he said. "His numbers this week aren't where we'd want them."

"What's the timeline."

"Weeks. Probably." He held her gaze. "Maybe less, depending on the next few days."

She thanked him. He went back toward the nurses' station and she stood in the corridor with the fluorescent light and the antiseptic smell. The second floor was doing its ordinary business around her: a cart going by, a door opening and closing, a conversation at the nurses' station that had nothing to do with Arthur. She stood in the middle of all that ordinary business and held what the doctor had said until it was the right size to carry, and then she carried it.

Then she went back in.

She sat in the chair beside his bed while he slept. The sky above the parking structure had gone the pale gray of late November afternoon, the color of a day that has given up on brightness without going dark, and the room was quiet around his breathing. His hands were on the blanket. The chess problem was on the bedside table with the answer still in it.

She had five days.

She did not think about that in this room. She sat with him, and the light did what November light does, and she stayed until the floor changed shift and someone came by to check the IV, and then she drove home through the early dark.

The petition pages were in her coat pocket. She had five days. She drove and did not think about the granola bars, which meant she thought about them briefly, and then she thought about what Leo had said in the Giving Spoon that morning, and what Noreen had said, and what Arthur had said with his eyes closed and the particular quality of a man who has been waiting a long time to say a true thing, and then she was home, and she went inside, and she put the kettle on.

Team and Truth

The Giving Spoon was dark when Mel arrived, the chairs still up on the tables, the morning unlaunched. She had left the hospital after midnight and slept four hours and driven back through a town going about its ordinary Thursday business without knowing the particular quality of the week she was in. She let herself in through the front door and stood in the threshold, out of habit now, checking the grammar of the room. The grammar was right. The room was as she had left it.

Noreen was already at the back table.

She had the supplies box on the chair beside her, the one she brought for the long kind of work, the kind requiring a second notebook and her own pen and the specific mechanical pencil she used for diagrams. Her coat was on the hook. Her coffee cup was half-empty. The notebook in front of her was nearly full on its current page, the handwriting small, organized the way a card catalog is organized because that is the way Noreen organizes everything.

Mel sat down across from her without an invitation.

"The folder," Noreen said, still writing. "Reconstructed. Suspect timeline here, chemistry summary here, the supplier printout from Leo's notes because I copied it into mine when he showed it to us." She turned the notebook so Mel could read the section headings. "I've also called Denise at Town Hall about the petition challenge. It's in process. The county attorney received the documentation Wednesday evening. We'll know Monday whether the grounds hold for reopening the council meeting as a real conversation."

"That's the best we can hope for."

"For now. Yes." Noreen turned the notebook back and made a note. "I made two more calls this morning before you arrived."

Mel waited.

"The first: a contact at the state beekeeper association about BeeLure Professional commercial availability. It's sold through agricultural supply networks and some hardware chains. No permit required below the hobbyist quantity threshold. Cash purchases leave no mandatory record." She looked up. "Which means anyone who knew what to buy could have walked into a store and walked out with it and left no trace."

"Or ordered it," Mel said.

"Under any name. Shipped to any address." Noreen capped her pen. "The people who manufacture BeeLure are selling it to beekeepers and orchard managers and fruit growers. They are not tracking individual buyers. It's garden supply." A pause. "This was not a hard product to obtain. What was hard was knowing to obtain it, and knowing the formulation that would work, and knowing where to put it and how."

"Or ordered online."

"Under any name, paid in advance, shipped to a post office box. Yes." She capped her pen and uncapped it again. "The second call was Tim Renshaw. He has information about Cheswick's rental car from Corbin's Athens thread. He said he'd come by today."

"Good."

Leo arrived at quarter past nine with his chemistry folder and his printouts in order and the paper bag still folded in the side pocket where it had been since the midpoint scene two nights ago. He sat down without taking off his jacket and put his folder on the table and looked at both of them.

"I need to tell you both something about the chess pieces," he said.

Noreen closed her notebook. "Go on."

He had started, he said, not with the chemistry but with the behavior.

What a colony does. How it moves when it is tracking a pheromone target versus how it moves when disturbed. Foraging or swarming naturally. He had gone back to his week-one notes and the witness accounts from the festival and looked at the swarm's trajectory, and the thing that had been bothering him was this: a compound applied to Bernie's person (his jacket, his hat, applied covertly in the hours before the match) would have required direct physical access to Bernie Travers. And Bernie Travers on festival day was not a man who was easy to approach without festival-goers noticing.

"He was the event," Leo said. He had his printout on the table, the festival map Mel had been looking at since October. "He was walking the grounds. He was performing. Everyone was watching him. Anyone who came close enough to apply a compound to his clothing or his skin must have been seen by someone." He set his finger on the map. "It's the wrong access point."

Mel looked at the cedar row, the pavilion, the hive rows behind it.

"The chess pieces," she said.

"The master's table is set up in advance. Hours before the tournament opens. The organizing committee and senior officials work the setup window before seven in the morning, before the crowds arrive. They place the pieces and leave the boards. The pieces sit there until play begins." He looked up. "Bernie opens the case. He takes out the white queen. He breathes on it and polishes it in slow circles and wipes the cloth across his palms. He does this in front of a full pavilion, the same as he has done before every match anyone in this county has ever watched him play."

"He carries it to his own hands," Mel said.

"And from his hands to his skin. The compound concentrates on him because he concentrates it on himself. The swarm tracks him because his personal scent load is highest. Not the pieces anymore, not the table, him." Leo squared the printout. "The swarm hits during play, not before. Before play, he's moving through the festival grounds, visible, dynamic, no consistent location. The bees aren't tracking him then. They respond when he sits down and begins handling the treated pieces, and the BeeLure transfers, and then he sits there for forty-five minutes not moving, the clearest possible target."

The room was still. Noreen had her mechanical pencil in her hand but was not writing.

"The slow-release question," Mel said.

"Right." Leo pulled a second sheet from his folder. "A surface-applied liquid on the base of a chess piece would volatilize significantly over several hours at room temperature. The active compounds would have dispersed well before the match. For the compound to still be meaningfully present when Bernie handled the piece, two or three hours after application, it would need to be in a slow-release carrier. A polymer gel or a rubber medallion or something similar. Commercial BeeLure products are often formulated this way." He set the sheet down. "Someone either bought the commercial slow-release product specifically, or they understood the chemistry of controlled-release formulation well enough to prepare one."

He let that sit.

"The pavilion in the early morning," Noreen said from across the table. She had her mechanical pencil in her hand. "Before the grounds filled. Who did they authorize to be there."

"Setup crew," Leo said. "Organizing committee. Senior tournament officials. Anyone with a credential for the morning prep window." He paused. "It's not a large group. It's a documented group. If someone checked the sign-in sheet from that morning, if there was a sign-in sheet, you'd have the list."

"Was there a sign-in sheet," Mel said.

Neither of them knew. Noreen wrote it down.

"This is not improvised," Mel said.

"No. This is someone who thought through every variable. How to get the compound onto the target. How to ensure it remained active. How to make the target carry it to himself. How to stay out of the crowd during the attack." He paused. "Patient. Precise. Working from real chemistry knowledge."

The closed Giving Spoon held the three of them and the problem they were working on, and the November morning came through the front window at its low angle, and somewhere up the block a truck was reversing with its beeper going, the ordinary Thursday world continuing outside.

"Before seven," Mel said. "Saturday morning. Before the grounds filled."

"Before the grounds filled. Yes."

Something crossed her mind: a line from Noreen's notebook, the canvass from the week after the festival, the morning-after walk through the park. A man with a small dog, moving back and forth near the chess area in the early hours, before the gates opened. Black and white, the dog. Little thing. The fragment surfaced and she felt the edge of something she couldn't quite hold, and then Leo was talking again about the slow-release formulation and she let the fragment go. She had a list to walk and four days left and Agnes at the top of a column that was becoming more documentable by the hour.

"Okay," she said. "Let's walk it."

Noreen spread her reconstructed notebook across the counter. The Giving Spoon wasn't open, and the afternoon light came in at the flat angle of November, and the three of them stood at the counter with the suspect columns in front of them and worked through them name by name.

Arthur Pumble: festival access, yes. Knowledge of bee behavior, yes, forty years of it. But the mechanism of the attack argued for his innocence in a way the investigation had been building toward since the midpoint: the swarm crossed the cedar line with precision and purpose that only served to highlight how unlike Arthur's working relationship with his colonies this was. He managed them gently. He understood their behavior at the level of years of observation. He would have known the risks to his own bees, that the attack would reflect back on them, on him, on everything he had been trying to protect. And he had no chemistry catalog. He ordered on paper through the co-op. No BeeLure purchase, no slow-release substrate, no synthetic formulation of any kind.

"He's the one it was designed to frame," Mel said.

"Yes," Noreen said. She wrote a note.

David Cheswick: absent from the festival grounds. The canvass had established his absence; Corbin's Athens trace had confirmed it; and when Tim Renshaw arrived this afternoon with the rental car detail, that would close it cleanly. Off the list.

Gregory Dowen: he had been at the pavilion early. Tournament director, or senior official, or whatever precise role had put him in the setup window: Mel had heard this from more than one source in the course of the investigation. He had the access. He had the twenty-four years and the hobby hive and the morning constancy and the chemistry correction he had made on Tuesday afternoon that she had not yet assembled into anything she could name aloud. She had all of those pieces, and she did not put them on the table. She had not assembled them into an accusation she could hand to Corbin. She had the chemistry fluency, filed. She had the twenty-four years, established. She had the timing, now established by Leo's analysis. What she did not have was a documented purchase. She did not have a compound she could trace to him. She had Agnes, whose supplier account was on record with a real address and a real order. She had the documentable case. She would work the documentable case and keep the other thing where it was, behind her attention, until she could do something with it.

She did not have a documented compound. She had Agnes.

"Agnes Moskov," she said.

Noreen wrote it first.

The case for Agnes, line by line. She had been at the festival, present from the early morning, her son playing the match. She had ordered a citrus-family attractant from a Nashville beekeeping supplier in the spring, the order on record with the forum account AMoskov and a Possum Gap shipping address. She grew lemon myrtle in her shop's south corner, the same chemical family, which had been visible to Mel since Scene 9 of the investigation. She had a documented public conflict with Bernie over her planning application, committee-declined, Bernie's objection on record in the county minutes.

And the line that closed it, the one Mel said flatly because it was true: "She's the only one whose compound I can actually document."

Leo had been quiet through the list. He was looking at his printout the way he looked at things he had not quite finished with.

"The compound isn't quite right," he said.

Both of them looked at him.

"What Agnes ordered was the citrus family. Geraniol and citral." He moved the printout a few inches on the counter, a small unnecessary adjustment, the gesture of a man organizing his thoughts through his hands. "An orientation signal. It tells scouts a swarm box is here, there is something worth investigating. You can attract a colony to a new location with it. It works for what her supplier account suggests she was trying to do." He looked up. "But what happened at the festival required 9-ODA. The queen mandibular component. You cannot direct a foraging swarm at a specific target across three hundred meters of open ground with geraniol and citral. It is not possible with that formulation."

"You're sure," Mel said.

"I've been running this since Tuesday. I believe it." He set the printout flat. "But I haven't confirmed it in the form I can present to Corbin. I want one more day."

"One more day," Mel said.

"Yes. Tomorrow morning."

She looked at the counter. She took the petition pages from her coat pocket, the three fraudulent entries and the cover page and the timeline that challenged the grounds for the shortened deadline, and set them on the counter beside Noreen's notebook.

“I’m taking these to Corbin this afternoon,” she said. “Get the challenge into the record before the weekend. Then tomorrow, when you have the chemistry confirmation, I’ll talk to Agnes.”

Noreen looked at the petition pages and said nothing about Agnes’s Saturday morning location, which was still an open entry in her notebook, not yet closed. She picked up her mechanical pencil and made a note.

Corbin sat at his desk when she came in, which meant he had been expecting her or had not left the building since morning. He looked up and said “Ms. Hunter” with the particular tone he used for things that did not surprise him.

She set the petition pages on his desk. Tree flagged entries: Russell Tate, who had not signed; Cynthia Pruett, who had left town before the petition began; Harold Pickett, who had died in August and signed in October. The filing date: September nineteenth. The timing, laid out plainly.

Corbin looked at the pages without picking them up. His expression did not change, which was his way of absorbing something significant.

“Where did these come from,” he said.

“Public record. Town Hall. I filed a freedom-of-information request.” She had done no such thing. Noreen had done it, through Denise, through a high school acquaintance and a working knowledge of what was and was not technically a public record. The answer was accurate enough.

He picked up the Harold Pickett page. He looked at it for a moment.

“Pickett,” he said. “He died in August.”

“August fourteenth. Before the petition went out. The signature’s date is October fourteenth.”

He set it back down. He aligned the three pages into a neat stack with the same automatic precision he used for everything else, and he looked at her.

"I'll be honest with you," he said, which was a phrase she had not heard from him before. "The council voted on grounds that they believed were solid. Sold to them that way. If the petition is invalid, the eradication order is as well." He paused. "I'll take this to the county attorney this afternoon."

"That's what I'm asking."

He nodded once. He did not thank her. He did not apologize for anything, either, which was appropriate, because an apology from Corbin would have felt like a different kind of wrong. He was doing what the evidence required. That was the correct response.

"The case is still open," he said, as she was standing to go.

"I know."

"If you have more of this kind of thing, bring it to me." He looked at the petition pages on his desk. "Bring it early."

She left. The afternoon was gray and cold and the street outside the police station smelled of exhaust and coming rain, and she drove back toward the Giving Spoon with something that was not quite relief but was adjacent to it: the petition was in Corbin's hands now, and he would do with it what the evidence required, and that was the most she had been able to say for certain all week.

Tim Renshaw's office had the warm smell of a building that had been in its current use for many years: floor cleaner and paper and the faint woodsmoke from the bakery two doors down. The gold lettering on the frosted glass door said *Renshaw Insurance & Financial Services* in a font his father had paid for when he opened the office, the letters worn to an almost-copper on the bottom curves where decades of hands had pushed through. Mel had noticed this before and had not, until this particular Friday morning, thought about what it meant to inherit a name above a door.

Tim stood when she came in, which was his manner. He did not make a production of it.

The church-league coffee mug was on his desk, the one he had been drinking from in the mornings for as long as anyone who used Renshaw Insurance had been coming here. His jacket was on the back of his chair. The desk had the organized clutter of a person who processes paper quickly and files it the same day, which was, Mel had decided some time ago, a form of competence that expressed character.

"I was going to call," he said. "I heard about the Giving Spoon."

"We're managing."

He received this the same way he received everything: without pressing it, without dismissing it, with the particular attentiveness of a person who has decided that what someone says about themselves is probably closer to true than what he might suppose about them.

He passed along what he had. The rental car Cheswick took out of Athens, Tennessee: a mid-size sedan, blue, returned clean, no damage report. The information had come to Martin Kenlee through the sheriff's department, and Tim had heard it from Kenlee when he called about something else entirely. He had been holding it since Noreen's inquiry earlier in the week, not sure when it was useful.

"Cheswick's closed," Mel said.

"That's how I read it."

They were both standing, which was the natural posture of a conversation that wasn't quite a visit. The mug on his desk had the chess club logo from a tournament three years back. A community sponsor contribution from Renshaw Insurance, his father's habit continued. She had not been inside this office before and she was cataloguing it the way she catalogued everything, storing it without knowing why.

At the door he said: "You're not going to stop, are you."

Not a question.

"No," Mel said.

He nodded once. Deliberate. As if he had expected that, and as if it was one of several things about her he had arrived at an understanding of, quietly, without announcement, the way a person learns what they need to know about someone they have been paying attention to without knowing they were paying attention.

She left. The November morning was cold and bright, and she drove back toward the Giving Spoon with four days left and Leo's confirmation coming in the morning and the nod still there somewhere behind her attention. She let it be. She had Agnes and the council and Arthur's clock and a chemistry confirmation she expected by seven the next morning.

She drove and thought about what Leo would find, and what it would mean when he found it, and whether she was ready for the aftermath.

Confrontation and Confession

Agnes Moskov's shop occupied the ground floor of a narrow building on Maple Street, sandwiched between a dry goods store and an insurance office that had been closed since September. The front window displayed dried herb bundles and small bottles of oil and sachets of things that smelled sharp or sweet depending on what you stood nearest to. The bell above the door was small and sounded more like a request than an announcement. The shop was open, which meant Agnes was there, which was what Mel had been counting on.

Noreen went in first.

The shop smelled of dried citrus and something older underneath, the smell of a room used for the same work for many years. Agnes was at the worktable in the back, sorting small glass bottles into rows and writing in pencil on small adhesive labels. She looked up when they came in and something in her face changed at the sight of Mel in a way she did not quite have time to conceal before the professional warmth closed over it.

"Mel." A beat. "Noreen."

"Agnes." Mel let her eyes move around the room. The drying bundles hanging from the ceiling hooks. The labeled shelf jars: rosemary, lavender, spearmint, something she couldn't name. The small refrigeration unit in the corner with the handwritten signs. And the lemon myrtle in its clay pot by the south window, growing in the corner where the afternoon light came in the longest.

She looked at it for the time it deserved.

The same chemical family. Geraniol, citral, the citrus orientation signal that Leo had explained in Act IIA and confirmed in Act IIB. The compound Agnes had ordered from the Nashville supplier. The compound that, in its commercial form with the right carrier chemistry, could orient a colony toward a target. Growing in a pot in the south window of Agnes Moskov's shop, where anyone could have seen it and none of them had thought to see it until now.

She kept her voice even.

Agnes had stopped sorting the bottles when they came in and had not resumed. The worktable between them was a workspace that doubled as a counter when needed, the kind of flat surface that accumulates the materials of a daily practice: a set of small funnels, a cloth, a pencil with a worn eraser, a notebook open to a page of inventory notes. It was the table of someone who had been doing the same careful work for a long time.

The stool she sat on was a working stool, the kind without a back, and the worktable between them held a row of half-labeled bottles and a cloth and a small glass funnel. Agnes's hands, when she folded them on the table, were a craftsperson's hands: particular, capable, a little rough at the knuckles. She had been doing this work for a long time.

She had come to ask, she said, not to accuse. There were things she needed to understand. She asked if they could sit.

Agnes gestured to the stools at the worktable. Her movements were the careful movements of a person who has decided in advance how to receive something difficult and is discovering that the decision does not make it easier.

Mel laid it out clearly and without rushing. The supplier order: the AMoskov forum account, the spring purchase, the citrus-family attractant compound, the Possum Gap shipping address. The festival timeline: Agnes had been at the grounds from early that Saturday morning, and the setup window in which a person could contaminate the chess pieces had been before seven. The conflict with Bernie: the planning application, the documented objection, the committee vote that went against her.

She watched Agnes receive each piece. Agnes's hands had gone still on the worktable. Her expression had the quality of someone watching a clock run backward: wrong, but each step internally consistent.

Mel asked her to explain the purchase.

She said it without inflection. She had laid out the evidence as she had laid out food quantities and pantry budgets for twelve years: without emotion that would confuse what was fact and what was commentary. The evidence was there. It was on the table between them, too substantial for anyone to ignore or wish away.

Agnes looked at the worktable for a moment. Then she looked at the lemon myrtle in the window. Then she looked at Mel.

"I didn't do it," she said.

"Agnes—"

"I didn't." Her voice broke cleanly. Not loudly. The kind of break that comes before a larger one, the kind that has been building for a while and finally finds a place to open. "I know how it looks. I have known exactly how it looks since the day after the festival, and I've been going over it every night, and I can't—" She pressed her fingers to the space between her eyebrows and held them there for a moment. "I have not been able to find the version of this that sounds like what it actually is."

Mel waited.

"There's a hive box," Agnes said. "Behind the shop. In the corner by the back fence, out of sight from the alley. I set it up in July." She stopped. She looked at the wall for a moment, then at Mel. "Arthur said once that I had the kind of patience bees require. He said it the first time he showed me the apiary, years ago, before all of this with Bernie. I had been thinking about it ever since." She looked at her hands. "I found the compound online when I was researching. I thought if I could attract a swarm naturally, without purchasing a nucleus hive, I could start small. The way Arthur started." She paused. "The package arrived in early October. I held it for a few days. Then I decided I couldn't use it. Not while all of this was happening. I threw it in the bin the night before the festival." She stopped again. "And then I took it back out. I could not stop thinking about what it looks like. I put it back in the box behind the shop. It's still there. I never opened it."

The words had come out in fragments, out of order, with the shape of truth assembled by someone too frightened to put it together correctly. The hive box behind the shop. Arthur's words about patience. The unopened package.

Mel heard the recognition arrive: something Arthur had said once, something from the early visits when he could still come to the Giving Spoon, a comment about Agnes Moskov's patience and her quiet curiosity about the hives that came to the Giving Spoon's clover corner in summer. She held the recognition against what was in front of her. The recognition was real. It was not sufficient. Agnes was crying now with the specific quality of someone who has been holding something too long and has finally set it down, but setting it down in the wrong place. The explanation had come out in fragments and out of order, and the fragments were plausible in isolation and implausible in combination, and Mel had been looking for a coherent exoneration and had not received one.

She had received an explanation. She could not tell, in this room, with this evidence on this table, whether the explanation was true.

She filed the distinction in the place where she filed things she could not act on yet, and she did not take it out again.

"I'd like to see the package," Mel said.

Agnes took them through the back of the shop and out through the rear door into the cold alley, to a corner where the fence met the building wall and a wooden box sat half-covered with a piece of tarpaulin. She lifted the tarpaulin. Inside: a cardboard shipping box, taped shut, unopened.

Mel looked at it. She looked at the address label. She looked at Agnes.

Agnes wiped her eyes. "I kept it because I thought, if I threw it away, and it showed up, there would be no way I could prove I never used it. Keeping it seemed like the safer choice." She gave a short, terrible laugh. "I understand that it's not, now."

Mel thanked her. She and Noreen left through the back door.

Corbin's office showed the flatness of official space that she had been in enough times now to know by smell. She sat across from his desk and told him what she had. The supplier order. The chemical match. The festival timeline. Agnes's presence at the festival. The conflict in the planning records. The confrontation this afternoon, and Agnes's account of it: the hive box, the unopened package, the explanation that had not come out in any coherent order. She gave him the words Agnes had said without interpreting them. The hive box behind the shop. The unopened package. The explanation that had not coalesced. The claim: I didn't do it. She said all of this neutrally, as a record.

He listened as he had not been listening for two weeks. He asked questions. He asked if there was independent verification of the chemistry. She told him yes. He asked about the physical evidence. She told him the package existed, confirmed in person: shipping box, still taped, behind the shop in a corner covered with tarpaulin. She had looked at it herself. He could verify it. He wrote something down and asked if she knew the lot number or the supplier batch code. She did not. He noted that.

He asked if she had any reason to believe Agnes had access to the chemical knowledge required for a slow-release preparation. She told him about Leo's analysis: the slow-release matrix, the chemistry required, the narrow group of people who would know to use one. She did not say that Agnes's compound, if it was what the label said, was probably the wrong formulation for what had happened at the festival. She didn't say that because she did not have that from Leo yet in confirmable form. and She made the decision not to mention it until Agnes did.

He wrote something else.

"If the order confirms and the package tests positive for the compound," he said, "that establishes procurement. Combined with the timeline and the documented conflict, it's sufficient to proceed." He looked up. "I'll move on it."

She left Corbin's office and sat in her car for a moment in the parking lot. The case was in official hands now. She had done what she could do with what she had, and she had handed it to the person with the authority to act on it, and he had said he would act. The transaction was complete in the way that necessary things are complete even when they leave you uncertain.

She drove to Silver Oak in the early dark of the November evening, through streets that smelled of cold exhaust and the particular emptiness of a Friday evening in a small town.

Arthur was awake. His window had the parking structure and its strip of sky, which was dark now, and the room had the fluorescent quality of a space that does not know what time it is. She sat in the chair beside his bed and told him that Corbin had taken Agnes Moskov in for questioning, that the evidence pointed to her, and that the charges against him were being held pending the outcome.

He was quiet for a long time. She waited in the quiet.

"Agnes," he said, finally.

"Yes."

He looked at the window. "Agnes Moskov." He said the full name, the way you say a name when you are checking whether you have the right person, whether the information and the person match. "She brought Derek to the Community Center. For his chess lessons, when he was small. She sat in the corner and let him work and never once rushed him."

He stopped. He turned his head on the pillow and looked at Mel.

"Are you sure," he said.

"The evidence holds," she said.

He looked at her the way he looked at things when he was holding two things at the same time and did not have the energy to resolve them. He had the particular stillness of someone who has run the arithmetic and does not like the answer but does not have the strength to run it again.

"She sat in the corner of your pantry," he said, "for three years, while Derek had those Thursday afternoon sessions. She never once interrupted."

"Arthur."

"I know." He turned his head back toward the window. The parking structure was dark beyond the glass. "I know. You've been careful."

He was quiet for a moment. Then: "You'll make sure they look at the package."

"Corbin will look at the package." She paused. "He's thorough."

Arthur made a sound that was not quite agreement and not quite skepticism but something between them, the sound of a man who has been thorough for seventy-three years and knows what thorough costs. He looked at the window. The parking structure sat in its sodium-lit quiet beyond the glass.

He nodded once. He closed his eyes.

Mel sat with him until his breathing changed and the room settled into its hospital quiet, and then she sat a little longer. The question he had asked was still there in the room. She held it the way you hold something you are not going to put down yet, that you know you will need to pick up again.

The police formally arrested Agnes that evening.

The news had been through the chess community before it reached the Giving Spoon's regulars, and through the regulars before it reached the rest of the town. By the time Mel opened the Spoon on Saturday morning, it was already flowing in the way small towns process significant news: with coffee, and in company, and with the particular energy of people who had been waiting for something definitive and had received it.

Mel had called the lawyer the night before. Arthur's charges would continue in place pending an outcome of the new development. Not dropped. Held. The phrase the lawyer used was "pending review of the new evidence," which meant the machinery had paused but had not reversed. It was not freedom. It was the right kind of pause.

Agnes arrested, Arthur still under suspicion. Mel felt a headache coming on. She wasn't sure she had done anyone a favor. She wasn't sure she had done the right thing. She didn't even know how to tell.

Derek called the Giving Spoon at half past eight to ask if she was all right. She told him she was, and thanked him for asking, and asked about the hives. He said the keepers from Friday's visit had declared the colonies stable. The queens were intact. He was doing the Saturday morning checks as usual. He sounded like someone who had decided what his job was and was doing it.

Noreen heard from a Town Hall clerk by mid-morning: the council had informally agreed to stay the eradication vote pending the arrest's outcome. No formal resolution, but they would hold the deadline of November thirteenth until they had more from Corbin. Three days had become something else, something open, and Mel felt the opening in her chest as pressure changes before a storm breaks.

The relief was real and she didn't argue with it. She let it arrive the way exhaustion lets relief arrive when the thing holding it back goes away. She had been running on something close to empty for two weeks, and the immediate pressure was off. She allowed herself to feel that. She told herself it was okay, it was true. She mostly believed it.

There was a note underneath it. A grain she could not smooth away. She had felt it since Corbin's office, and since the question Arthur had asked in the hospital room. She did not examine it directly. She had earned the morning.

The Giving Spoon filled up with its Saturday crowd, but with a particular quality she recognized: some of the people who came in were processing the arrest the way people process things they have been expecting and have now received confirmation of. They ordered their usual things and stayed slightly longer than usual and talked in the way of people who are not gossiping, exactly, but are placing a new thing in their understanding of the town they live in. Mel listened to some of it and let the rest go past her. She had heard all the versions already.

The Mercer brothers were in for the first time since the ransacking, sitting at their usual table and not talking about the investigation, which meant they were thinking about it. Mrs. Lund had heard the news from her neighbor and wanted to know what Agnes had said. Mel gave her the version that was public record and let the rest go. Sheila Baxter came through on her Saturday route and said she had never quite trusted anyone who grew that much lemon myrtle in a shop that small. Mel said she appreciated the sentiment and moved on.

Noreen worked the morning with efficiency and warmth in equal parts. She moved between tables with the quality of a person who has been doing this specific work in this specific space for a long time and knows the texture of it. She did not feed the processing crowd more than it needed. She gave people exactly the conversation they came in looking for and no more, which was a skill Mel had observed and respected across two weeks and many conversations.

Leo made the coffee. He had come in early and he was working the morning with the specific quality of quiet that meant he was still inside a problem and not yet ready to emerge from it. He did not mention Agnes. He did not mention the chemistry he had been running. He moved through the Spoon with the rest of them and the morning shaped itself around the three of them, and Mel let herself be in it.

The community's acceptance of the Agnes solution had a quality she recognized from other endings: the quick natural subsidence of something held under pressure too long. A tide going out. The ground appearing. That clean feeling of resolution settling over a community that had been waiting two weeks for something definitive. She felt it in the room and she let it in.

The grain underneath it was still there. Quiet, patient, not going anywhere.

The morning did what Saturday mornings do in a place where people come to be ordinary: it accumulated. Coffee cups and conversations and the texture of a community processing something significant at a comfortable remove. By eleven the first wave had thinned and the Spoon had settled into its quieter mid-morning character, the light coming through the front windows at its November angle, the radiator making its small ticking sound.

She was at the coffee station mid-morning when Leo looked up from the far end of the counter.

He looked at her across the room with the expression she had learned to read in the course of two weeks: not the expression of a man who wants to say something, but the expression of a man who is still inside a calculation, patient and careful, not finished. Running numbers. Waiting until he was sure.

She held the look.

She knew what the look meant. She could ask. She could cross the floor to where he was standing and say: tell me where you are. And he would tell her, because he always told her, and she would have the answer before she had decided whether she was ready for it.

She looked back down at the coffee station and finished what she was doing.

He would tell her when he was sure. She put the coffee back on the warmer and watched the room do its Saturday morning work, and let that be enough for now.

The Clouds Fade

Noreen called at eleven with the measured quality of someone delivering information she has verified three times.

"Agnes has an alibi," she said. "An extremely unglamorous one."

She had gone to the waste collection service's records first thing Saturday morning. Agnes had called the service the week before the festival to schedule an early-morning Saturday pickup, because she was attending the festival grounds that day and wanted to have the bin collected before she left. The driver had a log. He had come to Agnes's address on Cochran Street at six fifteen in the morning. Agnes had been home: dressing gown, half-awake, apologized for the time. He remembered her specifically because it was early enough that having someone awake to wheel the bin out had been an inconvenience he had been prepared for and had not needed to prepare for.

"Six fifteen," Mel said.

The geography told its own story. Cochran Street to Miller's Hollow Park: by car, twelve minutes in that hour. On foot, twenty-five. Agnes would have needed to leave her address no later than five forty-five in the morning to reach the chess pavilion by six fifteen, which was the time the waste truck arrived. The setup window itself did not fully open until nearer to six. She would have needed to be in two places at once.

"Six fifteen. Leo's setup window begins before seven. The chess pavilion is twelve minutes by car from Cochran Street, more on foot. Agnes would need to have been applying a compound to the master's chess table at some point between five thirty and six forty-five in the morning, and simultaneously in her driveway in a dressing gown at six fifteen. Those two things cannot occupy the same body."

Mel looked at the counter. "No."

"She cannot have done it," Noreen said. "Not with the timing. Not with the product she purchased. Not with any construction of the available evidence that holds up to examination."

Mel called Corbin immediately after she hung up. She gave him the information: the service log, the driver's name, Agnes's Cochran Street address, the six-fifteen timestamp. She did not interpret it. She gave him the facts and waited while he wrote them down.

He said he would follow up.

She set the phone down and stood at the counter with it.

Agnes had been in her dressing gown at six fifteen in the morning. The driver remembered her. The driver had a log. Agnes's compound was the wrong formulation. Agnes could not have done it with what she had, and she had not been where she would have needed to be. The case against Agnes, which Mel had assembled from reasonable evidence and presented to a professional with the authority to act on it, was wrong. Both legs of it were wrong. She had been right that the investigation had been right, and she had been wrong about everything that mattered.

She stood at the counter and let that be true for a moment.

Leo had his printout folded in thirds and he set it on the counter and smoothed it with the back of his hand before he spoke. He had the manner of someone who has been waiting to say a true thing and has been making sure it would hold before he said it.

"Agnes's compound has geraniol and citral," he said. "No 9-ODA. She can attract scouts. She cannot direct a swarm."

Mel looked at the printout.

"The bee attractant at the festival required the queen mandibular component. That's not available in commercial lemongrass extract. It's not available in her lure." He folded the printout again. "Whoever did this knew the difference."

"Who would know the difference."

"Someone with chemistry training. Or someone who did enough research to understand the specific mechanism." A pause. "It's a narrow group."

"I know," Mel said.

She said it and she meant it and she set it next to the other things she was not quite ready to examine directly.

The kitchen was quiet. Leo had his hands flat on the counter and was looking at the printout the way he looked at things when he was making sure they were as certain as he believed them to be.

"It's a narrow group," he said again, after a moment.

"The people who would know about 9-ODA as distinct from general citrus chemistry," Mel said.

"Bee scientists. Entomologists. Agricultural chemists. People who have specifically worked on swarm behavior." Leo paused. "Or someone with a strong enough chemistry background who had reason to research it carefully. If you know what question to ask, the specific mechanism is findable. But you'd need to know the right question." He squared the printout. "Most people asking about the festival's bees would find Nasonov. The 9-ODA question is a second level of looking."

"Someone who already knew where to look."

"Or who already knew the answer and was working backward to confirm it."

"Chemistry training, or enough research."

"Research to the level of understanding the specific mechanism. The 9-ODA distinction is not something you find in a general-interest article. Someone who read about the festival and the bees and the pheromone question afterward would find the Nasonov compound. They would not necessarily find the queen mandibular distinction unless they were specifically looking for it, or unless they already knew." He paused. "Knowing the difference between attracting scouts and directing foragers is a specialist's distinction."

Mel looked at the counter.

"Leo," she said. "Who would have been in the pavilion before seven on a Saturday morning."

"Someone with a reason to be there. A credential. An official role."

"A tournament director."

He was quiet for a moment. "Or a senior official. Someone whose presence at that hour, before the grounds filled, would would have been natural. Unquestioned." He looked at her. "That's a short list."

"Yes," she said.

She would need proof. She had not moved anything closer to proof. But the short list had, for the first time, a shape she could name.

Agnes's shop had its ordinary smell of dried citrus and worked herbs and the older smell underneath, and Agnes herself had the composed exhaustion of someone who has been through something and has not yet decided how to think about it. She was behind the counter when Mel came in. She did not look surprised to see her.

Mel told her that the rubbish collection had cleared the timeline question, and that Leo's chemistry analysis had cleared the compound question, and that Corbin had released her on the basis of the trash bin alibi that morning. Agnes listened. She listened as if she were hearing it placed in order for the first time.

"I know why you came to me," Agnes said. "The evidence was just as I said it was."

"It was."

Agnes looked at the lemon myrtle in the south window. It was catching the November afternoon light, which was the pale flat light of a sky that gave up performing for the day and was closing shop. "The swarm box is still behind the shop," she said. "I set it up in July, when Arthur told me that I had the patience for it. He said it the first time he showed me the apiary — years ago, before all of this. I thought I could attract a wild swarm naturally, without buying into a nucleus colony. The way he started." She paused. "The package arrived in October and I kept it because I was afraid that throwing it away would look like destroying evidence, and keeping it looked just as bad, and I could not find a version of saying any of it that didn't sound like I had assembled it in the last five minutes." She looked at Mel. "I should have said it the first time you asked."

"It would have made things better," Mel said.

Agnes took a moment with that. "I know that now."

They stood in the shop for a little while longer, not saying anything useful, because there was nothing useful left to say. Both of them had made reasonable mistakes. The reasonable mistakes had cost time and dignity and a degree of community trust that would take longer to repair than either of them wanted to think about. Mel thanked her for her time and Agnes nodded and Mel left.

Outside, the November afternoon was gray and cold and the street was quiet in the particular way of a Saturday afternoon when a community is processing something it didn't want to have to process. The arrest had created the feeling of resolution, a long breath released, and the release of Agnes had created something more complicated: a community that had exhaled and now had to inhale again, and wasn't sure what it was breathing in.

She had heard two reactions on the walk to her car. One was sympathy for Agnes: she never seemed like the type, did she. One was sympathy for the investigation: they were only working with what they had, weren't they.

Both were correct. Both were also insufficient.

Mel walked to her car and sat in it for a moment with her hands on the wheel.

Agnes was innocent. The investigation had produced no result. The real killer was still free. The council met Monday evening. Arthur was in hospital.

She started the car. Three days of investigation had just become no days, and Monday was tomorrow, and she had to start over with something better than what she had left.

The apartment had the particular quiet it always had when she did not want to be in it. She made dinner and ate some of it and washed the plate and stood at the kitchen window looking out at the alley between her building and the one behind it. The November dark settled in completely, the temperature in the alley turning one's breath to something almost visible at the edges of the streetlight's reach.

She went through the list one more time. She went through it as she had been going through it for days, name by name, and the conclusion had not changed.

Arthur: innocent. The pheromone theory had argued for his innocence before the case against Agnes seemed real, and it argued for it still. He had not done this.

Cheswick: definitively not there. Confirmed by the rental car, by the canvass, by two weeks of investigation. He had built a wall in his apartment and fled the county and neither of those things was the behavior of the killer.

Agnes: now definitively exonerated. Both legs: the rubbish collection at six fifteen and Leo's chemistry confirmation. She could not have done it. Agnes had not been where she would have needed to be.

Dowen: twenty-four years of documented grievance. A hobby hive. A morning walking route that took him past festival grounds. Chemistry knowledge she had filed away on a Tuesday afternoon and had not opened since.

And the dog. She had been at Haven Terrace, in Dowen's doorway, and Trixie had come to greet her, and she had crouched to receive the greeting, and she had held the left front paw for a moment, and she had counted, without meaning to count, without knowing she was doing it: five pads where there should have been four.

She did not know what she had in that. A dog's paw. A canvass entry about a man walking a small dog before seven in the morning near the chess area. No one had gotten a good look at the man. No one thought anything of a man walking a dog at a festival where people brought dogs. No one had thought anything of the paw prints in the soft ground near the table leg, either, because nobody had knelt down to look at them, and even if they had, what would five pads on a left front paw mean to someone who did not have a reason to count?

She tried not to follow it. She had one day. She had a chemistry connection and a motive and a detail about a dog that she couldn't prove to have been near the chess pavilion on October twenty-eighth. Not by anyone's testimony; only her memory. She did not have enough.

She went to bed.

She tried not to follow the thought. She did not have enough. She had the paw and a morning dog walker no one had gotten a look at and a chemistry correction that was plausible as idle reading-after-the-fact and twenty-four years that proved a motive and not a method. She did not have enough.

She went to bed.

She had been carrying it all day.

She had visited Arthur in the morning. She had done the Giving Spoon's Sunday afternoon run. She had called Derek about the hives. She had tried to read. She had done the ordinary things that needed doing and had felt the unresolved thought sitting just below the surface of everything like a stone below moving water, present, not going anywhere, waiting.

By evening she was at the kitchen table with Noreen's canvass notebook in front of her, going over what she had one last time before she allowed herself to stop. She had been through it four times. She would go through it once more and then she would put it away for the night and start over Monday with fresh eyes and whatever she could think of to do with twenty-four hours before the council meeting.

She opened to the morning-canvass section. Noreen's handwriting: precise, small, a librarian's catalog hand. The morning after the festival. The walk through the park, door to door, vendor to vendor, anyone who had been there early.

She read the entry.

Man walking small dog, black-and-white, near the chess pavilion, early morning, before 7. Nobody got a good look at him. Dog was small. Man had a jacket, maybe. Gone before the grounds filled.

She put the notebook down.

She picked it up.

She closed her eyes.

Trixie in the doorway at Haven Terrace. The greeting, the warm weight of her, the small body in motion. Mel crouching to receive it. Holding the left front paw for a moment. Counting, not deliberately, just the natural arithmetic of noticing: the pads on the left front. Four. And then the extra one, sitting snug against the inner side of the paw, a supernumerary digit, one more than the expected count. Five.

The canvass notebook on the table.

The chess pavilion in the morning. The soft ground from Friday's rain. The table leg, the low foot traffic near the base of it, the prints that the crowd had not pressed flat. A small dog's paw. The left front, one too many. Five pads where four belonged. She had looked at it and moved on.

The man with the small black-and-white dog, before seven, near the chess area. Nobody got a good look at him.

She put the notebook flat on the table with both hands.

Haven Terrace. The apartment with the economy of objects, the chess board, the game in progress. The hazel eyes. And on Tuesday of the week before, in that same apartment, the answer to a question she had framed loosely on purpose:

The compound that matters isn't the Nasonov component. It's the queen mandibular element. Without that, you attract scouts. You don't move a colony.

Said without prompting. Said with the reflexive precision of a man who cannot let an inaccuracy stand even when the cost of correcting it is visible in the room.

Twenty-four years. A startup in 1998. Cambridge Mathematics, first-class honours. The dot-com collapse and the patents and the life the patents took with them when they walked out in another man's briefcase.

She reached for her phone.

Leo answered on the second ring.

"Cambridge Mathematics," she said. "First-class honours. If someone had that background, would the pheromone chemistry be accessible to them? Could they have synthesized a proper BeeLure preparation, understood the slow-release formulation, applied it correctly?"

No hesitation. "Yes," Leo said. "Absolutely yes."

She thanked him and ended the call.

She sat with the kitchen in its Sunday evening quiet.

Cambridge Mathematics, first-class honours. The chemistry was accessible. The slow-release formulation was within reach of someone who had the mathematics background and the motivation to understand what he was preparing. The compound applied to the chess pieces in the setup window, before the grounds filled, by a man walking his dog back and forth near the chess area the way you walk a dog, unhurried, back and forth, when you are doing something else. The dog with the polydactyl left front paw, the prints of which were in the soft post-rain ground near the table leg where the crowd did not press in.

The twenty-four years. The precision of that number: no rounding, ever. The man who kept exact accounts.

He had taken Bernie's queen in 1999, in a filing cabinet somewhere with a government seal and an attorney's signature. It had taken him twenty-four years to work out an answer. The answer: the queen was the delivery system. Bernie's own queen, from the set he polished before every match, in the ritual that anyone who had ever watched him play had seen a hundred times.

His rite did the delivering.

Leo had said that, weeks ago. Leo had said it and she had used it to understand the mechanism, and the mechanism was correct, and she had pointed it at the wrong person. The November night darkened the window, and somewhere down the block a car passed, and then the street was quiet again. The notebook lay flat on the table in front of her with Noreen's handwriting on the open page.

The picture was complete. No more questions. No more uncertainty,

She knew who had killed Bernard Travers at the Possum Gap Fall Festival on the twenty-eighth of October. She knew the mechanism and the motive and the particular patience required to plan it, and she knew it the way you know a thing when the last piece settles into place and the shape is finally visible.

She did not call Corbin. She had a connection, not evidence. She knew she could have it all wrong, but her heart wouldn't believe that. What she needed was something that would hold in court, and what she knew from two weeks of watching a chess master in a small town was that what chess masters cannot resist is explaining their best game to someone who almost understands it. That was not a strategy yet. That was the beginning of one.

She closed Noreen's notebook.

Tomorrow she would call Corbin. Tomorrow she would explain what she had. Tomorrow, with one day left before the council met and sealed the apiary's fate. She had to figure out how to turn a connection into a case.

Tonight the picture was complete, false or true, and she held it, and the November dark held the town.

Derek had said on the phone: the colonies are stable. The queens are intact. He was doing the Saturday morning checks as usual.

Somewhere out at Mashburn Creek the bees were in their hives in their rows, patient, waiting for the spring she was trying to give them. She had one day to give them a path to it. One day, and what she had was not yet evidence, but it was the beginning of a plan that understood its subject: a man who had been patient for twenty-four years and who could not resist the endgame, and who would, she was nearly certain, want it recorded.

She sat with that for a while longer. Then she set it down and went to get ready for Monday.

First Principles

She wrote it out.

Not in a notebook (the stolen materials included her last notebook) but on a piece of paper from the supply drawer, with a pen from the counter, at the Giving Spoon kitchen table before Noreen arrived. It was still dark outside. She had been awake since five. She wrote the list and read it back to herself and wrote it again, not because the list changed but because writing it helped her know exactly what she had and what she didn't have.

The prints at the chess table: she had seen them on October 28. She could testify to that. A small dog's left front paw, five pads where four belonged. Corbin hadn't written that up. They were not in the official record.

The morning dog walker: verbal descriptions from the festival canvass. Inconsistent. No names. A man, a small black and white dog, near the chess area, before seven. Nobody had looked at him.

Trixie's extra toe: she had held the paw herself. She could testify to it. She could describe the count, the specific arrangement of the extra pad. It was not evidence of crime. It was a detail that mattered only if everything else held.

The prints at the vandalized apiary: ground too disturbed by the time of discovery. Suggestive, not probative.

The chemistry fluency: a correction given in an apartment on a Tuesday afternoon in November. She heard it. Leo heard it second-hand from her account. She could say what they had discussed and what it meant for someone with a Cambridge Mathematics background. Corbin would ask how she knew the fluency was unusual rather than the result of ordinary research. She would direct him to Leo.

The twenty-four years: motive. Documented by Eleanor Vance's account and the Historical Society archive. Duncan Vance's role, on record. Bernie's patents, on record. Strong.

Cambridge Mathematics, first-class honours: Leo had confirmed that the pheromone chemistry was accessible to someone with that background. Leo's confirmation, on record in his own verbal account.

She put the pen down. She looked at the list.

The kitchen was quiet and the Giving Spoon smelled of last night's coffee and the particular closed-space smell of a building not yet opened to the day. She had turned one lamp on. The paper sat in front of her and the list on it was as complete as she could make it.

There was a separate column, on the right side of the paper, which she had not written in the list section. In that column she had written a single question: *what will hold under cross-examination?* And beside each item she had put a word. The prints: seen. The canvass: verbal. Trixie's toe: tactile. The chemistry: Leo confirms. The motive: documented. The mathematics: Leo confirms.

She had put "seen" and "tactile" next to the physical evidence because those were hers to give. The rest required Leo or the paper trail Eleanor had walked her through. None of it, individually, constituted proof of murder. Together, it was the shape of the truth. A prosecutor would need more. A jury would need more. What she needed was the one thing that would make the shape solid: the specific person at the specific place at the specific time, confirmed by the specific person who was there.

Him saying it.

Noreen arrived at seven thirty with her coat on and her notebook already open. She set down a thermos of coffee she had made at home. She had done this exactly twice before in the course of the investigation, both times when she had driven straight to the Giving Spoon from somewhere else. This morning she had come straight from home. She sat down across from Mel and looked at the piece of paper.

She didn't read it aloud. She read it silently, line by line, and set her mechanical pencil down beside her notebook and looked at Mel.

"So what would hold up."

"Him saying it," Mel said.

Noreen picked up her pencil. "Then we need him to say it."

"Yes."

She folded the paper along its thirds and put it in her pocket. It was the fourth version of the case she had written down. The fourth was the right one.

"And you have a way to make that happen."

"I have a way to give him the opportunity. Whether he takes it depends on who he is." Mel looked at the list. "I think I know who he is."

Noreen nodded once, as if that answered a question she had been holding since Sunday evening, and opened her notebook to a fresh page.

Tim Renshaw's office had its Monday-morning quality: the coffee half-brewed, the first appointment not yet arrived, the gold lettering on the frosted glass catching the gray November light at a horizontal angle that made it look like something from another era.

He looked up when she came in and read something in her face. He had been getting better at reading her face across three weeks.

She asked a direct question: Did Tim know Gregory Dowen's morning routine? Specifically: did he walk his dog at Miller's Hollow Park early?

Tim set his coffee down. He thought about this for a moment, not stalling but actually checking his knowledge.

"Every morning," he said. "As long as I can remember him being in town. He's a creature of habit that way. East path, the one that runs along the cedar screen toward the tournament grounds. Usually there and back before six thirty, sometimes before six. He's gone before the dog-walkers with day jobs arrive." He looked at her. "He told me once that Trixie likes the east path because of the smells near the cedars. Something about the resin."

Mel said: "Has he walked there every day this month?"

"As far as I know. I've seen him twice from the road on my way in." A pause. "Early this week he was there Tuesday and Thursday. I didn't look for him today."

She nodded.

Tim didn't ask why she was asking. He looked at her for a moment, and then he said: "If you're going to talk to him there — early, before anyone arrives — be careful."

He didn't say careful of what. He didn't need to.

"I'll have company," Mel said.

He looked at her. The "company" answer satisfied something he had been worrying about without saying so.

At the door she paused. She had said "thank you" to Tim so many times across this investigation that the phrase had worn thin. She said it now anyway. She meant something different by it than she ever had before. Not gratitude for a specific piece of information, but for the larger thing, whatever it was, that Tim Renshaw had been doing for three weeks without needing to.

He nodded. He understood what she meant.

She left. The morning was gray and still cold and the gold lettering on Tim's frosted glass door caught the flat light as she pushed out onto the sidewalk.

She sat in her car for a moment.

She had a confirmed walk route and a confirmed time window. She had a target who was a creature of habit by his own description. She had a plan with one moving part and a single condition for success: that the person she was planning to trap was who she believed him to be.

She had been wrong once already.

She had been wrong about Agnes for reasonable reasons, from reasonable evidence, using reasonable judgment. She had put an innocent woman in custody for two days and been unable to say so without a physical record to back her up. And now she was going to build a second case against a second person, and the only thing standing between her and a second failure was her read of a man's character.

She started the car.

She had been right about his character before. She had been right about the correction in the apartment. She had been right about the precision. She had heard what precision cost him on a Tuesday afternoon when she asked a general question about bee lures and he corrected an inaccuracy he had no reason to correct.

She drove.

The Giving Spoon had its between-service quiet: the lunch crowd gone, the afternoon crowd not yet arrived, the steel counter clean and the chairs back in their positions. Leo was doing prep in the kitchen and Noreen had her notebook on the back table.

Mel sat down with them and walked them through it.

The east path at Miller's Hollow Park, confirmed: Dowen walked it every morning before six thirty, sometimes earlier. The cedar screen to the east. Tim had seen him twice this week already.

Noreen: "So tomorrow morning."

"Pre-dawn. Before he arrives. I'll be on the path."

Leo had stopped what he was doing in the kitchen and come to lean against the door frame with his forearms on the upper sill, listening. This was how he listened to things he found technically interesting.

"The mechanism," Mel said. "He cannot let an inaccuracy stand. I've seen it twice. In how he talks about the twenty-four years — never twenty-five, never almost a quarter century, always twenty-four, exact. And in his apartment, on Tuesday, when he corrected my description of the chemistry." She looked at Leo. "He couldn't stop himself."

Leo: "He'll say the exact time."

"That's what I'm counting on. I'll present the full case. The prints, the dog, the chemistry knowledge, the twenty-four years. And I'll say I believe he was at the chess pavilion around six in the morning on October 28."

A moment.

"Around six," Leo said.

"He was there at 5:47. If I say around six and I'm right about him, he'll correct me. He cannot let a wrong time stand on the record, even the record of his own confession."

Leo was quiet for a moment. He was running the logic as he ran chemistry: not looking for a flaw to dismiss, but checking for one he needed to account for.

"And if he doesn't correct you," Noreen said.

The question she always asked when a plan had a single moving part.

"Then I'm wrong about him," Mel said. "And I go back to the beginning."

Leo set his folder down. "You're not wrong about him," he said, carefully, not quickly. "The correction in the apartment. I've been thinking about it since November eleventh. You're not wrong." He picked the folder back up and squared it on the table.

She said it without drama because it was true and she had accepted it. She had one shot and one mechanism and the mechanism was Dowen's character. That was the plan. She had looked at it from every angle she could find and it was still the plan.

"The recording," Leo said. "I can—"

"Corbin will want control of that."

Leo nodded. He had expected that.

"I'm going to him this afternoon," Mel said. "If he agrees, the confrontation is tomorrow before dawn. If he doesn't—" She stopped. She didn't need to finish that sentence for either of them.

Noreen set her pencil down. She looked at the plan from the outside, which was her particular strength: not to build it, but to find what it missed. She had been doing this for three weeks and she had not yet found a hole Mel couldn't account for.

"The introduced inaccuracy," she said. "Around six."

"Yes."

"He'll know, when he hears that, that you don't know the exact time."

"He'll correct me before he can stop himself. That's the point." Mel looked at her. "If he doesn't, I have misjudged him, and we walk away."

"And if he does."

"Then he's placed himself at the chess pavilion at the specific time. Not approximately. Exactly. In front of Corbin."

Another silence. Noreen looked at her notebook. "The deliberate inaccuracy is elegant," she said, in the tone she used for things she found technically sound. "It requires no corroboration. It uses his own precision against him." She picked up her pencil. "I would like to have been wrong about him."

"So would I."

Noreen had been writing in her notebook. She looked up. "What do you need us to do?"

"Stay here. Open the Spoon tomorrow morning at seven." Mel looked at both of them. "If everything goes the way I'm planning it, the news will reach you before the coffee runs out."

Corbin waited at his desk. She had called ahead. He wore his best poker face. Mel took a deep breath.

She sat across from him and presented the case in the order that would land with the most weight, starting with what was strongest and moving toward what she needed him to believe.

She led with Leo's chemistry: what the compound required, why Agnes's lure could not have done it, why the person who did it understood the specific 9-ODA distinction without additional explanation. She moved to Agnes's exoneration (the trash collection, the wrong compound) and to Cheswick's elimination: the rental car, Pikeville, the obsession wall that contained not one word about bees.

Then: what remained. A man with a Cambridge Mathematics first-class honours, who had spent twenty-four years trying through proper channels to correct a documented wrong. Eleanor Vance's account of her father's role. The patent filing in Duncan Vance's handwriting, Bernie's instructions, the deliberate exclusion. She had Eleanor's confirmation; Corbin could verify it through the Historical Society if he wanted.

And then the physical evidence: a small dog, black and white, walking the east path of Miller's Hollow Park in the dark of October 28 before the festival crowds arrived. A man no one had gotten a good look at. The prints near the master's chess table in the soft post-rain ground, a left front paw with a toe count that was wrong by one. And in Dowen's apartment doorway on the third of November, a Cavalier King Charles Spaniel, female, named Trixie, left front paw: five.

Corbin was quiet for a long time when she stopped speaking.

She had learned, across fifteen chapters of working against and occasionally alongside him, that Corbin's silences were not empty. He processed in them. She had watched him do it in the Giving Spoon on day one, when Noreen laid out the pheromone theory and he had stood with his notebook and given nothing away. She watched him do it now.

Then: "The prints at the chess table." He said it without inflection. "I said dogs everywhere."

"Yes," Mel said.

She didn't offer him any more than he'd given her. He had identified the error himself, without prompting, without invitation. That was a different kind of accounting from someone telling you that you were wrong, and she understood the difference.

Another silence. He wasn't reviewing the evidence she had just given him; he was reviewing what he had said on October 28 in a park full of festival debris, looking at prints he had assigned to the ordinary noise of the day. He was doing what precise people do when they confront the evidence they got wrong: they hold it exactly, without flinching, until they know what it means.

"The dog is at Haven Terrace," he said.

"He lives at Haven Terrace. He walks the dog at Miller's Hollow Park every morning before six thirty. East path, along the cedar screen."

Corbin looked at his desk. He picked up his pen and put it down without writing anything.

"If he corrects the time," he said, "and I'm present with a recording device, that constitutes an admissible statement."

"Leo believes so. I would want your assessment."

He was quiet again. She could see him checking the legal architecture of it as he checked everything: looking for what would break under load before he committed to standing on it.

Then he said: "My conditions."

He said it as he said everything factual: without inflection, as if the conditions were already standing facts and he was now reading them into the record. She had the impression, not for the first time, that Corbin had been running this meeting in his head for longer than she had.

He said it without drama. She had expected conditions. A man like Corbin did not take risks he hadn't calculated.

She waited.

"I control the recording. I determine the position. I make the arrest if he says something actionable. I decide what 'actionable' means." He looked at her. "If it doesn't work, we walk away. No public accusation.

No arrest on theory alone." A pause. "And you do not approach Dowen alone. I am there before he arrives, and I remain concealed throughout."

"Agreed."

"All of it."

"All of it."

They had been in this room together five or six times across three weeks. Each time she had come with evidence and left without a result. This was the first time she was leaving with something she hadn't brought in: his agreement. It sat differently than anything the investigation had produced so far.

He looked at her for a moment longer. He had been looking at her across a desk for three weeks with the particular expression of a man who has not yet decided whether this person is a problem or a resource, and it was possible that he had not yet fully decided even now. But he had looked at the evidence she brought him and done the arithmetic on what he had said in a park on October 28, and the arithmetic did not leave him room to say no.

"I'll be at the park by four in the morning," he said. "Before he arrives."

"He usually comes between five and six thirty."

"Then I'll be there by four." He stood. The meeting was over, in the way Corbin's meetings always ended: not with warmth, not with a handshake, but by him standing up. He was ready to act on their agreement, on their plan.

At the door: "If you're wrong about this—"

"Then we're both back where we started," Mel said.

"Yes."

He nodded once. She left.

The Monday afternoon was gray and cold outside, and the council was meeting in four hours to confirm the eradication order for Tuesday, and tomorrow before the sun came up she was going to be standing on the east path of Miller's Hollow Park in the dark with a plan that had one moving part and a fifteen-chapter adversarial relationship converted, in forty minutes, into a professional partnership.

Outside, the council was meeting in four hours. The Monday November 13 session, the one the council had been waiting to hold since they shortened the deadline, would vote tonight. The eradication order for Tuesday would pass. It would pass because the council had voted on compromised grounds and then been told the arrest had resolved the matter, and when the arrest fell apart the council had paused but not revoked.

Tonight they would stop pausing.

Tomorrow before dawn, Corbin would be behind the cedar screen on the east path of Miller's Hollow Park, concealed, with a recording device. Tomorrow, if the plan worked, the council's Tuesday vote would be something that needed reversing rather than enforcing.

She drove back to the Giving Spoon. She turned off the parking lights and sat in the alley for a moment. She had run the plan from every angle she could find. It had one moving part. The moving part was a human being's inability to let an inaccuracy stand. She had seen it twice. She was betting the investigation on a third time.

She went inside. She had work to do before morning.

She opened a new piece of paper and wrote down the order in which she would present the case. Not because she didn't know the order (she had known it since Sunday evening) but because writing it steadied her, as it had always steadied her. She had been writing things down for thirty days and someone had stolen the notebook and she had reconstructed it and the reconstruction was better than the original. Tomorrow she would say it aloud in a dark park to a man who had spent twenty-four years keeping exact accounts, and the only version of the future she could commit to was the one in which he corrected a thirteen-minute inaccuracy in front of a detective with a recording device.

She wrote the order. She put the paper in her coat pocket. She made herself a cup of coffee she didn't particularly want and sat with it until it was late enough to sleep.

5:47

The park was dark.

Not the dark of deep night, which has its own settled quality, but the dark of the last hour before light when the sky has made a decision it hasn't yet delivered on. The festival was long gone. The chess pavilion tent was taken down in the first week of November; the grass near the eastern edge was recovering, the impressions of the tournament setup fading back into ordinary ground. The cedar screen stood black against a slightly lighter sky to the east, and to the west the park was open and empty, the vendor spaces bare, the silence of a place that has supported a special event and has gone back to being a park.

Mel had arrived first, as agreed. She had walked the east path from the lot and found her position in the spot where the path bent nearest the space where the master's chess table had stood. She could see the ground where she had stood outside the crime tape on the twenty-eighth of October, where she had seen the prints in the soft post-rain earth and then moved on.

Somewhere in the shadow of the cedar screen, to her left, was Corbin. She did not look.

She waited.

Arthur was here, in her mind, in her thoughts. In her heart. Not the Arthur in the hospital bed, but the Arthur she had known for four years: the deliveries, the tremor starting in his right hand, the particular care with which he set honey jars on her counter. And the print she had seen here in October: five toe-pads where four belonged. And the words Corbin had used when she pointed it out. Dogs everywhere. She had agreed, because that was the reasonable reading of the evidence.

The cedar screen was a presence in the dark, the same boundary it had always been. She had stood on this side of it looking at the pavilion; she had stood on the other side looking back through the gap. The distance between the hive rows and the chess table was three hundred meters and a favorable wind and a man with a slow-release compound and twenty-four years of practice at patience.

This was not a place she had expected to end up when she opened the Giving Spoon three weeks ago on a Monday morning in October and Arthur delivered his honey and said something she hadn't known how to hear correctly until later. She had been trying to feed people and keep the lights on. Her main efforts were to help a friend whose bees were weaponized against him in a murder she had not yet understood. She had not been trying to be a detective. She had been trying to be accurate. Accurate had led her here.

She did not think about what she was going to say. She knew what she was going to say. She had been over it with Noreen and Leo in the Giving Spoon kitchen on Monday afternoon, and she had been over it alone on Monday night, and she had been over it on the drive here. There was nothing left in it that she needed to find. What she needed now was to be standing on this path at this hour in this cold, present.

The cedar screen was a presence she had been thinking about since October. From the west, it looked like a boundary and a barrier, the thing Arthur's bees had crossed that shouldn't have been crossable, the windbreak that had made the whole investigation's chemistry theory feel impossible until it wasn't. From the east side of it, looking back through the gap toward the park, you could see exactly how far the chess pavilion was and exactly how a man walking a dog before the festival grounds opened would have moved along this path without being noticed, because a man walking a dog early in the morning at a park is not a thing anyone looks at twice.

She had walked this path twice herself. Once in October, the morning after the festival, with Noreen. Once just now. It was flat and well-kept and ran parallel to the cedar screen from the parking area on the north side to the meadow on the south. At a normal walking pace you covered it in three minutes. Dowen had been covering it every morning, according to Tim, for as long as anyone in the chess community could remember.

The air smelled of frozen grass and cedar resin and the cold particular smell of November before first light. Somewhere in the shadow of the cedar screen Corbin waited in his chosen hideout. She did not look.

She shivered and waited.

At half past five, Trixie came around the bend.

She came with her nose down, working the east path the way she always worked it, her small black-and-white body moving in the grey before-light with the unhurried expertise of a dog on familiar ground. Then she found Mel and her whole manner changed: the greeting, the warmth, the uncomplicated recognition of a person she had met before. She reached Mel and put her feet up and Mel crouched and held the left front paw for a moment.

Five.

Then Dowen came around the bend.

Dressed for the cold, unhurried, a man in his habitual routine. He walked with the particular economy of a person who has made the same route so many times it requires no attention. He saw Mel and stopped.

Not with alarm. With assessment. The calculation of a man reading a position on a board.

Trixie went back to him, briefly, and then returned to Mel.

"Ms. Hunter," he said. Not a question. Not surprise. The voice of a man who has been expecting something and is now measuring whether this is it.

"Mr. Dowen." She straightened. "I'm sorry to interrupt your walk."

"No you're not."

A pause.

"No," she said. "I'm not."

She presented the case.

She had spent three weeks assembling it and two days verifying that what she had would hold, and she had been over the order of it enough times that it had the quality of something load-bearing, a structure that would take the weight. She delivered it standing on the east path of Miller's Hollow Park in the dark of a November morning, without histrionics, to the man she believed was a killer.

She led with the chemistry.

What BeeLure Professional Swarm Attractant does: the compound in its full formulation attracts and directs foraging bees toward a target by simulating the presence of a queen. It requires both the orientation signal and the queen mandibular component: geraniol and citral for the scouts, 9-ODA to move the colony. Without the queen mandibular element, you can attract scouts. You cannot direct a swarm.

What a properly formulated slow-release preparation requires: a carrier chemistry (polymer gel or rubber medallion) that keeps the active compound volatile over a three-to-four-hour window. A surface-applied liquid would have dispersed before the match began. Whoever prepared the compound understood the specific delivery mechanism, not in general terms but in working detail. Why the compound Agnes Moskov purchased could not have directed a swarm across three hundred meters to one specific man: because it lacked the queen mandibular component, without which you attract scouts but cannot move a colony. Why the compound used at the festival required a chemist's preparation and a chemist's understanding of the specific mechanism. Why Cambridge Mathematics, first-class honours, would give a person exactly that access.

She presented the twenty-four years. The startup co-founded in 1998. The algorithm built over four years that became a patent filing in 1999 naming one inventor. Duncan Vance's role, on record in the

Historical Society archive. Eleanor Vance's knowledge of her father's involvement. Bernie walking away with the intellectual property and the career and the credit when the company dissolved. She named the twenty-four years specifically, with no rounding.

She presented the eliminations. Agnes Moskov: the rubbish collection at six fifteen, the wrong compound, the timing impossibility. David Cheswick: the rental car, Pikeville, the obsession wall that contained every record of the chess betrayal and not one word about bees.

What remained. A man with Cambridge Mathematics and a documented twenty-four-year grievance and access to the east side of the festival grounds in his capacity as a tournament official. A morning walk route confirmed by multiple sources: east path, Miller's Hollow Park, before seven, daily.

She described the canvass Noreen had run in the week after the festival. The morning-after walk through the park, vendor to vendor, anyone who had been there early. A woman from the setup crew who had been at Miller's Hollow Park before six thirty on the morning of October 28, counting chairs. She had looked up once. A man walking a small dog, black and white, near the chess area, back and forth as you walk a dog when you are doing something else and the dog needs the time and you need the path to stay near. Nobody had gotten a good look at the man. The dog was small. It was a festival venue; there were dogs. Nobody had thought anything of it.

She had filed it as you file a receipt you expect never to look at again.

She said this to him now, standing on the east path in the dark. She said it without apology. There was no version of what had happened that required her to apologize for not understanding a case with missing pieces. She had assembled the pieces in the order they became available. That was all she had ever had to work with.

She described his apartment doorway in November, and the dog greeting her, and the left front paw she had held for a moment, the extra toe, five pads where four belonged, sitting snug inside the others.

She described what she had seen in the soft post-rain ground near the master's chess table on the twenty-eighth of October: a small dog's left front paw, one too many pads. She had looked at it and moved on. She had moved on because at that moment she did not have the frame to make it mean anything. She had not yet met the dog.

She described Derek Moskov's finding at the vandalized apiary in November: prints in the soft ground with a toe count that was wrong by one.

She described what the vandalized apiary meant. The timing: the same night of the break-in at The Giving Spoon. Coordinated. A message sent to two places simultaneously. Someone who knew enough about the investigation to know where the notes were and what the hives meant. Someone who had been watching, or been told, or both.

She described Corbin's own investigation thread: the Cheswick rental car, the obsession wall at Pinewoods Apartments, a man who had spent a decade building a case for exposure rather than death. She said: David Cheswick wanted Bernie alive and wrong on the public record. The wall was a courtroom, not a funeral plan. Cheswick had not been at the festival.

She described the mechanism. How she knew the compound had been on the chess pieces rather than on Bernie's person. How the setup window worked. How Bernie's polishing ritual had moved the compound from the piece to the cloth and from the cloth to his hands and from his hands to the bees' target. She was describing things she had worked out with Leo across three weeks of investigation, things that had been speculative until the timeline of the swarm made them certain.

Throughout the presentation, Dowen had said nothing. He stood on the east path with his hands in his jacket pockets and his face in a configuration that gave away nothing, and he listened. He did not interrupt. He did not deny. He did not look at the ground or at the cedar screen or at the parking area behind Mel. He looked at her, with the attention that she had first read as chess-player focus and then, over weeks of encountering it, had come to understand as something more specific: the attention of a man who has decided something and is waiting for the correct moment to act on it.

He had made his decision, she now understood, the moment he saw her on the path.

Then she stopped working the list and looked at him.

She said her planned speech directly: the morning dog walker was him. The prints were Trixie's. The chemistry fluency in his apartment on a Tuesday afternoon in November was not the result of reading a general-interest article about the festival's bees. She could not prove any of it to a standard that would satisfy a court. She could describe what she had observed and what it added up to, and she could name the person it added up to, and she could say the one thing she was not sure of: the exact time he had been at the pavilion.

She said: "You were at the east side of the pavilion at around six in the morning."

Dowen stood very still.

Trixie sat beside him, watching Mel.

Mel stopped speaking. The silence was the invitation.

She described the chemistry correction he had given her on a Tuesday afternoon in his apartment. The specific distinction between the Nasonov component and the queen mandibular element. The reflexive precision of a man who could not let an inaccuracy stand even when the cost of correcting it was visible in the room.

She said it again: "You were at the east side of the pavilion at around six in the morning."

The silence after she stopped was long enough to feel like its own event.

Then Dowen said: "It was 5:47."

He said it the way he said everything precise: not as a boast, not with any hint of emotion. A correction of a factual error. Because he cannot let an inaccuracy stand, even now. Even in this.

The silence after that was different in kind.

Trixie stood and put her nose briefly against Dowen's hand. He didn't look down at her.

Mel: "Why?"

A long pause.

Then Dowen spoke.

He had built the algorithm over four years starting in 1994, the work of a twenty-four-year-old man who had found the problem he wanted to spend his career on. He had watched Bernie Travers file the patents under his name alone in 1999 and walk away with the intellectual property and the professional recognition when the company dissolved in the collapse that took most of the dot-com sector with it. He had spent twenty-four years attempting to correct the record: attorneys, arbitration, academic review boards, three separate applications to invalidate the patents, each one closed by the combination of expired legal deadlines and a dead man's careful paperwork. Duncan Vance's name had appeared in every channel. Eleanor Vance had known what her father had done and had not been able to make it matter.

He said it without inflection. He was not unburdening himself. He was explaining, because a precise man does not leave his own motivation imprecise when there is someone present to give the explanation to.

He looked at the chess pavilion ground for a moment, the space where the table had stood.

"I was not going to watch him win the Silvergrove tournament with a program built on my mathematics."

The sentence landed in the cold air and stayed there.

Mel had been thinking, for three weeks, about what a man does with twenty-four years of documented injustice. She had been thinking about the difference between wanting Bernie exposed and wanting him dead. Cheswick had wanted exposure: the wall, the letters, the decade of drafts, a courtroom verdict that would have required Bernie to be alive to receive it. Dowen had wanted something nobody could give back.

But the Silvergrove tournament sentence was something else. It was not twenty-four years in the aggregate. It was one specific, final, intolerable instance of it. The program he had built was going to win a tournament under Bernie's name. Dowen had sat with twenty-four years of imprecision in the public record and then this had been the one he could not tolerate. Mel understood that distinction.

She did not say that she understood it. There was nothing useful to say about it.

Another silence.

"Arthur Pumble has been in custody for two weeks," Mel said.

"I know." A pause. "I'm aware that's my fault."

He did not look at Mel when he said it. He looked at the ground near the east path, the frozen grass, the place where the festival had happened seventeen days ago. He had stayed at the festival all day. He had sat in the crowd and watched the swarm and watched the aftermath and walked away at the end of the afternoon the same color he had walked in. He had been precise about that too.

He said it as he kept all accounts: accurately, precisely, with the particular tone of a man recording an entry on a ledger. Regretted. Not quite enough.

Corbin came out of the shadow of the cedar screen.

He had been there since before four in the morning. Mel had not heard him arrive. She had not been meant to. She had known only that the agreement was that he would be there, positioned, with the recording device, before the subject arrived. She had trusted that he had honored the agreement because Corbin honored agreements, not out of warmth for the person making the ask but because he was a man who did what he said he would do. He had been in the cold for three hours and forty-seven minutes, by her calculation, waiting for a man to correct a thirteen-minute inaccuracy on a November morning in a park.

Dowen turned to look at him. His expression did not change.

Corbin identified himself. He read Dowen his rights in the procedural voice of a man who has done this many times and does not make it into a performance. Dowen listened without expression. He didn't resist and he didn't speak and he didn't look at Mel again.

He handed Trixie's leash to Corbin.

Corbin looked at the leash, then at Mel, with the expression that asked a question he didn't say aloud.

Mel took the leash.

They walked Dowen toward the parking area. His footsteps on the frozen grass were precise and even, diminishing.

Mel stood on the east path and watched them go. The parking area was across the mowed ground, a hundred meters, and the sound of a car door and an engine diminishing was the sound of twenty-four years of a man's life arriving at its consequence.

The sky to the east was beginning to show the first grey differentiation of a day coming. Not light yet, just the suggestion of it, the sky deciding. The cedar screen was still dark. Behind it, three hundred meters, the hives sat in their winter rows along Mashburn Creek, the bees inside quiet and patient, doing what they do.

Trixie sat beside Mel on the path and watched the parking area.

The day came in. The hives were three hundred meters away, and Derek would be at the apiary by seven, and the bees did not know what the morning had cost.

Deliverance

The woman at the reception desk looked up when Mel came through the front door of Town Hall and said nothing, which was its own kind of message. The building had already received its version of the morning's news before the morning was half over. The corridor outside the council chamber had been rearranged by it: two people stood where they usually sat, a cluster of three near the water fountain had the compressed quality of a group mid-exchange, and a planning department clerk Mel half-recognized met her eye and looked away with the expression of a man who has been wanting to say something since nine o'clock and has not yet found the words.

She had come with Noreen and Leo. Noreen had her notebook open before they reached the chamber door. Leo had said nothing since the parking lot, and the silence was right.

The chamber was fuller than a standard Tuesday morning warranted. Word had traveled, as it traveled in Possum Gap, not through any organized channel but through the ordinary human mechanism of people telling other people things they needed to know. The room had the quality of a room that has been holding its breath.

The session opened at nine. The mayor read the agenda in order.

When Patricia Coldwell reached item three, she stood. She had been mayor through two contested elections and had the expression of someone who had learned to hold institutional news still in her face before delivering it. She announced that agenda item three, the eradication order for the apiary located at Mashburn Creek, Redbud County, belonging to Arthur Dariel Pumble, would be withdrawn, pending review of the case against the recently charged party. The formal language was bloodless. She delivered it in the same tone she used for zoning variances and budget line items, which was the correct tone for a body reversing itself under observation.

The room's response was not bloodless. There was something collective in it: not a sound, exactly, but a change in pressure, the same quality a room has in the moment before someone speaks and in the moment after. A collective breath, or the near-equivalent of one.

Noreen stepped forward when the floor opened. She submitted her documentation to the record without preamble: the timeline, the petition collection dates, the public filing that established Harold Pickett's name in the September–October 2023 signature window. Harold Pickett had died on the fourteenth of August, 2023, at the age of eighty-one, of the cancer that had been present in his blood for four years before it finished what it had started. He had brought Miriam's crabapple preserves to the Giving Spoon's pantry shelf every October for as long as Mel had been running the place, and he had opposed every county development proposal in living memory. Dowen had used his name after he was no longer around to object to its use.

The council received the documentation. Their expressions were the expressions of an institutional body that has acted on falsified grounds and is finally seeing the accurate record. Mel did not give them the satisfaction of watching too closely.

Someone near the back of the room, a man she had seen at the festival and once at the Sunflower whose name she did not know, said quietly: "What happens to the bees now?"

She said: "They stay."

She said it before the thought was fully organized. It arrived in her mouth as a fact she had apparently already decided, and she let it land without adding to it, and the room received it in the particular way that small rooms receive statements that are both specific and general at once.

He was on the steps when she came out. Not waiting in any formal sense: he had a folder under his arm and the manner of a man who has concluded his business in the building and has not yet committed to the next thing. She came down the steps and they were both briefly on the landing, with the cold November air between them and the parking lot beyond and a crow on the far fence doing nothing specific.

She stopped. He looked at her.

"The confession will hold," Corbin said. "The chemistry evidence and the warrant are procedurally clean. Dowen's attorney will look at the recording — that's standard practice. It'll hold."

She said she understood.

He adjusted the folder under his arm. She had watched him make that small movement across a kitchen counter and a conference table across the past six weeks, and she had learned it was not habitual in the nervous way but deliberate, the movement of a man transferring something between columns in an internal accounting. He was doing one now.

"I wrote the prints into the supplemental report," he said. "Details seen at the chess table. By whom. On the morning of October twenty-eighth." He looked at her steadily. "They're in the record."

She took a moment with that. She had been in a park three weeks ago and crouched in the soft ground near a table leg and looked at what was there and noted it, and the person with the authority to put it in the official record had said dogs everywhere and moved on. Now it was in a supplemental report. Now it was where it should have been from the start.

"Thank you," she said.

He held her gaze with the expression she had been cataloguing since October, the one that was not warmth and was not its opposite, but was something precise and direct, the expression of a man taking an accurate reading of a situation and returning it unchanged. What she read today was different in one specific quality: settled. The particular look of a case moved from the open column to the closed one, of a man whose accounting had come out clean.

She could read it because she was standing on the same steps and could see his face, and what she saw was not warm but it was honest, and honest was what she had needed from him across the whole of the investigation.

"You built a solid case," he said. A professional assessment, delivered without inflection. An accurate statement of fact.

He nodded once and walked toward the parking lot.

The steps were cold under her shoes and the November morning was flat and pale. She had been awake since before four and the most significant thing she had to do today was still ahead of her.

She went to get her car.

The Giving Spoon had its mid-morning quiet: the early crowd gone, the lunch crowd not yet arrived, the surfaces clean and the kitchen at rest between services. Leo was at the prep station when she came in through the back. He read her face in the two seconds it took him to look up.

Trixie had arranged herself on the folded towels in the corner near the dry goods shelf with the settled authority of a dog who has found a good spot and decided it is permanent. She raised her head when Mel came in and lowered it again.

"The vote was pulled," Mel said.

Leo set down what he was holding. He said: "Good." One word, plainly. She heard in it the accumulated weight of seventeen days of chemistry research and early mornings and the specific care of a person who doesn't make speeches about the things that matter.

He moved to the counter and made her sit down. He made coffee as he made it on mornings she hadn't asked for it, stronger than the service carafe, in the heavy cups from the back shelf, and set it in front of her without ceremony.

Noreen came in eight minutes later, took her coat off, and looked at Mel with the particular inventory of a woman who checks a room before she decides what it requires. Then she opened her notebook and began writing something. Mel drank the coffee. The silence between the three of them was the silence of people who have been through the same thing from different angles and do not need to debrief.

The twenty minutes passed in the ordinary rhythms of the Giving Spoon between services: Leo's prep movements, the specific sounds of a kitchen at rest, the November light through the rear window. Trixie slept. The coffee was exactly as good as it needed to be.

When the cup was empty, Mel got up and set it in the rack and reached for her keys.

Noreen looked up from her notebook.

"He's been waiting long enough," she said. Flat. Factual. The tone she reserved for things she had already concluded and was now simply stating.

She put her pen back to the page. Mel went.

The nurse on the third floor recognized her. She didn't ask, simply waved. Mel had been here four times since October thirty-first, and the corridor was familiar now as places become familiar through the specific practice of walking them with purpose. She knocked at the door she knew and stepped in.

Derek was in the chair beside the bed. He had the look of someone who had arrived early and made his peace with the room. Arthur's room had settled into itself over two weeks: the water pitcher in its position, the blinds at the angle Derek had set, his jacket over the chair back. The deputy was long gone. The hospital's official quality of detention had been softened, through use, back to simply a room.

Derek looked up when she came in and read her face before she had crossed the threshold.

Arthur's eyes were open. He had been resting when she knocked and had heard the door.

She told him.

She told him in the correct order: "Corbin arrested Down. His confession is on record. The charges against you are invalid and will be dropped. The council has reversed their vote. The hives are safe.

She said each thing once, plainly, with the same economy she had brought to every other delivery of fact across the preceding eighteen days. No interpretation. No performance. The facts carried what they carried. She watched his face while she spoke.

His eyes were open and very still. He received the information with his whole attention, with the specific quality of a man awaiting a long-expected accounting from a source he had trusted to be accurate. He had been in this room for two weeks on a charge that was not true, in a body running its own separate and longer accounting, and he listened to her with the same settled patience he had brought to forty years of knowing what bees need and what bees will tell you and what you do when neither can tell you anything more.

When she finished, the room was quiet for a while.

Arthur closed his eyes.

She waited. She had learned to wait in this room.

Then: "Derek."

He said it the way you say a name when you have been carrying it all morning and are finally setting it down. Derek leaned forward. His chair moved an inch without his noticing.

Arthur said: "You know what to do with them."

Not an instruction. Not a plea. A statement of what was already true, a recognition spoken aloud, of what Derek had been making true in the hive rows at Mashburn Creek for two years, in the winter checks and the feeding logs and the specific kind of attention that an apiary requires and rewards. Arthur had been watching. He had seen what was there. He only said it now because it needed, finally, to be said.

Derek said: "Yes."

One word. Said as a true thing, the way you say a true thing when it has been true for long enough that saying it aloud is simply the last motion of something already decided.

Arthur's face settled. The accounting was complete and the columns balanced, and the quality of the room became the quality of a man who has been carrying something at considerable expense and has set it down. Not diminished. Arrived.

His breathing was slow and even.

Mel stayed. She stood at the foot of the bed and was present in the room and looked at Arthur and at Derek in his chair and understood what the room held and what it did not need from her. She touched the rail at the foot of the bed, a brief contact, and left.

The corridor was the same corridor it had always been. She walked it toward the elevator, and while she waited for it she held what she had just delivered: not the words, which were already settling into the particulars of the day, but the fact of what they had moved. Dowen had said five words in a park before sunrise, and those five words had traveled from a recording device to an official record to a council chamber to a man in a hospital bed in the space of six hours. That was how it worked when it worked. She pressed the button and the elevator came.

Silver Oak Hospital in the mid-morning had its flat November light, the institutional windows making the most of what the sky offered, and the sky not offering much. She came out through the lobby and stood on the sidewalk for a moment with the November air on her face and the quality of a day that has completed its main work and still has hours left to run.

Derek was with him. The hives were safe. The accounting balanced.

She drove back to the Giving Spoon.

The Giving Spoon filled up without any invitation or notice.

It happened the way Possum Gap moved when important matters had been sorted and the town needed somewhere to put itself. People came in twos and alone and in the familiar configurations of an afternoon crowd, and some of them were the usual Tuesday afternoon people, and some were not usually Tuesday afternoon people but were this afternoon because the day had warranted it. Word had been traveling since the council session, and what word does in a town of this size is give people a reason to end up where they were already half-inclined to be.

Leo made coffee. He had been making it since six in the morning and he made it now with the same precision he brought to every task he considered worth doing well, which was every task. Noreen moved through the room with the ease of someone in her element, the ease that comes not from the absence of effort but from long practice that has made the effort invisible. She knew who needed refills and who was waiting to talk and who she should leave alone. She attended to each with the proper degree of attention and no more.

Mel was at the counter.

She was tired in the specific way that comes when sustained tension releases and the body does not immediately know what to replace the organization with. She let the afternoon happen around her. People said things and she responded, and the responses required nothing exceptional. The day's exceptional work was already done.

Mrs. Lund came in at two with her usual order and asked for it without checking whether it was available, because in sixteen years it had always been available on a Tuesday. The two men from the electricians' shop took the far table, the claimed territory of long habit. A woman Mel knew only by her order, chamomile and no honey and a blueberry muffin, came in at half past two and settled into the window seat with a book and did not look up except to acknowledge the order's arrival.

The ordinary held. Mel was grateful for it in the way you are grateful for things you have taken for granted until the day you needed them to be exactly as they have always been.

Trixie had moved from the back storage room to a corner near the kitchen door where she could observe the room without being underfoot. She had been in an unusual situation since before sunrise and had managed it with the equanimity of a well-adjusted animal. Leo had handled the logistics of a dog in a working kitchen with the efficiency he brought to practical problems, and Trixie had accepted the folded towels and the water bowl and the proximity to human activity as a reasonable arrangement. A few of the afternoon customers noticed her and asked, and Mel said she was minding the dog for a day or two, which was accurate.

Tim Renshaw came in at half past four.

He came in without an appointment to keep, found a stool at the counter, settled into the room in the manner of a man who has come for one cup and is in no hurry about it. He ordered coffee. Mel poured it.

At the counter, with the cup in front of him, he said: "Arthur?"

"Stable," she said. "Derek's with him."

Tim nodded. He picked up the cup and held it and looked at the counter for a moment. She could see him doing the arithmetic she recognized: the math of what stable meant today and what it meant in stages; the calculations of a man who understood the situation from what she had said, and from what remained unsaid. And from what he understood on his own. He did the arithmetic and he set the cup down and he did not say what the answer was.

He stayed for one cup. He left without lingering. At the door he looked back once, not at her specifically, but at the room in its afternoon state, at the Giving Spoon as a person looks at a place that has been through something and is on the other side of it. Finally, he grinned and gave Mel a parting wink.

After Tim left, the afternoon had its full-tide hour: the period when the room was as full as it was going to be, the conversations at their most sustained, Leo in constant motion between the counter and the kitchen. Noreen had taken the back table and was writing, occasionally, and mostly listening, which was its own form of taking notes.

Mel worked. She made the drinks and cleared the tables and acknowledged the faces of people she had known for years: Mrs. Lund's habitual economy of order, the electricians' companionable silence, the woman with the blueberry muffin still in the window seat, turned now to watch the street rather than read. She knew these people as a person knows the specifics of their own life: not by cataloguing them but by having been present for them repeatedly, long enough that their particulars had become part of the texture of the days.

The investigation had been in this room too. She had worked this same counter while everything else was happening, and the Giving Spoon had been open through every day of it. The regulars had come. She had made their orders and listened to the room with part of her attention and kept the other part for what needed keeping. The room had held, as it always held, and she was grateful for that the way she was grateful for all the things she had taken for granted until the day she needed them.

She put the last afternoon order in front of Mrs. Lund, who received it without comment, which was how Mrs. Lund received things she considered correct.

The afternoon wound down the way Tuesday afternoons wound down, by degrees, the last customers taking their time, which was their right. When the last one left and the door closed on the November evening outside, full dark now, arrived between one cup and the next without announcement, the sound of the lock was ordinary and complete.

Mel, Noreen, and Leo were alone in the Giving Spoon.

Leo put three cups on the counter. The heavy ones from the back shelf, the cups kept for the end of long days. He set them down and climbed onto a stool and folded his arms on the counter. He looked at nothing in particular, with the expression of a man who has worked since before dawn.

They sat together.

The room had its end-of-day quality: the wiped-down surfaces, the chairs turned on some of the tables, the low light over the counter. The coffee was the last of the pot. The November dark blacked out the windows, and somewhere behind the building the alley was quiet. The town had gone about the remainder of its Tuesday.

Nobody said much. There wasn't much that needed saying.

The rum cake sat on the shelf behind the counter. It had been there since Noreen arrived, three weeks ago, and put it there. She had brought it from Jamaica. It had sat on that shelf through days and nights of investigation, through the wrong arrest and the right one, through the long preparation for the morning that had finally come and gone. It had waited, as a thing waits when the time has not yet been right.

Noreen looked at it.

She got up from her stool, reached up, and took it down from the shelf. She set it on the counter. She found the knife from the third drawer and cut it.

Changes

Derek arrived at the apiary before the light had fully settled into the cedar screen, as he had arrived every Wednesday for two years. The apiary in November had a different quality from the apiary in any other month: quieter, the ambient hum that ran through the warm seasons gone, the colonies pulled down to their winter configurations, the entrance reducers in, the hive bodies compressed to hold heat. The November apiary was a place that had made its preparations and was waiting.

He pulled on his gloves at the gate and did what he always did first: walked the row and looked. Not for specific problems but for the general picture: whether anything was different from how he had left it Monday, whether the overnight had changed anything. The cedar screen behind the eastern row had shed most of its leaves in the past week. The creek was lower than October, the bank exposed further, the stones at the near bend visible now where summer rains kept them covered. The morning was cold and still with the quality of a morning that intends to stay cold.

The hives were Arthur's design: twelve boxes in two rows, each colony positioned for morning sun, the spacing generous enough for easy inspection, tight enough to be efficient. Derek had not changed the spacing. He had not changed anything that was working, and everything was working. The two boxes in the fifth and sixth positions of the western row, the ones he had repaired after the vandalism, had gone into winter with their populations intact. He had been watching them since mid-October and they had not faltered.

He moved through the checks: entrance reducers in place, all twelve. He did each one twice when he was uncertain, once when he was sure, and today he was sure. Winter stores: he lifted each inner cover briefly, mentally recorded what was there, replaced it carefully. The colonies did not appreciate disturbance in cold weather and he kept the inspections as short as accuracy allowed. Eleven of twelve had laid in enough to carry them to March without supplemental feeding. The twelfth, the furthest east in the second row, had stores he would not have been comfortable with going into December.

The eastern box had been like this in its second autumn too. The colony was productive in spring and summer and characteristically reluctant about late-season stores. Something in its particular genetic line, Arthur had said once, prioritized foraging over consolidation. You could spend years trying to correct a hive's character, or you could accept the character and manage for it. Arthur had accepted it. Derek had watched him accept it and had understood, over two years, why that was the correct approach.

You just feed it more in November, Arthur had told him. Some of them are like that.

He added the eastern box supplement to his Saturday list.

At the far end of the eastern row he stopped and looked through the gap in the cedar screen toward the park. The tournament grounds were visible: the mowed rectangle, now brown and going brittle with frost, the empty area where the pavilion had stood, the chess table cleared away weeks ago. The ground was doing what November ground does: withdrawing into itself, closing up, going quiet. It looked like any ground. Ordinary.

He looked at it for a moment. Then he looked back at the hives.

He finished the eastern row and started the western again, moving in the other direction this time, checking what he had already noted and checking for what he might have missed. The second box from the northern end of the western row had a lighter cluster than he preferred. He put it on the list. That was three things for Saturday: the eastern box supplement, the cluster check on the light western box, and a general winter-feeding review of the whole row. A reasonable Saturday for mid-November. Not bad.

When he finished his tasks he stood at the gate with the morning around him and the creek running quietly behind the cedars. The bees inside their boxes did what bees do in winter, which is conserve what they have and wait for the conditions to change. He had been doing apiary work long enough to find this posture recognizable. The patience of it.

He reached into his jacket and took out the beekeeper's log. Not Arthur's. Arthur's logs went back to 1984 and held forty years of observations in a hand that had grown steadier with age rather than less so, and those logs belonged to the archive and would stay there. This was his own: a standard composition notebook with a green cover, his name written on the inside front in plain block letters. He had bought it last week.

He opened it to the first page and wrote the date.

November 15.

He put the pen back in his pocket and stood there a moment longer, the notebook open in his hand, the date at the top of the first entry, and the rest of the page blank and waiting.

He closed it and walked back through the gate.

The call came at six forty-eight in the morning. Mel had been awake since six, in her kitchen with coffee she had made and not yet finished, looking at the alley in the early light. November light at this hour was almost no light: just the suggestion of the world outside, the shapes of the building opposite and the bins along the wall and the sky above the alley deciding what kind of gray to be.

A woman from Silver Oak Hospital. The woman checked her record: Melissa Hunter was listed as a close contact. Was this the same Melissa Hunter?

She said yes.

The woman continued. A careful voice, carrying the specific burden of someone who has delivered this kind of news professionally many times. Trained to hold it with kindness without pretending it was anything other than what it was. Arthur Dariel Pumble had passed during the night. Peacefully, his chart said. He had no next of kin to notify.

She thanked the woman. The call ended. She set the phone on the table and placed her chin and mouth in her hands.

She sat with it in her kitchen for a few minutes, rocking back and forth on her chair. Her coffee was still warm; she did not drink it. Her first thought, the one that arrived before she had organized herself to have thoughts about anything, was the eastern hive box at Mashburn Creek, the one with the reluctant late-season stores. Whether Derek had put the Saturday supplement on his list: she was certain he had, because Derek always put the things in order. He had been doing it for two years without being asked. The apiary in the morning cold, the colonies in their winter clusters, the entrance reducers doing what they were meant to do.

This was the proper form of grief for this particular morning. Arthur had spent eleven years learning the language of the apiary and she had spent three weeks learning its edges, enough to think in. Thinking about the hives was not deflection. It was what he would have thought, and thinking it was the closest she could come to him now.

Peacefully, his chart said. Derek had been with him. Tears dripped on her forearm.

She sat in her kitchen and held that against her heart. The mercy of it: that Arthur had died in the night, with someone who knew the apiary beside him, without having to wait any longer for the thing he had been waiting for. The bees were safe. He had known it. The alley outside was filling with the flat gray of a November morning that was not going to offer much. A car passed on the street somewhere.

The coffee cooled.

She swiped at her face with a paper napkin. She picked up her phone and called Noreen.

Then Leo.

She opened the Giving Spoon on Friday morning with both of them there. Leo was at the prep station when she came in, an hour before opening. Noreen arrived fifteen minutes later with her coat on and her notebook already out, and the three of them went through the opening routine in the specific silence of people who are doing what they do because it is what they do, and because the doing of it is the correct response to a morning like this one.

They did not put a sign in the window. They did not make any announcement. The Giving Spoon opened on Friday mornings and it was a Friday morning.

The ordinary mechanics of opening: chairs down from the tables, the register counted, the front windows cleared with a cloth Noreen produced from somewhere, the first carafe of coffee drawn. Trixie was in her corner. Leo had settled her there when he arrived and she had accepted it, her chin on her paws, watching the kitchen with the patient attention of a dog that has decided to be useful by staying out of the way.

People came in by degrees. The first few arrived not knowing, just their usual orders, their usual tables, the usual economy of a regular's routine, and then word traveled, as it always traveled in Possum Gap, and the arrivals changed in character. The faces that came in after eight had heard something. They came in more carefully, sat more quietly, made their orders and let the room have its weight.

When people asked, Mel said he was a good man.

He was.

Mrs. Lund came in at nine-fifteen, her walking coat still buttoned. She sat at her usual corner table and looked at Mel for a long moment without speaking, and Mel looked back, and that was sufficient. Mrs. Lund ordered her usual. Leo brought it over himself.

The two electricians came in together, not their usual Friday, their work jackets still on. They sat at the counter and ordered coffee and when one of them said "We heard about the beekeeper" Mel said yes and that was all she could muster. They drank their coffee and left more money than the bill and did not wait for change.

By mid-morning the room had what she recognized from the weeks of the investigation. People aware of each other, aware that something they held in common and they could now let go. She had watched Possum Gap do this over the years. The specific attention it paid to its own. The way a small town closes ranks around grief not with noise but with presence, with the ordinary things done in the ordinary way and a certain careful fullness of attention laid over everything.

Noreen moved through the room with the ease of a woman in her natural environment. She filled cups. She remembered which of the regulars took cream and which didn't. She had the skill of someone who has spent a long time reading rooms and knowing what people needed before they said it.

Leo stayed at the prep station and the counter, doing what he did, making what he made. He did not talk much. He did not need to.

She said it to the woman from the post office and to the man who ran the hardware store and to the retired schoolteacher whose name she could never quite hold on to. She said it because it was accurate, and because accuracy was what the question deserved.

The Giving Spoon on Friday morning had its ordinary rhythms and its extraordinary undertow, and the ordinary held the way it had held on Tuesday, and Mel was grateful for it in the specific way she had become grateful for ordinary things over the past three weeks. The room did what it had always done. That was what she needed it to do.

Eleanor called at ten. She had waited two days since their brief Friday conversation to say something more. Two days, Mel understood, of deciding what more to say and whether to say it at all.

She said she was sorry. For what she had known about her father's role in the patent situation and had not said sooner, when saying it sooner might have mattered. For Arthur, who had deserved better from the people and the institutions that should have protected what he built. She said both things in Eleanor's unique voice: considered, precise, without self-pity, with the quality of a woman who has examined a thing carefully before speaking it and is now delivering the examination rather than the emotion.

Mel let her say it.

She told Eleanor that Derek was tending the apiary. That the winter preparations were complete and the colonies were well. That there would be bees at Mashburn Creek next spring, which was what Arthur had worked to ensure.

Eleanor was quiet for a moment. Then: "Good."

A pause.

"I'll be in touch soon about something. Not today. When I've had the weekend." She didn't explain what the something was. Mel had been her friend long enough to understand that Eleanor Vance had been carrying something for a long time and had decided, after this week, that she would no longer carry it alone.

"Whenever you're ready," Mel said.

They said their goodbyes and the call ended and Mel went back to the counter.

Agnes came in just before noon.

She brought a jar of spiced citrus preserve, something from her shop's fall batch: a small amber jar with a hand-lettered label and the smell of clove and orange peel when Mel opened the lid. Agnes set it on the counter with the brevity of a person who has brought a thing and does not want to make a production of having brought it. A small gesture, offered as a gesture rather than as currency.

Mel thanked her. Agnes nodded and ordered coffee and a muffin and took them to the back window table, and that might have been the whole of it: two women who had been wrong about each other, briefly, in ways both of them now understood, sharing a room without incident. Which would have been enough.

But when Agnes finished her coffee and brought the cup back to the counter, she paused.

"I'm going to try again with the hive box," she said.

Mel looked at her.

"Arthur told me once I had the patience for it. Years ago. I thought, after everything, that it was still true." She looked at the counter. "I still have the equipment."

"Talk to Derek," Mel said.

She was direct, but not unkind. It was the correct sentence. Derek was at the apiary and he knew the apiary and he had two years of experience and the patience of someone who has learned something from the man who was good at it. Agnes Moskov already knew who Derek Moskov was. If she was going to learn to keep bees, he was the right teacher.

Agnes said she would. She said it with the manner of someone who has already decided and is simply confirming the decision aloud, which was how Agnes said most things once she had arrived at them. The jar of preserves stayed where she had set it, Mel understood, as a thing for the Giving Spoon's pantry shelf rather than a thing for Agnes to take back. Agnes said goodbye and left.

The jar stayed on the counter. Mel would put it on the shelf later.

Leo found her in the kitchen after the lunch crowd had thinned. He had the look of someone who has been carrying a piece of information for several days and has settled on today as the right day to set it down.

“I got an email on Tuesday,” he said. “While everything else was happening. I didn’t want to bring it up until—” He stopped, and the stopped sentence contained the whole of the week, and Mel understood it.

“A researcher at the University of Tennessee extension program,” he continued. “He studies directed foraging behavior in honeybees. He followed the case coverage and reached out about the queen mandibular pheromone mechanism — the specific directed-swarm application. What I worked out for the investigation.” He folded the dish towel he was holding and set it on the prep counter. “He wants to co-author a paper on the delivery system. The chess piece application, the slow-release formulation at ambient temperature. He says the controlled delivery of 9-ODA in that specific concentration hasn’t been studied outside of lab conditions. He thinks there’s a publishable paper in the mechanism, separate from the criminal case.”

Mel said: “He wants you as co-author.”

“My name on the paper,” Leo said. He said it as a fact. It was, she understood, a significant fact, not because Leo didn’t know his own worth, but because the academic world had not previously offered to confirm it in the particular way that a published paper confirmed it. He had come to Possum Gap with a scholarship timeline and a knife roll and two years of cooking experience and the kind of chemistry knowledge that lived in his hands and his father’s phone calls and the library of papers he had read because they interested him. Now a researcher at a university was going to put his name next to his own on something that would reach other researchers.

“My advisor will grant a program extension,” Leo went on. “There’s a formal process for research opportunities that emerge during a fellowship. The paper will take a few months: drafting, review, revisions. Most of that I can do from here.” He picked up the dish towel again and set it back down. “I do have to go back first. Get everything set with my advisor, meet with the UT researcher. A few weeks. Then I’m back.”

She took a moment with that. Not with the leaving, which she had made her peace with a long time ago, but with the coming back. She looked at Leo Cortez, who had been at the Giving Spoon’s prep station since before any of this started and who would be back at it before the year was out, and she felt something loosen in the specific way that things loosen when you have been afraid of something you were not quite admitting you were afraid of. The fellowship would do what fellowships did. The Giving Spoon would not need a permanent replacement. Both of those things were true at once, and she could hold both.

"The coffee gets better when you stay," she said.

"The coffee is always good," he said.

An old argument, delivered without heat, which was its own form of saying what neither of them was going to say any other way.

Tim came by at four, as he had on Tuesday, without a specific announced purpose. He asked whether there was anything she needed for the weekend, for Saturday's memorial, for the Giving Spoon, for herself.

She said no.

He nodded. He was in his coat, keys in hand, on his way out the way he was on his way out every time he came by at four on a Friday. He was a man of regular habits and he had made the Giving Spoon a regular habit, somewhere in the past three weeks, and it did not seem to be a habit he was in any hurry to revise.

At the door he paused.

He had the look of a man who has been thinking about something since Tuesday morning and has decided that a quiet Friday afternoon, at the end of the particular week this had been, was a reasonable time to say it.

"The Trixie question," he said.

Mel looked up from the counter.

"If you can't keep her." He met her eyes for a beat that lasted just slightly longer than the sentence required, the kind of beat that is not quite neutral, that carries the shape of something without stating it. "I know someone."

He left it there.

The door closed. Mel stood at the counter. The Giving Spoon was quiet with the quality of a late Friday afternoon when the day is done and the week is done and the light through the front windows is the low amber of a November sun making its exit. Trixie was in her corner by the kitchen door with her chin on her paws, watching Mel with the calm attention of a dog who has decided that this is where she belongs and is waiting to see if the person across the room has reached the same conclusion.

Mel looked at her.

Trixie had her left front paw tucked under her chin. The paw that had been through dog shows and a murder investigation and a park at five forty-seven in the morning. Five toes where there should have been four.

Mel looked at her for a long moment.

Then she went to get her coat. There was a memorial to prepare for, and a dog that needed her walk, and the Saturday list was not going to write itself.

A New Balance

The apiary gate was open when Mel arrived, which was as it should be. Derek had unlocked it that morning and left it that way, and the crowd that had gathered along the creek bank stood in the particular way that people stand at outdoor gatherings in cold weather: close together, coats buttoned, the particular stillness of people who are present on purpose.

Fall winds had stripped the eastern row of cedars to its branches. Through the gaps where leaves had been, the park was visible: the tournament area, the brown rectangle of the mowed field going brittle with frost. The space where the pavilion had stood for a week and a half before it was packed away. It looked like any field in November. Ordinary. The creek ran low and clear over the stones at the near bend, unhurried in the way of water that has been running over those stones for a long time and intends to continue.

There were perhaps seventy people. Mel had not expected seventy. She had expected the people who had known Arthur closely, Derek and Noreen and Leo among them, a handful of the chess regulars from the centennial as well, and there were those people, but there were also others: faces she recognized from the council chamber, from the Giving Spoon's regular tables, from the tournament grounds on the morning of October 28 when everything had not yet come apart. A woman who had been in the spectator area when the swarm crossed the pavilion. Two men from the regional chess community who had driven in for the occasion. The retired schoolteacher whose name Mel could never quite hold onto. Mrs. Lund, in her good coat.

The contrast with the other November memorial, the one at Christ Lutheran two weeks earlier, was present in the field. That gathering had been obligatory. A room of people who had come because one was expected to come. This field was a choice. These seventy-odd people had looked at their Saturday afternoon and decided to be here, which was a different kind of gathering entirely.

Derek stood at the apiary gate with the hive rows behind him. Twelve boxes in two rows, the entrance reducers in, the colonies in their winter clusters. He had unlocked the gate and taken his position at it and that was where he would stay. He was wearing the same jacket he wore to the apiary every morning, which was the right thing to wear.

The afternoon settled around them. The sky was the flat white of a November sky that has made its decision about the light and will not be changing it. The creek ran. The cedar branches moved in the occasional small wind off the meadow.

On the warmest part of the afternoon, just before three, a sound came from the nearest hive box: low, continuous, barely audible over the water. Not the summer hum, not the full-colony sound she had come to know over three weeks of standing near Arthur's property: something smaller and interior, the sound of a colony doing what colonies do in winter. Someone near Mel said: "They're still going." She did not respond. The sound was sufficient and required nothing added to it.

Several people spoke. A woman who had known Arthur since before the chess community had organized itself into anything formal said that he had brought hives to the east meadow before there were entrance reducers, before the modern equipment, before any of the things that make it manageable now, and had figured most of it out by watching, which was how he had approached most things. A man from the county who handled the wildlife corridor grants said that Arthur had been the most reliable steward of the Mashburn Creek watershed for twenty-three years without anyone asking him to be, without any committee or designation, and that the grant paperwork would miss his signature more than it had words to say. He had been the person who showed up. These were rarer than the county tended to acknowledge.

Leo spoke last among the others, before Mel. He said only that Arthur had once told him you could tell the health of a colony by its smell in winter, not by its sound, not by its activity, but by the specific smell at the entrance in cold weather, and that he had been right about that, and that he had been right about most things, and that being in the presence of someone who is right about most things is something you recognize only afterward, when you are trying to figure out how to go forward without them.

The crowd was quiet for a moment after that.

Mel had not planned to speak. She found herself speaking.

Harold Pickett had given two hundred and fifty dollars every quarter to the Giving Spoon's pantry fund, in Miriam Pickett's name, for as long as Mel had been running the place. He had never mentioned it. He had never asked for acknowledgment or recognition of any kind. The quarterly transfer came through the donor account and she had kept it private in the way she kept all donor information private, because that was what the work required and because it was plainly what Harold wanted. She was saying it now because Harold Pickett was the kind of person Arthur Pumble kept company with: the kind who did what the situation needed without requiring anyone to notice. Arthur had liked people who kept their own accounts and didn't ask the world to balance them. She believed Arthur had known about the fund. She believed he had approved.

She stopped there. She had not planned to say more and did not.

A few faces she recognized as people who had known Harold saw this without visible reaction. A few others looked surprised. A woman near the back put her hand briefly over her mouth and then took it away. Near the front, a man she recognized from the Giving Spoon, one of the regulars whose name she had never caught, nodded once, in the manner of someone confirming something they had long suspected. Mel did not dwell on any of it. She had said the thing that belonged to the occasion and the occasion could have it.

Tim was somewhere toward the middle of the crowd. At some point, before Derek spoke, after a brief silence in which nobody moved, Mel looked up and found him looking at her. She did not look away first. It lasted a moment and was enough, and they both understood that everything else was for another time.

When the others had finished, Derek spoke.

"I'm going to take care of them."

He said it simply, in the manner of a person who has no need to announce a decision. He simply confirmed, for the record, what was already true. He was looking at the hive rows, not at the crowd. The hive rows were what he was responsible for and they were what he was talking about. Whether the crowd understood he was also talking about something larger was their business. He had said what was accurate and that was enough.

Nobody spoke after that. The gathering held the line for a moment in the way a piece of music holds its last note before the silence takes over, and then people began to move in the small incremental way that means a gathering is ending.

The afternoon wound down. The November light did what November light does: lower and flatter, the cedar screen throwing its shadow across the eastern row, the temperature dropping two degrees in twenty minutes. Mel moved through the dispersing crowd, exchanging what there was to exchange: a hand held briefly, a look, a sentence or two with the wildlife corridor man about Derek's plans for the spring. Noreen had found someone she knew from the county and was talking with the focused efficiency of a woman who does not waste conversations. Leo was near the gate, waiting.

The three of them walked out together. The apiary gate clicked shut behind them. Nobody said much on the walk back to the cars, which was right.

Eleanor arrived at seven with the box.

It was a legal archive box, the standard size, worn at the corners in the way of a box that made moves from storage to closet to shelf and back again over the course of fifteen years without ever being thrown away and without ever being opened. It was heavier than it looked. Eleanor carried it with the careful grip of someone who has been carrying it in her mind for longer than she has been carrying it in her hands.

Mel held the door. Eleanor brought it in and set it on the kitchen table and stepped back from it the way you step back from something once you have set it down in the right place.

She said it quickly, because she had decided beforehand to say it quickly. Her father had kept meticulous records, which she had always known, a quality she had inherited and had understood as organizational precision, the mark of a man who valued accuracy and order. She now understood it also as something else: as the behavior of a man who needed to know that what he had done lived in documents, somewhere, in his own hand. When he died she had found the archive in the course of settling the estate and had understood immediately what she was looking at. She had tried twice to bring it to legal attention. Once in 2011, once in 2014. Both times she had heard the same thing by different lawyers. The patents had expired. Dowen had no more legal remedies. The company hadn't existed for fifteen years. There was nothing to correct. There was no venue that had jurisdiction over a wrong this old.

She had kept the box since 2010 because she could not bring herself to throw it away.

She looked at the table. "I don't know what you'd do with them." A pause that had some weight in it. "I couldn't throw them away." She looked at Mel directly. "I couldn't keep them anymore."

After everything that had come out in the past three weeks, the weight of knowing had changed its character. Dowen's story was public. Everyone in the county talked about what had happened to him. They reported it, argued about it, and picked it apart just like they always did. None of it cleared Eleanor of blame. She only felt a little lighter.

Mel could see both of these things in her face and said nothing about.

"Do you want tea?" Mel said.

Eleanor said no. She had another stop. She said goodnight and left, and the door closed, and Mel was alone in her kitchen with the box on the table.

She sat with it for a little while. Then she took the lid off.

She read enough to confirm what Eleanor had described. The patent filing, the dates carefully recorded, the correspondence in Duncan Vance's handwriting that traced the exclusion of Dowen's name from the documentation: clear and methodical, the work of a man who knew exactly what he was doing and saw fit to write it down in the way careful people write down the things they have done, for their own accounting if no one else's. Forty years of proper channels that had led nowhere, because the same name had appeared at every door, politely closing each one.

Gregory Claude Dowen's grievance had been real. Documented. Legitimate by any standard she could apply to it. He had then killed a man with a swarm of bees in a public park in the middle of the afternoon, and a seventy-three-year-old beekeeper had spent two weeks in a holding facility and a hospital bed while the truth found its way to the surface.

Both of those things were true. Neither cancelled the other. The box held both of them in a dead man's careful handwriting, and there was nothing anyone could do about that now except know it.

She put the lid back on the box.

She would take it to the Giving Spoon in the morning and put it on the shelf behind the counter. She did not know what she would eventually do with it. She had kept harder things than this. She would know when the time came.

Trixie was under the desk at Mel's feet when Leo came out of the kitchen with his bag. The knife roll was in his hand, the same one that had lived on the prep station for three months, zipped now and going with him. He set it on the counter while he checked that he had everything, and Trixie came out from under the desk to investigate it with the thoroughness she brought to all objects that arrived at counter height, and Leo crouched briefly to let her and scratched behind her ears.

He stood up and looked at Mel.

"You're good," she said.

"I'll call when I get in."

"Drive safe."

He picked up the knife roll. The Giving Spoon on a Monday morning in late November was not a place that called for extended goodbyes. What needed saying had been said on Friday over coffee, in the old-argument style that was how they shared things. He went to the door.

Noreen was on the front step with a paper bag when he opened it. Something from wherever Noreen found things at seven in the morning in a town she had been in for three weeks. She looked at Leo and the bag and the knife roll with the expression of a woman making a rapid assessment.

"Goodbye," she said.

"So long," Leo said. "For a bit."

He went around her and down the step and got into his car, and Trixie watched from just inside the doorway as the car pulled out, and then Noreen came in and the door closed.

Trixie greeted Noreen with the conviction of a dog who considers every arrival an event worth noting and then went back under the desk. Noreen set the pastries on the planning desk and pulled out the chair across from Mel's.

She looked toward the door. "Is he coming back?"

"A few weeks. He needs to get things sorted at school. The extension paperwork, the research arrangement, and spend some time in the teaching kitchen. He'll be back before the year's out."

Noreen processed this in her usual way, which was warm and did not waste motion. She opened the paper bag and put a pastry in front of Mel. They were small and glazed and smelled of orange peel, which was the right smell for a Monday morning at the end of November when there was work ahead.

The teapot was already on. Two cups. The Eleanor box was on the shelf behind the counter where Mel had put it when she came in, and she had not looked at it again and did not need to.

They settled.

"Thanksgiving Thursday," Mel said.

"Thursday."

Mel looked at the pantry shelves. They were the same shelves she had been looking at since October, through all of it, and the shelves said what they had been saying for weeks: not enough. The demand that came with the last week of November would arrive in three days and the inventory did not reflect what three days meant.

"We don't have enough," she said.

It was not a complaint. It was the shelves, accurately reported.

Noreen looked at the list Mel had started on the legal pad between their cups. She looked at the shelves. She put down her pastry, clearly done with portion of the morning that involved pastries.

"We'll find a way," she said. "We always find a way."

Trixie's tail moved once under the desk, in agreement or in some other opinion.

Noreen glanced down at her. "Speaking of." She looked at Mel. "Are you keeping her?"

"No decision's been made," Mel said.

Noreen accepted this with the composure of a woman who recognized the sentence and understood that pressing it would not improve matters. She picked up her phone.

"I can make some calls. There are people I haven't tried. Give me the morning."

She opened her contacts list.

That was when they heard the truck.

It was a bobtail with no markings on the side panels, nothing to indicate where it had come from or who had sent it, pulling up on the street outside with the deliberateness of a driver who had the address right and knew how close to park. Mel noticed it through the front window in the way she noticed things that arrived out of the morning's expected order: the size of it, the blankness, the specific care with which it positioned itself at the curb.

The driver came in. A man in a plain uniform, manifest board under his arm, the manner of someone with a straightforward job who wanted to do it and move on.

"Pantry manager?" he said.

"That's me."

He had a delivery. He was going to need some help unloading it.

Noreen was already on the phone before Mel had her coat on. Not the call she had been about to make, but a different one, faster. "I need hands at the Giving Spoon," she was saying. "Twenty minutes. Anyone you can reach, bring them." She was dialing the next number before the first call finished.

Mel went out with the driver to the back of the truck.

He rolled up the door.

She looked at pallets. Floor to ceiling, filling the box from the roll door to the cab wall: canned goods, stacked with the efficiency of a commercial order assembled by someone who knew exactly what they were doing. She stepped up on the bumper to read the nearest label. Standard pantry items: beans, corn, tomatoes, green beans, stew, soup.

Brand names she recognized. Commercial quantities. Case after case after case, more than the Giving Spoon's pantry had ever held at one time.

She looked at the driver. He looked back at her with the neutral patience of a man whose job was the driving.

"How much is this?" she said.

He told her the pallet count and the case count per pallet. She did the arithmetic.

She stood on the bumper in the November morning and looked at the largest single donation the Giving Spoon's food pantry had received in its history.

The first volunteer arrived in eleven minutes: one of the electricians, work jacket on, having apparently left a job site when Noreen's call came through. Three more followed within the quarter hour. Noreen directed traffic from the back step with the easy authority of a woman who has organized operations considerably more demanding than this one, and the canned goods came off the pallets and through the back door and onto the shelves and into the storage room and onto the tables pulled out to serve as staging area. Trixie was in the middle of it all: curious, tail in constant motion, threading between legs and hand trucks with the cheerful confidence that whatever was happening here was happening correctly and she was part of it.

The shelves that had been short an hour ago were not short anymore.

When the truck was empty and the driver had his signed manifest and the volunteers had found the coffee and Noreen was reorganizing the storage room with the particular satisfaction of a woman doing work that is exactly suited to her, Mel went back out to the driver.

"Who sent this?"

He went through his manifest with the care of a man checking for something he already suspects is not there. He turned the board toward her.

No name on the delivery slip. Shipper listed as anonymous. He was sorry; that was all he had. He was a driver. He delivered what the paperwork told him to.

He thanked her for the signature, climbed back into the cab, and drove away.

Mel stood at the back step of the Giving Spoon with the door open and the November air coming in around her, looking at the full shelves and the canned goods stacked three rows deep where the gaps had been that morning. Inside, Noreen's voice moved through the storage room, easy and practical. The volunteers talked among themselves at the coffee station. Through the kitchen pass-through she could see Trixie's corner, where the dog had settled back into her spot by the kitchen door, chin on her paws, watching Mel with the calm attention of a dog who has decided where she belongs and is simply waiting for the other party to arrive at the same conclusion.

She didn't know who had sent it.

She would think about it. She was already thinking about it.

She closed the door.

The Giving Spoon filled up. The day began.

The End of

Dead to Rites

Other White Jade Books

Brannigan Mysteries

Secrets of Silvergrove

Forget-Me-Nots and Forgotten Graves

Blue Iris, Blood Morning

Lotus, Lilies, and Last Courses (Summer 2026)

Roses are Red, Violets are Murder (Winter 2026)

Summers Rose Investigations

End in a Dead Heat

So Easy It's Criminal

Tacos, Sunsets, and Murder

The Drowned Duck (Summer 2026)

Cascade Agency Thrillers

Warm Taipei Rain

New Delhi Monsoon (Summer 2026)

Science Fiction

Samarqand: Prelude

Samarqand

Blue Stone, Black Water

Redeeming Lost Pegasus (Fall 2026)

Lost and Fallen (Winter 2026)

Bloodwine Warriors Trilogy (2027)

ABOUT THE AUTHOR

P. J. Kozeman: Finding the Plot at Mile 18

P. J. Kozeman has a theory about storytelling: the best plot twists, the most elusive clues, and the perfect motives don't reveal themselves at a desk. They appear on the dusty, sun-drenched roads of the Texas Hill Country, usually somewhere around mile 18 of a long marathon training run.

"There's a rhythm to it," she says, her voice warm and thoughtful, with the faintest hint of a Midwestern accent that has stubbornly refused to be baked out by the Texas sun. "The steady beat of your feet on the pavement, the landscape rolling by… your mind just goes to a different place. It's the perfect state for untangling a knotty plot. Or, more often, for deciding who the next victim should be."

At a striking 5' 11", with a cascade of light blonde hair streaked with distinguished silver, P. J. is a woman in constant, gentle motion. Now in her mid-fifties, she possesses a serene energy that seems to fuel a life rich with creative and compassionate pursuits. She and her husband, a retired geological engineer with a passion for birdwatching, settled in a quiet corner of the Hill Country over two decades ago, trading snowy winters for bluebonnet springs. It was here they raised their two children, and it is here they now welcome the happy chaos of their three young grandchildren.

For years, P. J.'s professional life was spent in the hushed, story-filled aisles of a community library. She was a librarian, a curator of worlds, a guide for readers young and old. It was a role she cherished, but she always harbored a desire not just to shelve stories, but to create them. When her younger child left for college, the quiet in the house became a blank page, and P. J. decided it was time to write.

Her love for the traditional mysteries of Agatha Christie and Dorothy L. Sayers, combined with her deep appreciation for tight-knit communities, naturally led her to the cozy mystery genre. Her fictional towns, while often plagued by a surprising number of murders, are always places of comfort, populated by quirky, loyal characters inspired by the very real people she meets every day.

Her writing life is a study in disciplined balance. Mornings begin before dawn, with a headlamp cutting through the pre-dawn darkness as she logs her daily miles. As an accomplished amateur distance athlete, she completes several half-marathons and at least one full marathon each year. This isn't just a hobby; it's an integral part of her creative process. The solitude of the run is where she works out the scaffolding of her novels.

After her run, and fortified with a strong cup of coffee, her focus shifts to a completely different kind of creation. In a small, light-filled studio behind her house sits a potter's wheel. Here, P. J. spends hours with her hands covered in clay, transforming shapeless lumps into elegant, functional pots and mugs. "Centering the clay on the wheel is a lot like centering a story," she muses. "You have to apply firm, steady pressure, but you can't force it. You have to feel where it wants to go. It teaches you incredible patience, which is something every writer needs."

But her home is not just a place of solitary creativity. It's also, frequently, a nursery. As a dedicated kitten foster for a local animal rescue, P. J.'s writing is often accompanied by the pitter-patter of tiny paws and the surprisingly loud mews of orphaned kittens. She and her husband have socialized and cared for dozens of litters, giving them comical, mystery-themed names like "Hercule Purr-ot" and "Miss Marbles." This work, she says, is pure joy and a constant reminder that even the most fragile beings can thrive with a bit of warmth and care.

That same spirit of community care extends beyond her front door. One day a week, every week, P. J. can be found at her local food pantry, sorting donations, packing boxes, and chatting with clients. It keeps her grounded, she insists. It's a powerful dose of reality that fuels the authenticity and heart in her characters. "Everyone has a story," she says. "In a place like the food pantry, you see the whole spectrum of human resilience and kindness. You can't invent characters better than the real people you meet."

P. J. Kozeman's life is a tapestry woven from long roads, spinning clay, purring kittens, and the quiet act of putting words on a page. It's a life built on discipline and empathy, a perfect reflection of the cozy, clever, and heartfelt mysteries she shares with her readers.

White Jade Books thanks you for purchasing "Dead to Rites" and hopes you enjoyed this story. For other great books, scan the code below.

www.ingramcontent.com/pod-product-compliance
Lightning Source LLC
LaVergne TN
LVHW091044080826
845145LV00002B/620

* 9 7 8 1 9 6 7 8 9 2 1 3 6 *